NORTH
OF THE
CRAZIES

JESSICA McCLELLAND

RED SKY INC.

Red Sky Inc.
Grand Junction, Colorado.

First printing: 2014
Second printing: 2018

PRAISE FOR THE KILLDEER SERIES

You'll be compelled to race through North of the Crazies by Jessica McClelland's easy and addictive prose, but that means you'll lose the detail and the accuracy that make her a truly fine writer. Her knowledge of the contemporary West and her abilities as a storyteller makes her a welcomed addition to the new class of crime fiction authors.

-Craig Johnson, author of the Walt Longmire Mysteries, the basis of A&E's hit series Longmire

Jessica McClelland's Snow at Midnight bursts out of the chute with a fresh new voice an authentic Montana sense of place, and a flawed but endearing protagonist readers will cheer for. Welcome aboard, Marley Dearcorn.

–C.J. Box, New York Times bestselling author of Force of Nature.

Snow at Midnight highlights not just a murder, but the nuances of Western culture: the conflict between old ranchers and new money, the independent self-sufficiency that comes from living an hour down a dirt road from the nearest hospital, the power struggles, the endless sky arching from the jagged horizon.

-The Daily Sentinel

NORTH OF THE CRAZIES

CHAPTER 1

Growing up in rural Montana taught me a few simple rules most folks never needed to know. If there are kids or cats in the house, before you sit down always check the toilet for snakes, just in case. Never shove a fully charged nine-volt battery in your pants pocket with a bunch of .22 shells, and never try to take a raw steak away from a forty-pound raccoon, no matter how close you were to him when he was a cub.

One thing I'd never bothered to learn was what to do if a couple of strangers from the city suddenly showed up, uninvited, inside your house. It wasn't something that happened enough to warrant a protocol.

I was blowing my nose on the sleeve of my T-shirt when I came up the stairs into the living room and saw two Mafia guys standing by the sofa. The thought popped into my head before I really had time to process the situation. I took one look at them and instantly thought it. Mobster.

They hadn't knocked, and they hadn't bothered to ring the doorbell. They'd simply walked right in without asking, and there they stood, looking at me.

My first thought was that I wished I'd taken the time to find a Kleenex.

There were only two of them, but that didn't stop them from sizing up the place like they were considering it as a time-share investment.

The fat one hitched his designer slacks up and over his beach-ball stomach and said in an unmistakably Eastern accent, "Mrs. Gable home? 'Cause my associate and me, we'd like a word."

Definitely Mafia.

Who else would show up in the middle of southwestern Montana wearing polished wingtip shoes and a salmon-colored silk tie, and walk into somebody's house unannounced? Well, someone who wasn't afraid of a hostile welcome, that's who.

I glanced down at myself, coming to the conclusion instantly that there was no way these two men would ever believe that I was, in fact, Mrs. Gable. Well, technically I was still Marley Dearcorn since I'd kept my maiden name, but either way, I was Leif Gable's wife and I doubted these two men would be interested in technicalities.

My strawberry blonde hair was shoved under a blue bandanna, my clothes were old and torn, my sneakers had holes in them and I clutched a mop and a dust rag in one hand. Hoping that to them I seemed more like the hired help than the lady of the house, I shifted the mop and tried to look clueless. "Mrs. Gable's not home."

I had actually been married to Leif for a little more than a month now, but they didn't need to know that, because I'd noticed that the fat man had a bulge under his left arm about the size and shape of a heavy pistol. The two men were stuffed into their expensive suits, looking the way retired football players look when they stopped tackling huge men for a living and tried to go into broadcasting. Neither one of them had a neck to speak of. They bristled with contempt.

"She's not here," I said again. "She's out shopping."

The fat man glanced around, his small eyes working the room like a ricocheting bullet. He smelled like treated leather, like the interior of a brand-new car. His black hair was dusted with a whisper of gray, and both hands flashed with gold. For late September he looked incredibly tanned.

The second man was a slightly slimmer version of his fat companion, but sported the same buzz haircut and had a similar taste for garish jewelry. He scanned me once, took in my appearance, and instantly dismissed me as unimportant. He looked irritated. He also looked like he could stop a speeding truck with one hand.

Being married to Leif Gable had been a joy, so far. But he had warned me repeatedly that the work he did sometimes forced him to knock up against people with sharp edges. I had an awful feeling that I was currently looking at two of them.

The fat man's small eyes came to rest on the fabric of his sleeve and he made a face. Using his thumbnail and stubby finger, he picked a speck of dirt off his jacket cuff with delicate precision. "In that case, tell Mister Gable that we dropped by to have a chat about his wife."

I had to get rid of them.

"You want me to call him?" I asked. "He can be here in five minutes."

Which was a total lie but I was betting he wouldn't know that.

"Sure," said the stocky man, smiling like a weasel sniffing the air for field mice. "Call him and tell him we want to talk about financial planning."

Since they didn't seem to know me, I gave them a subservient nod. "You want to leave a message?"

The fat man laughed. "Yeah, tell Mrs. Gable we are concerned about her credit score."

I shifted my feet backwards, which managed to get me one step closer to the stairs directly behind me. If they lunged, I'd make a run for the basement and try to put a door between us.

The stocky gangster shook his head, pivoted on his heel and headed outside, mumbling. "I said this was a waste of time."

The fat man stared after his companion, blinking with disappointment. "Bobby," he called. "Take an antacid."

He watched as the younger man heaved his bulk down the porch and out of sight. Then he swiveled his wide frame towards me and I froze.

"Here's the thing," he said, talking to me but not bothering to actually look at me. Instead he addressed the coffee table at his feet, giving every impression that he didn't consider me important enough to make eye contact with. "Mrs. Gable hasn't been keeping current on her interest payments. Maybe you could deliver that message to Mr. Gable for me?"

"Yes. I will tell him." I nodded my head up and down like the handle on a butter churn.

He spun one slow circle, taking in the house, and pulled a face that suggested he wasn't very impressed.

He glanced up the stairs that led to the master bedroom. "You sure Mrs. Gable isn't here? Could have sworn she'd be."

My mouth was so dry I could barely speak. "Nobody but me."

His beady eyes shifted to me and he squinted, thinking.

The last thing I should have said was that I was alone in the big house. Leif and I lived literally at the end of the road, in the middle of a thick forest of tall pines, and no matter how loud I screamed there wasn't a soul who would hear me. Pointing out that fact to my unwelcome guest wasn't the smartest thing to do. But I didn't want him to see me as a threat; I wanted him to see me as someone he could dismiss without a thought.

After a moment that seemed to last an eternity, the fat man reached quickly inside his sport coat pocket and I felt my knees nearly buckle.

Here we go . . .

Instead of pulling out a gun, his thick fingers fumbled around, eventually locating a bright tube of ChapStick. He leisurely smoothed a generous coat to his bottom lip, all the while staring at me. When he replaced the tube, he seemed to have come to a conclusion.

The fat man gave me a stern look and waggled a finger in my general direction. "Tell Mr. Gable we will be in touch and maybe we will let him work out a payment plan."

My heart was beating like a pair of flapping bird wings. I managed a weak nod.

When he finally turned and walked out, navigating his wide frame down the stairs, he sauntered with ease and didn't bother to look back.

I dropped the mop and dust rag and scrambled for the front door. Since the two of them were leaving I wasn't about to go charging after them demanding answers. Deciding that caution was the better part of valor, I slammed the front door and locked the dead bolt. I watched from the window as the fat man went to a long, cream-colored and sparkling Lincoln Continental. The car sagged when he climbed inside.

The two of them sat in the driveway for a moment, arguing. The stocky gangster seemed impatient, and the fat man seemed to be attempting a negotiation. Finally they settled whatever it was they were trying to work out. Neither one of them looked very happy, but they had come to a decision about something. The stocky man reluctantly nodded, and the car roared to life.

I studied the license plate. Illinois.

As the car rolled backwards I memorized the plate number. They backed down the driveway, narrowly missing the rows of pine trees on either side.

After they'd managed to get the long car turned round, they eased down the gravel road, and as their taillights faded from view I was already dialing the phone at the sheriff's station.

He answered on the third ring. "Sheriff Shucraft."

I squeezed the receiver with relief. "Loy, I'm really happy to hear your voice just now."

"Marley. What's up?"

His voice was low and raspy from lack of sleep. He had been without a deputy now for about as long as I had been married. Just over a month. Loy had been holding the entire town of Killdeer together single-handed since then. He'd been run absolutely ragged, and now I was about to throw a fresh bag of rattlesnakes on his desk.

"Two men from Illinois just broke into my house," I said.

There was a slight pause. "Are you alright?"

"I'm alright. They just left. I have their license plate number."

He sounded wide-awake now. "Give it to me."

I repeated the plate number, still watching the driveway for any sign the two men were returning.

"Alright, which way did they go?" asked the sheriff.

His sleep deprivation must have been worse than I'd originally thought. Leif Gable's house, well, our house, was the very end of the line in the valley. When you left our driveway there literally was only one way left to go and that was back towards the tiny town of Killdeer.

"They left a couple of minutes ago. They should be passing my father's ranch soon and if you just sit out in front of the sheriff station they will probably drive right by. It's a big cream-colored Lincoln."

"Stay there, keep the door locked and I will call when I locate the car." He hung up without another word.

I set the phone back in the receiver, still feeling shaken.

I paced back and forth for a few minutes, and it seemed clear that they were not coming back. At least, I dearly hoped that was the case. I really didn't want to think about what might have happened if I'd panicked and made a run for it.

It wouldn't do a bit of good to call my husband yet because he was currently in the air. Leif had his own airplane, which allowed him to travel quickly to business meetings, and he was on his way to Billings at the moment. I glanced at the clock and guessed that he wouldn't land for another twenty minutes.

Had the two men waited for Leif to leave before showing up unannounced? Probably. The point had obviously been to scare the hell out of his wife.

It had worked perfectly.

I sat down hard with my back against the door and tried to get my heartbeat to slow down.

7

I thought about my new husband, and about his repeated warnings after we had been married that his work occasionally led him into some very dark corners of the business world. Leif Gable was the president of a company that did international imports, but he was also something called a forensic accountant. From time to time, he told me he did investigative work for the government, and that involved locating and seizing great sums of money from crooked businessmen who sometimes used corporate funds for illegal purposes. He wouldn't elaborate, but I knew from all of our talks that if anyone ever arrived unannounced at the house I should be immediately suspicious. Leif's work had pitted him against some ruthless men. Although he took steps to remain anonymous he'd cautioned me that I should always be alert to strangers.

I would be taking that advice to heart after this incident.

Sometime soon I would need to sit down with my new husband and ask him to elaborate on his activities a bit more. Coming face-to-face with large, angry men wasn't what I had expected after we'd gotten married. If disgruntled businessmen were going to make it a habit to drop by in the future it was something I'd like to know about.

But if these two guys were angry with Leif, why did they ask for his wife? That didn't make sense to me now that I had a chance to think about it. I got the impression the two men weren't simply a couple of businessmen Leif had helped to convict. There was a lot more to it than that.

It seemed like forever, but finally the telephone rang. I jumped at the sound, shook my head at myself, and snatched the phone.

"Did you find the car?" I asked.

"Since when do you ever answer on the first ring?"

Not the voice I had expected.

It took me a second to realize who it was. "Allen?"

He cleared his throat, gearing up for a lengthy conversation. "Listen, I need to come talk to you about something."

Allen Hunter. My ex-husband and probably the last person I wanted to talk to at the moment.

I craned my head around to check the driveway again. "This isn't a good time."

"We can't do this on the phone," he said. "I need you to meet me in Helena."

"I can't meet you in Helena," I said. "Look, I really can't talk to you right now."

"Dang it, Marley. I mean it. It's important." He was dangerously close to whining.

"Allen, I've got to go. I'm getting another call and I can't miss it."

The second after I slammed the phone down, it rang again. "Hello?"

"Marley? I never saw the car, are you sure about the color?" Loy said, not bothering with identifying himself.

"Haven't you hired a new deputy yet? You can't be everywhere at once."

"All the applicants are goons. Would you explain to me, please, what two guys were doing breaking into your house while you are currently occupying it?"

"They didn't exactly break in. The door was unlocked. But they weren't what you would call the Mormon missionary type."

"I ran the plate number and it's registered to a plumbing company in Chicago," Loy said.

"A plumbing company?" That didn't make any sense to me, but the Chicago connection did.

"Hun, did they say anything to you?" he asked.

"They wanted to talk to Mrs. Gable," I told him.

"You are Mrs. Gable," he reminded me.

"Now that I think about it, they probably didn't want me." I paced back and forth. "I think they wanted Leif's ex-wife. She is from Chicago. I didn't recognize either one of those men and they didn't seem to have the first clue who I was."

"Virginia Gable, huh?" Loy asked. "Why would someone come all the way to Killdeer from Chicago to talk to his ex-wife? Leif divorced her a couple years ago."

"Something tells me they don't know that."

It was speculation on my part, but I had gotten the impression from the two gangsters that they were not looking for me, but for the woman who they knew as Mrs. Gable.

That would be Virginia, Leif's firecracker ex, and source of nothing but trouble for me since the first day I'd met her.

"Okay, what did these two men look like?" Loy asked.

"Like they would be right at home sitting in the front row of a fixed boxing match while some lackey sold illegal hooch out of a back room," I said.

"Marley, I need you to be serious."

"They also said they wanted to talk to Mrs. Gable about her credit score, because she hadn't been keeping up on her interest payments," I told him.

"Holy hell," Loy said. "Have you got a shotgun in the house?"

"What do you think?"

"I'm on my way. If they come back, don't let them even get to the bell, just shoot them through the door."

There was nothing for me to do but wait, and after I checked to make certain no vehicles were pulling up, I hunkered down by the front door again, listening for the sound of tires on gravel.

We had a shotgun propped up inside the closet a few feet from where I sat, and if I needed it in a hurry it was easy to snatch. Knowing it was there gave me a little more confidence, but not much.

The two men had surprised me while I was right in the middle of cleaning the huge house, top to bottom, and I felt ridiculously relieved that if I'd been murdered in my living room at least everything would have been spotless when the investigators arrived.

The first thing I'd done after our back-yard wedding a little over a month ago was fire Leif's housekeepers. Having strangers care for my new home wasn't how I was raised and I'd taken over the responsibility. It was fortunate for me that my part-time job working as a librarian only took me out of the house a couple of days a week, because the rest of the time I spent cleaning the three-story mansion.

It was a mansion by my standards. I'd grown up on a cattle ranch, so by definition I'd been poor my entire life, and now that I was living in a house with six bedrooms it was sinking in at last just how much money my new husband actually had. I still hadn't gotten used to the idea of driving a BMW sport-utility to the grocery store. Maybe someday I would.

After leaning against the door for another ten minutes I started to feel so jumpy, sitting still was no longer an option. I retrieved the mop and dust rag from the floor where they'd landed and stowed them back in the cupboard in the utility room, all the while keeping my ears tuned for any sounds of trouble.

Loy should have arrived already. What was taking him so long?

The thought of standing around doing nothing was unthinkable and I fidgeted, my adrenaline still pumping.

I rummaged around the utility room impatiently, gathering the garbage into a pile of four white bags. Since it was only a dozen steps to the bear-proof Dumpster outside by the garage I cracked the door and peered out. When I poked my head outside, everything looked normal. The tall pine trees surrounding the house whispered in the fall breeze, and aside from the flash of bird wings, nothing moved.

My fingers strained around the four heavy garbage sacks as I lifted them and scurried down the steps towards the Dumpster.

After shoving the garbage inside the big green container and locking it tight, I darted back inside the house, scanning the trees nervously, but there was no one in sight.

Maybe Loy had stopped down the road to look for signs of the Lincoln? For the life of me I couldn't think of a good reason why he would do such a thing, but hiding inside the house like a trapped rabbit was not my idea of dealing with the situation. What was taking him so long?

It was probably the worst possible move I could make, but I decided to drive the short distance to the mailbox at the end of the road. It might give me a clue about what was keeping the sheriff. At least I wasn't foolish enough to walk, leaving myself totally vulnerable.

I headed through the living room and fished the keys out of the bowl by the front door, stepped cautiously out onto the front porch and locked the dead bolt behind me. The air was crisp with early fall, but still warm enough that a T-shirt was all the clothing I needed.

My dirty sneakers kicked up pebbles as I headed across the driveway and made my way behind the house. The air was eerily still.

As I drove out of the garage my eyes fell on the steps leading to the back door. Had I remembered to lock it before coming outside? Thinking that it was inconceivable I'd forget something that important with two strangers lurking around, I hit the gas and drove down the gravel road. Of course I'd remembered to lock it.

When I reached our mailbox I saw Loy's sheriff truck parked in the center of the lane. He glanced up with irritation when he saw me.

"What are you doing out here?" His heavy frame cast a broad shadow on the ground.

"I really doubt they dropped a business card as they drove off," I said.

"I wanted to see if they had gotten out of the car and walked around," he explained.

"Because?"

Loy gave me a hard look. "Because if they did, it might tell me that they were checking to see if they had a clear shot at your house from here."

A wave of dread washed over me.

We both turned to look up the long driveway, trying to see if we could make out the house clearly through the thick trees. From where we stood, it was impossible.

I turned back to Loy and shook my head. "You almost have to be sitting in the driveway to see the porch."

Loy nodded as he scanned the ground. "And I can't see any sign that they stopped."

"Well, that's the first good news I've had all day."

"Where's Leif?" the sheriff asked, abandoning his track search and resting his palm on the butt of his pistol.

"Billings. He flew out a little while ago and said he will be back tomorrow."

"Maybe you should stay with your father tonight, just until he gets home."

I didn't say anything, but Loy could see from my face that I wasn't too keen on the idea of scampering back home every time there was some sort of commotion in my life. If I did that, I'd spend three-quarters of my time at my father's ranch house hiding under the bed. My life had been a series of disasters over the last few years.

Loy opened his mouth to argue, but then his face twisted with confusion as he looked over my shoulder. He peered up at the sky, his eyes lifted high as he focused on something that had caught his attention.

"What is that?" His broad forehead wrinkled and he pointed towards the treetops.

I spun around. "What?"

I felt my stomach twist with shock. "Ohmygosh."

A black plume of heavy smoke filled the pale autumn sky above the tree line. It was coming from the end of my driveway.

Loy's blue eyes fixed on me. "Marley," he said. "I think your house is on fire."

CHAPTER 2

I was so stunned at the sight of smoke billowing up in an angry black column towards the heavens I sprinted right past my SUV and started running up the long driveway in a blind panic. I made it halfway up the drive when I heard the roar of an engine.

The sheriff tore past me in his truck and I could hear him shouting into his radio as he raced by. When I reached the end of the driveway my heart nearly stopped when I saw the upstairs window belching sparks and angry red fire. The massive window had shattered and the remaining stubs of wooden frame glowed hot. Tall flames began curling out from the windows and licked the steel rooftop.

When I reached the yard Loy jumped out of his truck and lunged on the front porch. He tried the front door but it was locked. He started struggling to pull out a screen from the open window.

"Got to starve it of air!" he shouted. "I'll get this window shut and you check the back door!"

Without a second thought I ran to the back and nearly sobbed when the doorknob turned in my hand. I'd left it unlocked after all. Someone had gotten inside; there was no doubt about it.

I threw the door open and it crashed against the wall. I sprinted through the utility room and headed for the upstairs, thinking that I might be able to grab a fire extinguisher and quell the blaze. But when I reached the top of the stairs leading to the master bedroom I could see at once the fire was completely out of control. Heat like a blowtorch hit my bare face, forcing me to back away. Smoke rolled across the high ceiling only a few feet above my head. In a matter of moments, the entire upstairs of the house would be engulfed. I had only a few seconds to salvage what I could.

"Leif's computer." I stumbled backwards down the stairs. As I backed away from the growing tide of flames, I could see that the fire had started in the master bedroom. The bed was nearly destroyed.

My feet slipped as I sprinted down the steps, but I stayed upright and tried to think. There wasn't much time. I had to grab what I could.

I managed to locate my wallet on the table by the front door. As I snatched it and crammed it in my back pocket, Loy Shucraft glanced up from his task of slamming shut the windows and saw me inside the house.

His face lit up with fury. "Marley Dearcorn you get out of there now!"

The flames hadn't started rolling downstairs yet. I still had a few moments to spare. I backpedaled away from the door and scampered to the basement. The door to Leif's office was unlocked and I almost fell inside the room, and when I saw Leif's laptop computer sitting on the big oak desk I lunged for it. His entire life was on that laptop. Bank accounts, business contracts, legal documents, everything. With shaking hands I ripped the laptop off its docking station and tore the power cord free.

"Hurry, hurry."

I chanced a frenzied glance around the office, looking for anything else that might be irreplaceable, but the only thing of value other than Leif's laptop in the office was his beloved, huge oak pool table. I took one look at the massive thing and shook my head with regret. "Not a chance."

I sprinted up the stairs.

The laptop was snug underneath my arm and I felt the reassuring pressure of my wallet in my back pocket. At least I'd still have my driver's license and credit card when this was all over.

I was about to make a run for the back door when the realization hit me.

"My wedding ring!"

I'd set it inside the soap dish by the kitchen sink while I cleaned the house. There was no way I was leaving without it.

Just as I hit the swinging door to the kitchen I heard Loy burst through the utility room shouting my name. I dashed through the swinging door and dove for the sink. The soap dish was shiny and perfectly polished, just the way I'd left it. My wedding ring, a platinum band circled with diamonds, lay inside the dish gleaming. I managed to cram the ring on my finger and turned to make a run for the door when I crashed right into the sheriff's chest. He was so angry he couldn't even speak.

Without a word, Loy wrapped both arms around me and heaved me off my feet. I yelped once and struggled but to him I was hardly a burden. He bulldogged me through the kitchen door and when we pushed through it into the living room a wall of flames was rolling down the stairs like a tidal wave. It seemed impossible, but the fire actually seemed to walk down the stairs like a living thing. It was striking, beautiful and completely terrifying. For only the second time in my entire life I actually screamed with fear.

The flames rolled across the floor like they had been poured from a giant cauldron. Great plumes of black smoke boiled on the ceiling. The fire spread so quickly it was only at that moment I realized we were completely cut off from the utility room.

The front door was locked and if we stopped long enough to turn the dead bolt and rotate the knob we would be washed in flames.

There was no way out.

I felt Loy's big arms lock around me like a vise and my feet left the floor. He sucked in a huge breath and heaved us towards the picture window.

"Shut your eyes!"

My stomach lurched as the burly sheriff lowered his shoulder, took two running steps and dove for the glass.

We crashed through the window, spraying glass and splinters in a cascade, and landed hard enough to knock the wind out of my lungs.

I felt myself pulled to my feet and dragged down the stairs away from the burning house like a rag doll. When I finally dared open my eyes, I was sprawled on the ground and Loy was propping me against the tire of his sheriff's truck. He was saying something. I blinked a few times, willing my eyes to focus.

"Marley, are you hurt?" His face was inches away, but I'd barely heard a word. My ears were ringing from the fall.

Finally I managed to shake my head. "I don't think so."

The laptop was still clutched in my arms, and when I relaxed my grip and let it slide down onto my legs it looked like it was in one piece.

"What in the hell were you doing in there?" Loy demanded. "It's just a computer, for crying out loud. You ran inside a burning house to save a laptop?"

I swallowed, my mouth tasting like burned plastic and soot. "I had to get my wedding ring."

"Jesus, a child I could understand," Loy said, fighting to regain his temper. "I could even forgive you for a dog. But a piece of jewelry?"

"I'm sorry." I reached over and squeezed his arm with gratitude.

"Don't ever do that again." He dropped to the ground beside me. His broad shoulders fell back against the side of the truck and he winced with pain.

"I don't know what I was thinking," I told him. "I've never seen a fire move that fast before. I was sure there was enough time."

Loy cast a pained look towards the house. "I called the fire department and they should be here any minute. Maybe they can save it."

My lungs felt bruised on the inside, and when I coughed a smattering of dark drops smudged my palms. The air had been laced with scorched nylon and singed wood and no doubt I'd inhaled a lungful.

We sat shoulder to shoulder on the ground, leaning against the wheel of the truck, and helplessly watched as fire chewed its way through the first porch window. When flames began to spiral out the top of the window frame in tiny tornados of heat and ash, my shoulders slumped and I let my head drop into my hands.

Loy gave my knee a sympathetic nudge. "They're coming. Hang in there, Hun."

"I just polished all the chrome bathroom fixtures," I said miserably.

"I hear them. Maybe they can save the garage." Loy got to his feet. He walked towards the road as the sound of a single siren echoed against the trees.

Our all-volunteer fire department had mobilized their single engine crew in record time, and the five men who held down day jobs all over Killdeer leapt from the old truck as they rolled to a stop beside the house.

The truck was capable of pumping a full blast of water for more than twenty minutes and the five men scrambled frantically to get into position. They had water flowing in moments, but even the quick response and frantic efforts from the firefighters couldn't save my house. Hot ashes rained down on the garage as the back steps heaved a column of sparks. Unlike the house itself, the garage lacked a steel roof and in minutes the flames had taken hold. Both structures were soon ablaze. The entire garage was enveloped rapidly, so instead of wasting water on two buildings that were obviously destined to be a total loss, the firefighters wisely concentrated on preventing the flames from making it to the trees.

Leif had purposefully positioned the propane tank a safe distance from the house, and by some miracle, it didn't explode. One of the firefighters had already disconnected it, and it was out of danger. After several close calls and mad dashes into the trees to pound out small fires started from falling embers, the crew managed to contain the blaze and kept the forest from lighting up. At least the trees were safe.

We'd been incredibly lucky. There was no wind today.

Loy stood facing me while he watched the crew battle the blaze. It wasn't until he turned his back on me that I saw streaks of red crisscrossing his left shoulder and back.

"The glass." I dropped the laptop and got to my feet. "Loy you've been cut."

He shrugged me off, acting more like a cowboy than a sheriff. "It's not bad."

It looked awful, but I wasn't about to accuse him of being stubborn. He'd just saved my miserable hide, after all.

The sound of tires on gravel caught my attention and I saw a white four-door sedan pull into the long driveway, rolling slowly until it eased to a stop. The driver was a man, but other than that I couldn't see clearly who he was. Loy hurried away to intercept the car and as he bent down to speak to the driver, a cloud of dust appeared from the road behind him.

My father's old pickup truck roared into view. His face changed before my eyes from frantic to relieved when he saw me standing beside the sheriff's truck. He jumped out and marched towards me, not bothering to shut his door. His old cowboy boots and faded jeans were splattered with drops of white paint, and it was clear he had been working on a painting project only minutes before.

"Kiddo, please tell me that Leif Gable is not inside that house." He wrapped me in a tight hug.

I shook my head and managed a wan smile. "He is flying to Billings, Dad."

He heaved a sigh and stepped back to take me in. "When I saw the fire truck come tearing down the road I went up on the hill behind the ranch house to see what was going on. You can see the smoke from the pasture."

Loy was taking a long drink from a bottle of water, talking to the man inside the white car. Whoever he was, the sheriff seemed familiar with him and they spoke back and forth in short sentences.

Loy ambled away from the car and stopped beside my father, wincing a bit as he walked.

My father surveyed Loy's current state. "Sheriff, you're missing an eyebrow."

"Miracle I'm not missing more than that."

My father looked back and forth between us, taking in our stained clothing and the heavy coat of soot on our faces. His eyes fixed on the smoldering house. "You two want to explain why you both look like you were inside that thing when it went up?"

"Your daughter felt compelled to go back in to save her wedding ring," Loy said, a touch of anger in his voice.

My father looked at me with disbelief. "Marley, I can see you doing that for a dog, but a—"

"I know, I know," I said miserably. "I really did think I had enough time or I never would have done something so stupid. The fire moved a lot faster than I expected."

The man in the white car retrieved something from the floor of the sedan and slid out through the driver's side.

He was a slender man, and wore a crisp white shirt, his black hair thick as a rug.

He stood beside us and stared at me with an unreadable expression. The official patch sewn on the sleeve of his shirt indicated that he was from the Parkman fire department.

Since Parkman was at least a half hour away, even at top speed, this man must have already been close to Killdeer when he heard the call over Loy's radio.

He pulled off a pair of generic sunglasses and looked at me with a blank expression. "Mrs. Gable? Is this your residence?"

I simply nodded at him. "This is my house."

"Could you hold out your hands for me please?" he asked.

Thinking that he wanted to check me for injuries, I lifted my hands, palms out, and held them up for him to examine. They were grimy and stained.

Instead of looking at the skin for burns or injuries, he leaned down and smelled my palms, sniffing them like a bloodhound.

When I started to pull away, he snatched my left hand and turned it over, smelling it carefully like he was taking in the aroma of a fine wine.

"Ah . . . ?" I said, watching him with confusion. "What are you doing?"

"Craig McCumber. I'm the arson investigator from Parkman," he said, as if that would explain everything.

"Nice to meet you?" I said hesitantly.

"Could you lift up your feet for me, please?" he asked.

Reluctantly, I propped myself against Loy's truck and held up my right foot so that he could see the bottom.

To my astonishment he sniffed the bottom of my shoe exactly like he had my hands.

Loy was sucking down the last of his bottled water and watching the investigator. He hadn't uttered a word. After I shot him a scathing look, he shrugged. "Craig was up on Highway 89 looking at an old grass fire. Thought he might be useful, so he came by."

"And why is he sniffing my shoes?" I asked.

Loy tossed the empty bottle in the bed of his truck. "You were the last person inside before the fire started."

After dropping my right leg, the arson investigator reached down and scooped up my left leg like he was shoeing a horse.

He sniffed the sole of my sneaker, his face wrinkling up with an expression of disgust.

"Accelerant." He dropped my foot to the ground.

"Like, gasoline?" I asked.

My father took a protective step forward. "Mr. McCumber, just what are you getting at?"

The slim investigator shifted his eyes back and forth between us, his tone matter-of-fact. "Someone poured kerosene inside the home as an accelerant. It's all over your shoes. This fire was set deliberately."

My mouth danced between open and closed a few times before I could get the words out. "You don't actually think that I would burn down my own house?"

His dark eyes met mine. "You'd be amazed at what people will light on fire if the insurance money is tempting enough."

"I just spent five hours cleaning the damn thing!" I shouted.

Loy held up a hand. "Easy, Marley. It's just procedure."

"And to answer your question," Craig said, "no, I do not think you set this fire. Your feet smell of kerosene, but your hands do not. Your clothes have no trace of liquid that I am able to detect, but you did run through the kerosene that had been poured on the floor. It's astonishing, really, that you didn't ignite yourself while you were inside the structure."

Loy shot me a stern look. "Astonishing."

I leaned against the sheriff's truck, my legs weak and my head spinning. "No wonder the fire spread so quickly."

"If the arsonist had used gasoline instead of kerosene, you and I would not be having this conversation," Mr. McCumber said.

"Why not?" I asked.

"Because you would be dead."

A wave of nausea forced me to lower my head and I took a slow, steady breath to calm my hammering heart.

"Mrs. Gable?" asked the investigator. "Do you have any idea who may have set this fire? You were apparently home at the time, based on what Sheriff Shucraft has told me."

"Oh, yeah," I said, my face burning hot with anger. "I have a pretty good idea who it was."

Loy jerked his head towards the cab of his sheriff's truck. "Let me get you the information I've got on an Illinois vehicle registration."

The arson investigator followed Loy and the two of them continued their conversation in low tones as they walked away.

My father glanced at me warily. "You know who did this?"

I bent down to the ground and picked up Leif's laptop computer where I'd dropped it.

It was a bit smudged, but seemed intact. I wiped the dust from the cover and hugged it to my chest.

The laptop, my wallet and my wedding ring were all I had left in the world.

At that moment the upper floor of the beautiful house collapsed, sending a plume of sparks high in the air, and the firefighters dashed to quell the embers as they drifted into the trees.

Everything I owned, my clothes, my shoes, all my jewelry and my library books that had been sitting on the nightstand beside the bed? All gone.

My father put a firm hand on my shoulder. When I met his eyes, it was impossible to keep the tears from coming.

"You always told me it wasn't a good idea to jump to conclusions," I said, wiping my face with the back of my hand. "But in this case, I think I have a pretty good idea who's responsible for this."

My father looked determined and furious, staying perfectly silent, waiting for me to tell him.

"You are not going to believe it," I said, realizing how crazy it would sound. "But I'm sure it was all Virginia's fault."

CHAPTER 3

He answered his cell phone on the second ring. "Leif Gable."

"Hey, I hope you are not in a meeting yet. I've got some bad news," I told him.

My voice must have been deceptively calm. He chuckled before he replied.

"Did raccoons break into the garage again? I thought I saw some suspicious paw prints in the dust when I left."

"Well, it's a bit more serious than that," I said. A sudden coughing fit seized me and I had to hold the phone away for a moment.

"Sweetheart, are you alright?" he asked.

After my father handed me a glass of water, I took a long drink and propped my hip against the kitchen counter, the same mustard yellow rotary phone clutched in my hand that had been in the ranch house since I was a child.

"I'm alright. No one was hurt."

"Now I'm worried," he said.

There was no easy way to say it, so I plunged in. "Someone burned down our house. The garage too. Both of them are a total loss. I managed to have the BMW parked at the end of the driveway, so it's alright, but everything else was wiped out."

"Oh, no. What happened?"

"Kerosene was poured on the floor. It was set deliberately," I told him.

"But you are alright." He enunciated each word carefully.

"I'm alright."

He took a breath. "Then we will be fine."

It did my heart good to hear him say those words, but the situation was finally starting to sink in. I was beginning to realize just how much work lay ahead. "We lost everything."

A fraction of a second passed.

He sounded determined. "Things can be replaced. People can't. This is fixable."

Even I was a bit surprised at how calm he seemed. "Leif, don't worry. We can stay at the ranch house until we can figure out what to do next."

"I'll have it sorted out by this afternoon," he said. "Do you have any idea who did this?"

"Two men came to see me right before it happened. They said they wanted to talk to Mrs. Gable about her interest payments. They were from Chicago," I said.

I could hear Leif rummaging for something. His voice was muffled and he had probably just tucked his cell phone under his chin. I heard a car door slam. "Listen carefully, Marley. I need you to go to your father's."

"I'm there," I said, my heart pounding all over again.

"Good. Were you able to save anything from inside the house? Anything at all?"

"I got your laptop out, and my wallet. I've got a credit card and my checkbook, but that's all. I'm sorry." I felt like crying, but that wouldn't do a bit of good so I settled for angry resolve.

"You did fine. Now, I will be there in three hours. It will take me a few minutes to chat with my attorney and cancel our meeting, but I will be in the air as soon as I can. I have to file my flight plan and do a preflight check of the plane and then I will come home. Don't worry about a thing, sweetie. Put your father on the phone, please."

Surprised, I handed my father the receiver and he took it at once.

"Nathan here." He nodded as Leif spoke, not realizing that Leif couldn't see him nodding on the phone.

My father listened intently for a few seconds. "Nope. Nothing left standing, not even the stairs. Took about half an hour and it was all over. What's the plan?"

Not for the first time, I marveled at the resiliency of the rural soul.

I heard Leif's muffled voice ticking off a list of instructions.

There was one thing I could say about my new husband. He was one cool cucumber.

I rubbed my forehead and it came away covered with black grime. I scooped up a bar of soap by the sink and went to work washing my face and hands.

Finally, my father pushed away from the counter and I could tell he was wrapping up the phone call. "I can do that. How much? Okay, I'm on it, Leif."

After my father hung up he stood next to me at the sink and rubbed his palms on the front of his paint-stained shirt. "Kiddo, are you feeling up to going over to Falcon Realty? I know this is all a big shock, but Leif asked me to help you handle this, and I think that things are going to move pretty darn quick this afternoon."

I paused from drying my face. "Falcon? He wants to rent a house or something?"

"Sort of," my father said, reaching for his truck keys. "He also said something about you being around other people out in public until he can get home."

Obviously the two men who had come looking for Virginia had set off the same warning bells for Leif as they had for me. "Okay. I'm up for it."

As if he was operating under orders, my father hurried outside and shuffled the vehicles around so that my black BMW was parked inside his old garage and his new pickup truck was stationed conspicuously in front of the ranch house, and as we clambered inside his ancient and battered work truck he wasted no time. We were bouncing down the rutted gravel road towards Killdeer in a matter of moments, my father driving like he was trying to make it to the county line while being chased by two redneck cops.

"Dad, you can slow down. We aren't delivering a kidney."

He slowed his pace fractionally, but still roared through Killdeer and zipped down Main Street oblivious to all posted speed limit signs, and turned savagely to the left down Dayton Lane. I reflexively tugged my seat belt tighter in case my father planned to roll the truck.

We screeched to a halt in front of Falcon Realty, and as I gratefully climbed out and put my feet on solid ground my father rounded the nose of the truck and hustled me inside the office, clutching my elbow and steering me along quickly. It was all happening so fast I didn't have time to feel anything other than numb shock. It was entirely possible my father was overreacting just a bit. What had Leif told him on the phone? I didn't have time to contemplate anything, because he practically dragged me inside.

The mayor of Killdeer owned Falcon Realty. David Jordan doubled as a politician and real estate broker. He ran the city while his agents ran the real estate business. When we walked through the front door, three people leapt up from their desks and rushed to assist us.

The youngest member of the team, a straightlaced boy of a man with a sharp suit, darted to my side and took my arm. He guided me towards the hallway. "Right this way."

He ushered me past the main reception area with care.

I gave him a grateful smile. "Thanks, Billy."

We walked through a set of double doors that led to a large office decorated with the utmost care.

I had recognized Billy Collins right away. He always dressed impeccably, and that was part of the reason David kept him around. Billy looked like a young attorney from Wall Street. Everyone at Falcon presented himself or herself as neat and efficient. It was their trademark.

Falcon Realty occupied a huge old Victorian-style house one block off of Main Street, nestled in a tidy neighborhood full of other stately old homes that had been built when Killdeer had been a thriving suburb for a local coal mine. The coal mine had closed years ago when a newer, larger mine opened up a two-hour drive away in the rugged mountains to the south. After the local mine had closed, the thriving coal community of Killdeer had reverted back to a small agricultural town. That had all happened long before I was born, but the brief surge of prosperity in our town's past had left it flush with dozens of huge old mansions that were now used for other purposes. Falcon Realty's office had probably been built around 1918, and its lead glass windows and crown molding above the doorways made it look like there should be at least a couple of servants running around fetching martinis for sparkling dinner guests.

My father and I sat down in two matching leather chairs. Across from us a massive cherrywood desk dominated the office.

Billy adjusted his sleek tie and gave me a sympathetic smile. He put one hand on the back of my chair. "Can I get you anything? Coffee?"

"Whiskey?" my father asked.

Billy laughed, nervous and high. "Debbie will be right in."

As he left, he carefully closed the double doors behind us, and I sat looking down at myself with disgust. I was dressed in the worst clothes I owned. I realized suddenly they were also the only clothes I owned. My old sneakers were covered in soot, my T-shirt was grimy and my hair was sticking out at all angles from underneath my old bandanna. I felt like something that should have been taken out with the trash.

But dammit, I still had my wedding ring.

Debbie, the senior agent, breezed in. "Sorry to keep you waiting." She paused long enough to pull the doors closed, giving the three of us privacy.

The entire office seemed to have been waiting specifically for us. "Did Leif telephone you?" I asked.

Debbie gave me a soft smile. "Oh, yes. It's all been arranged. Shall we get started?"

As I watched her roll down the heavy blinds behind our chairs, the two other real estate agents in the office, both women, were furiously scanning thick stacks of paper. I wondered if they were working so diligently on my account.

Debbie took her seat behind the wide desk. Her short black hair was trimmed expertly, and her lavender business suit was pressed and spotless.

"I am terribly sorry for all the inconvenience you are facing, Marley. And I am so sorry for your troubles. We are all here to make this process as comfortable for you as possible."

I knew Debbie, though not very well. In Killdeer it was practically impossible not to. You couldn't live in a town with a population of 901 people and not at least be familiar with all of its denizens.

Debbie Pritchett was Lewis Pritchett's cousin, once removed, and even though she was his only living relative, her share of the family fortune was considerably smaller than his had been. Lewis had discovered years before that his old, tattered ranch was sitting on top of one of Montana's richest coal bed methane deposits. He'd retired younger than he ever dreamed possible, and had spent his newly acquired vast fortune building a huge house on the grounds of Killdeer's recently built ritzy golf community. Debbie had garnered a tiny share of the profits by virtue of her blood relation to Lewis, but nobody knew exactly how much, and she had continued working as a real estate agent probably out of necessity. I'd always thought she was one of the classiest women I had ever met. Her soft voice was helping soothe my nerves.

I wiped my sweaty hands on my legs. My jeans were so filthy they instantly stained my palms. Funny, but being in shock didn't feel that bad. Then it occurred to me what I would feel like when the numbness eventually wore off.

I managed to keep from touching the expensive leather with my filthy hands. "Leif must have worked out a rental house with your office?"

Debbie nodded. "He and I have made arrangements for you, my dear. Things will be back to normal in no time. Mr. Gable instructed me to let you know that he will not be able to return home for another few hours. He mentioned that something had come up, and he would be detained. But don't let that concern you, he has made arrangements for you to have accommodations."

"Alright," I said, a bit confused. "But it's really no trouble for me to stay with my father."

Debbie smiled, her big brown eyes as soft as a whitetail doe's. "He has purchased a house that we have had on the market for some time. We have drawn up a contract. Billy should be coming in with it as soon as the ladies are finished, and you will be able to move in after you leave our office."

Most of the air suddenly left my lungs. "He bought a house?"

The clock behind Debbie's desk read 1:45. Our house had burned to the ground less than two hours ago and already Leif had managed to buy a new one, over the telephone, from a hundred miles away.

"Which house?" I asked, my mouth gaping.

"It's actually very close to your original residence. Sadly, there is no garage, only a toolshed in the back yard. But, with Mr. Gable's resources I am sure he can install a two-car detached garage shortly."

"It's only my father's ranch and that obscenely huge Nesbit property out our end of the valley," I said. "I know Leif didn't buy the ranch."

Debbie's cheeks colored slightly. "That is correct."

Realization dawned and I leaned forward with disbelief. "He bought Paul Nesbit's house?"

"Take a breath, Kiddo," my father instructed.

"Since he has agreed to pay in cash, we were happy to expedite the process," Debbie said smoothly.

How had Leif managed to do this so quickly?

Then I recalled that Leif's ex-wife, Virginia, used to be a real estate agent out of Falcon's office. No wonder they were all so willing to bend over backwards to help him in such a rush. He was probably a familiar face around the office, and the way things worked in Killdeer, folks usually bent the rules to the breaking point for a friend.

The double doors swung open quietly behind me. Billy Collins came in and reached across the wide desk discreetly. "Here you are, Ms. Pritchett." He handed Debbie a heavy black folder.

She set it carefully on her desk and pulled out an intimidating stack of papers. "Now, this is only the renter's contract. Since the house has sat vacant for two years, we were able to hurry the process, but the actual purchase will take place after we have title insurance. Until then, we have drawn up a lease agreement, which will allow you to move into the home right away. Leif has let us know that he will handle the closing personally, and until then all we need from you is a check for the first month's rent, plus fees."

I could see her lips moving, but I was having a difficult time understanding the words.

Paul Nesbit had been a close neighbor of mine who lived in a fabulously plush, monstrous log lodge not very far from Leif's house. Paul had actually died inside the home, which probably accounted for the fact that such a gorgeous piece of property failed to sell for over two years. The price might have had something to do with it too. I'd heard through the Killdeer grapevine the home was worth over a half a million dollars. I shuddered to think what the first lease payment would be.

"I will need a check for six thousand dollars," Debbie said gently.

I made a sound like a toad that had just coughed up a bowling ball. "I'm sorry. Did you say six thousand dollars?"

"It will cover the lease for the thirty-day period necessary to close the sale, accommodate the processing fees, and it will also cover the cost of title insurance. And Mr. Gable also mentioned that you could use the remainder of the funds he transferred to you for personal items that will need to be replaced."

"Remainder? I'm not sure I understand." I glanced between my father and Debbie.

My father cleared his throat. "I forgot to tell you. Leif wired you some cash."

"He wired me cash?"

Debbie explained it to me, her patient expression set like it had been poured in concrete. "Mr. Gable sent you an electronic deposit of ten thousand dollars. It should be in your account now. Of course, we will hold the check until this afternoon, to give the transfer time to clear."

"Ten thousand dollars?" I asked.

My father turned sideways to look at me. "Marley, you sound like a myna bird."

"Ten thousand?"

He leaned forward in his chair and propped one arm on the big desk. "Debbie, hand over those papers and we will be out of your hair. Don't suppose you have keys?"

Debbie smiled at my father, grateful that someone was with me who was able to form a complete sentence.

She gave him the keys. "The house is fully furnished. It still contains dishes and the bare essentials. We were hoping to rent it out but since there have been no inquiries the usual household items should still be fully stocked."

I pulled my checkbook out of my back pocket and wordlessly jotted down a transfer in the register for the money Leif had sent. I very nearly added the incorrect amount, because I wasn't used to writing down deposits in my checkbook that included so many zeros. But I managed to get it right after counting out the places on my fingers. Debbie was kind enough not to pay attention to the fact that when I gave her the check my hand was shaking. When my father had said things were about to start moving fast, he hadn't been kidding.

After I'd signed my name multiple times on multiple copies of legal-sized documents, initialed a few more times, and listened as she explained to me patiently and slowly that the water to the property was turned on, as well as the electricity and the propane, but that those things would need to be changed into our name within twenty-four hours, I felt as wrung out as I ever had in my life.

My father had the good sense to retrieve the house keys and ushered me back out to his truck with a steady hand. I sat in the passenger seat, buckled my seat belt and stared with disbelief at the keys resting in my palm.

The entire situation was surreal. I'd watched helplessly as my home and all my earthly possessions went up in flames, and now I was holding a set of keys to a freshly purchased house, all in less time than it took to get a new set of tires and an oil change. It was apparent my new husband didn't understand the concept of procrastination. At the moment I had been having a nervous breakdown, he had coordinated Operation Save-the-Day with nothing more than a cell phone.

We drove through town and I realized my father had been chatting the whole way, but I couldn't recall what he'd said. Finally he eased us into the parking lot of the Stock Market grocery store.

A row of shopping carts was corralled in the parking lot, and each one of the shopping carts had a pair of plastic steer horns protruding from the handles. The Stock Market was Killdeer's version of kitsch humor. It was supposed to call to mind a cattle market, and the parking lot spaces were painted with lines that looked like lassos. Usually its silly theme gave me a chuckle, but today it would be a hard task for me to feel amused about anything.

My father cut the engine on the truck. He stared out the windshield. "Well, I suppose you will be needing toothpaste."

It was as if I'd just awakened from a coma. "Right. Toothpaste."

The little grocery store was comfortingly familiar. I still felt numb, but managed to navigate the aisles without crashing into anything.

We filled the cart with things that I might need, things I would definitely need, a few things I couldn't live without, and by the time we had come back outside I'd spent over a hundred and fifty bucks on groceries and household items.

We packed the bed of the truck and my father kept a constant vigil, scanning the parking lot and keeping his eyes open for trouble. When we climbed back in the cab I sat motionless in the seat beside him, feeling like I could sleep for a month.

My father leaned back without starting the engine.

"How's about we drop by Lil's and grab a bite to eat?"

"After we just bought three packages of Oreos?"

He stared at his hands where they rested in his lap. "I thought you could use some normal, after everything that's happened today."

I was exhausted, dirty and shaken up, but also acutely aware that my father was deliberately trying to keep something from me. "Dad, what did Leif tell you on the phone that you don't want to talk to me about?"

After a tense pause he glanced over. "He's your husband. You two can talk about it after he gets home."

I managed to nod. "Alright."

"So. Off to Lil's?" he asked.

"Trying to take me someplace to keep an eye on me for a couple hours?" I asked.

He started the engine, but wouldn't look at me. "Yep."

"You want to tell me why?" I asked.

"Nope."

He pulled out of the parking lot and headed back towards Lil's café without another word.

CHAPTER 4

Irene Baker, my dearest friend and owner of the best café in Killdeer, took one look at me when I walked through the door of Lil's and nearly dropped her coffee mug.

"Nathan, what the bloody blue blazes happened to her?" she demanded.

Irene darted around the long counter like a barrel racer and was at my side instantly.

Her stern gaze raked over me, no doubt taking in the layer of soot and smell of charred wood.

She glanced at my father, who also happened to be her boyfriend, and she practically snarled.

"I told you two not to burn that heap of old barn wood down in the alfalfa field without the county having the fire truck there to supervise." She glared at us. "I just knew it would get out of hand."

My father, completely unfazed, gave her a peck on the cheek and took a seat at the long counter.

"It wasn't the barn wood." I eased myself onto a stool.

I could feel her glaring at my back.

"What did you two do this time?"

She stomped back behind the counter and stared at me.

My father stretched across the counter and snagged two water glasses from a tray, helping himself to a pitcher as well. He set a full glass in front of me and I gratefully gulped it.

When it was clear we weren't quite ready to talk, Irene crossed her arms. She called over her shoulder into the kitchen, her voice clouded with concern.

"Andy, I need two smothered roast beef sandwiches," she said.

"But I've got three pork roasts in the oven, Ms. Baker." The cook's pale round face appeared in the window opening.

"Multitask, Andy," she said, pulling out a small stool from underneath the counter and propping herself up on one hip.

Harvey Wilson was the only other customer in the café. Killdeer's own version of CNN and Fox News combined, he sat at the far end of the long counter like a disapproving and curious toad. His stained bib coveralls were stretched to capacity across his vast expanse of belly, and he eyed us with obvious interest.

Irene shot him a glare. "Maybe you should run along and see to that broken piece of haying equipment, Harvey."

The chubby rancher adjusted the ever-present toothpick in his mouth. He'd long since finished his lunch and was loitering over the newspaper, as usual. "I don't have a piece of broken haying equipment."

Irene tucked a strand of short blonde hair behind one ear. "If you don't get out of my café in one minute, you will have."

Harvey pulled his ancient John Deere baseball cap down to shade his eyes and stood up, grumbling. "You know someday I'll make good on my threat to call the Better Business Bureau on you, Irene."

She folded her arms, determined to chase him out so my father and I would explain ourselves.

Since Lil's was the best café within twenty-five miles, Irene could abuse her customers occasionally and it wouldn't make a bit of difference to her bottom line.

When Harvey finally ambled out, Irene waved both hands impatiently. "Well? What's going on?"

My father lifted his hand and gave my shoulder a sturdy squeeze. "Marley's house burned down."

Irene's eyes bulged. "Your house? Oh, honey." She lunged forward and squeezed my hand. "Not that big beautiful log home. That's horrible! Are you alright?"

That wasn't an easy question to answer. "Thanks to Loy I am."

"The sheriff was there when it caught fire," my father explained.

"What happened?" She dropped back onto her little stool. Irene never permitted herself to fully sit down while she was working, but she did allow herself the occasional boost. At the moment it looked like the stool was the only thing holding her up.

"Someone has it in for Virginia," my father explained. "It was deliberately set. Marley thinks they were looking for Leif's ex-wife."

Irene's eyes went from concerned to flaming mad in one blink. "Divorcing her was the second-best move Leif Gable ever made in his entire life."

"What was the first-best move he ever made?" I asked.

She stared at me. "Marrying you, of course. Anyway, what makes you think they were after Virginia? She hasn't been in Leif's orbit for over two years."

"Except that it looks like she has managed to find a way to make trouble for us anyway," I said.

Andy rang the order-up bell sitting in the window. He had been listening to us, but trying to look like he hadn't been listening.

Without missing a beat Irene scooped up both of our plates and set them on the counter.

Realizing that I was starving, I dug into the food gratefully.

Three bites in, I looked down and noticed a piece of glass sticking out of my pant leg. It hadn't cut me, but only by sheer luck. I pulled it out of the fabric and apologetically handed it to Irene. She pitched it in the trash and stared at me with concern.

"You can come stay with me." Irene slid her stool back beneath the counter.

"Leif bought Paul Nesbit's place," my father said around a mouthful of roast beef.

She gasped. "He didn't."

"I've already got the key," I told her. "But thanks for the offer."

Irene blinked at me. "Your husband's Indian name should be Chief-Doesn't-Screw-Around."

"You got that right," I said.

"Aren't you worried that whoever lit the fire will come looking for you there?" Irene asked.

"I'm thinking they weren't looking for me in the first place," I said, my loaded fork poised halfway to my mouth. "And I also think that Leif told my father something on the phone that he's not too keen on sharing with me."

Irene shot him a heavy glare. "That so, Nathan?"

He grumbled for a moment, but withered under the angry gaze of his iron-maiden partner and relented. "He said that Virginia left Killdeer after they got divorced so she could get a fresh start. She ended up back in D.C. for a while."

I set my fork down and folded my hands in my lap. Why was it that my husband knew so much about his ex-wife's personal life? Brushing the feelings of confusion and irritation aside, I took a deep breath and decided the best thing to do was keep my mouth shut and listen.

My father tried to break it to me easy.

"Leif said that a few months back, Virginia went off the radar and their son was mighty concerned about her," he told me carefully. "Turns out she was in Chicago, making a mess of her life. For the sake of Scott, Leif tracked her down and stuck her in a rehab clinic. She'd been hitting the pills again, pretty hard. He was sure this time the therapy would take, but after she got out of treatment she sort of vanished again."

"Owing some not-very-nice people a lot of money," I said bitterly.

My father looked at the counter, his voice low. "Yeah, something like that. At least it looks that way now."

"Not-very-nice people," Irene said. "What does that mean?"

I explained about the two men who had come to the house. My father's expression hardened while I spoke, and his anger flared up. He'd been hopping mad in the driveway back at my place when I'd explained to him about the two goons from

Chicago walking in on me. As I told Irene the same story I'd told him, he simmered with a scowl on his face.

"Nathan, take it easy." Irene put a hand on his arm to steady him.

It was still amazing to me that my father and my best friend were a couple. I hated saying the word girlfriend to him when I spoke about her.

Since Irene was a decade my senior and pushing forty-five, their relationship wasn't exactly a May/December affair.

More like August/November.

Most days I took comfort in the knowledge that they were the two people I cared about the most, other than my husband, and it seemed natural that they would care about each other as well. But other days, it only served to remind me that my mother was long gone from this world.

After a drunk driver had killed my mother when I was seven years old, my father had refused to get involved with any other woman in a serious way. Until Irene, that is.

In many ways I was grateful to her that she had helped drag my father back to the human race.

"So let me get this straight," Irene said, propping both elbows on the counter and leaning in. "You think that Virginia has pissed someone off, and they are trying to send her a message by destroying your home. What they think is still Virginia's home."

I took another long drink of water. "I know it sounds crazy."

"No, it sounds like Virginia." She stood up and rubbed her temples. "I think your father is right. You should come stay with me for a while."

"No way. I'm staying at the new house. I don't want anyone else involved in this mess."

The air crackled with tension. I hadn't realized it, but I was looking at the both of them with my hands clenched into fists.

"Leif said you might say that." My father looked at me with concern.

It took effort, but I managed to calm down long enough to take a deep breath and regain my temper. "I'm not about to get anyone else involved. This is my problem."

"Honey, don't be stupid," Irene said. "You need to be careful."

Had any other person said it, I would have been angry in a flash. But, since she was the queen of stubborn and pigheadedness and my best friend, Irene could get way with calling me stupid. I hated to admit it, but she was right.

"Look, I'll think of something." I held out my hands and heaved a sigh. "I'm sort of making this up as I go along."

"Leif said he would take care of it," my father said. "If he says he will take care of something, it'll get done no matter what."

I believed it too. My husband could handle things better than anyone I'd ever met. It still hadn't quite sunk in that he'd transferred to me what amounted to half a year's salary in the time it took other people to fill up their cars at Quickie-Mart.

The three of us were silent while I thought about what to do next.

My head was a jumble of conflicting thoughts and feelings. I wasn't entirely sure how a person was supposed to handle a disaster like losing everything she owned in one afternoon, but sitting around crying about bad luck had never worked out for me in the past.

"Dad, take me by The Big R, and after I get some new clothes, we are going back to your place and pick up my vehicle. I'm spending the night at the Nesbit house."

He watched me speculatively.

Irene shook her head. "Are you sure about this?"

I held up one finger. "First of all, they think I'm the Gables' housekeeper so they won't be interested in me."

"How did they get that idea?" my father asked.

"Second," I held up two fingers, "Paul's house isn't high-profile. Unless you know it's there, it's practically impossible to find."

I was reasonably confident that I was right about both of those things. Paul's house was invisible from the washboard dirt road snaking through the valley, and unless you drove directly to it, the huge structure was well hidden by the thick forest.

I held up a third finger. "Leif will be home in no time. So you don't need to worry about me being alone."

Both Irene and my father grumbled and argued, but after I made it perfectly clear I wasn't about to budge, they finally relented and agreed.

Uncharacteristically for her, Irene gave me a crushing bear hug as she walked us to the parking lot.

Just before she turned to head back inside her café, Irene snagged my arm. "I almost forgot to tell you. Allen called here wanting to talk to you. He said you hung up on him."

I let out a groan and rolled my eyes towards the sky. "Did he say what he wanted? And, I swear, if he thinks for one minute that I'm driving up to Helena to meet him—"

"He said he would come see you. I tried every trick I could think of, but he wouldn't even give me a hint about what he wanted." Irene prided herself on her ability to pry gossip out of anyone. Apparently Allen had some big news that not even she could get him to open up about.

"I don't have time to worry about him," I said. "Whatever it is. It can wait. See you later, Irene."

She cast a worried look at the two of us as we left.

My father didn't look very happy about it, but he dutifully drove me over to the Big R store and patiently held a shopping basket while he followed me through the clothing department. I hated shopping for clothes, but the selection wasn't so vast that I was overwhelmed.

I stuck to my old standby Wrangler blue jeans and bought a few new T-shirts. It was coming on winter, so I tried on a heavy coat, loaded up on socks and threw a half dozen pair in the basket. After replacing just the essentials, underwear and pajamas, it occurred to me that I wasn't the only one who had just lost everything in the fire. I knew his size, so while replacing my items I snagged another basket and chose a few key things for Leif, too. Since the aisle across from the clothing section was full of saddle tack, it was a given that Leif would need to do his own shopping in Billings to replace his business wardrobe. Finding a tailored suit in Killdeer was impossible. The Big R had never carried a selection of ties, so I grabbed him a few bare necessities: socks, jeans and T-shirts. For the time being at least he wouldn't have to walk around naked.

My sneakers were practically ready for the garbage can, and the last thing I bought before checking out was a sturdy pair of lace-up Justin Ropers. On impulse I threw in two heavy-duty pairs of gloves.

Cringing, I wrote out a check for everything and my father helped me cart it back to the truck. When we finally made it back out to the ranch house and I was shifting everything over into my SUV, the sun was dipping beneath the rim of the mountain and the valley was full of long shadows.

"At least let me follow you over to Paul's," my father said as he handed me the last bag of clothes.

"I suppose." I knew if I argued with him, he would just go and do it anyway.

As we drove in tandem my eyes darted everywhere, searching for a cream-colored Lincoln. But we were the only ones on the dusty road. As I pulled up in front of the place that had just become my new home, it was a relief that not even a squirrel was moving through the trees. Everything looked completely deserted.

I climbed out of my SUV and stood leaning on the door for a moment, staring at the ostentatious house with a mixture of awe and disdain. A touch of dread was thrown into the batch as well. I'd been the one to discover the home's former owner, Paul, dying inside on his kitchen floor, and not a few bad memories haunted me still.

Although most folks in the valley felt uneasy because of what had happened in the home in the past, my dislike stemmed more from my own personal ambivalence concerning the house's architecture. Paul's house had a nickname in the valley. The nickname was well deserved.

The entire east side of the structure was nothing but one long window. Actually, it was several windows, but they were so huge and packed together so tight the place looked like it was mostly made out of glass. Except that it was really a very pretentious cabin, constructed to look like it had cost a million bucks, and no expense had been spared. Paul had no concept of privacy when he'd built the home, but he'd certainly had a concept of showmanship.

"I can't believe I'm living in the fishbowl." I stared at the place.

My father stood beside me and adjusted his stained baseball cap. "Good thing you bought pajamas."

With the lights on inside, anyone standing outside the house would be able to see into the bedroom easily. "Maybe I should spray-paint the windows until I can find some drapes."

"You sure you don't want me to stay over?" He reached inside my backseat for the first load of bags.

"Tell you what, Dad. If Leif doesn't make it home tonight for some reason, I'll come over and stay with you."

He thought about that as he juggled four heavy sacks. "That works for me."

The key turned easily in the front door and I realized that I'd been holding my breath from the moment my hands touched the knob. After everything else that had gone wrong today it wouldn't have surprised me one bit if Debbie had given me the wrong house keys. But we managed to get inside with no trouble, and when I flicked on the lights the vast living room burst into view. Just as Debbie had promised, everything was exactly how Paul had left it, except that all of the bigger pieces of furniture were draped with drop cloths to protect them from dust.

I set my first load of bags inside the front door and headed for the kitchen. All the cupboards were full of dishes, the drawers were neatly packed with sparkling silverware and even the Cuisinart coffeemaker looked like it had just been washed and dried that very morning.

Three trips later we finished piling the groceries on the kitchen counter and hauling the clothes into the living room. I leaned against the door, grateful for a chance to catch my breath and take stock.

"It looks like everything is ready to go," I said.

My father gave the house one last critical examination and seemed satisfied. "Alright, Kiddo. But if you see anyone, anyone at all, hightail it out of here."

"Thanks for everything, Dad. Really, I don't know what I'd do without you."

He squeezed my shoulder with one hand, and as he jogged back to his truck, I was careful to lock the door behind him.

The heavy wood felt reassuring against my shoulder, and for several minutes I didn't move at all.

It would take time for everything to sink in, but at the moment I was safe and dry, and alive, and that was good enough.

The next hour flew by as I unloaded the groceries, checked that the water heater was functioning and made sure the thermostat was set correctly.

I was surprised to find a bag of coffee in the cupboard above the coffeemaker. Someone from the real estate office must have brought it by to prepare in case a potential buyer came to view the home.

The refrigerator was already plugged in, which annoyed me. Why run a fridge when nobody was home? And I noticed the garbage cans already had liners. Whoever had been responsible for taking care of this place was doing a fantastic job.

The groceries I'd picked out myself didn't remotely resemble the items I discovered in the sacks. My father had surreptitiously tossed a number of things into the cart, obviously.

A huge can of hot chocolate, six Hershey bars and a big bag of thick cut potato chips told me he had managed to load me up with some comfort food.

It was ridiculous, but for supper I finished off half the bag of chips and was working on my second cup of hot chocolate when I remembered all the sacks of clothing would need to be taken upstairs and put away.

Figuring that the second floor would be intact exactly like the living room, fully furnished and ready to go, I scooped up two heavy sacks of clothes, intending to stow them inside dressers, and left the bags containing toothpaste and shampoo for the second trip. I wobbled to the bottom of the stairs and used my elbow to flip on the light switch.

The ornate pine stairway gleamed when the light flickered to life, illuminating the spotless treads. There wasn't a speck of dust in sight, which seemed odd.

Everything about this house was over the top, and even the individual rungs on the banister had been handcrafted to resemble the twisting vines of ivy.

But every house, no matter how ornate, was subject to the forces of changing seasons. It was September 19th, and this time of year the miller moths made their biennial pilgrimage through Killdeer Valley in droves.

Normally, all the homes in the vicinity would be inundated with the corpses of the gray insects. It was almost like the moths all reached their expiration date at the same time each week, and a big house like this should have been littered with them.

But I didn't see a single dead miller moth anywhere. It was almost as if the entire place had recently been scrubbed.

The heavy bags bit into my fingers, and as I put my foot on the first step I froze when I heard the unmistakable sound of a dog barking.

Hearing a dog bark in Killdeer wasn't unusual. It happened all the time. The fact that someone's dog was barking wasn't what had made me stop dead where I stood.

It was the fact that it had come from inside.

CHAPTER 5

I dropped both bags of clothes to the floor and backed away from the stairs quietly.

Dogs couldn't turn doorknobs, so there was only one way it could have gotten inside one of the upstairs bedrooms.

I was not alone.

Both my father and I had been all over the first level of the house, but out of sheer carelessness we hadn't bothered to check anywhere else.

In spite of everything that had happened so far, I forced myself to stay calm and think.

Could the two men from Chicago have found me somehow? That didn't make much sense. They hadn't had a dog with them, and how could they possibly have known I would be here?

There had to be another explanation.

Trying to keep my head clear, I headed back to the kitchen and flipped on the light switch.

My eyes fell on the pristine coffeepot on the counter. Not a speck of dust marred its black surface.

For the first time I noticed that the entire kitchen was spotless. Not just the countertops, but also the floors, the sink, everything, had been cleaned so recently that everything gleamed.

I wasn't frightened any longer. That feeling was quickly being replaced by another emotion altogether.

There wasn't a garage for the house, but it did have a massive back yard that was large enough for a barrel racing competition, and with a growing sense of anger I marched to the back door and flipped on the outside floodlight.

As I peered through the window on the kitchen door my stomach flipped with shock when I saw a pearl-white sedan parked in the back yard, hidden behind the house. It would have been invisible from the road, and there was no way we would have seen it driving in. If only I had taken the time to simply look outside . . .

I unlocked the back door and went to examine the car.

I didn't even need to look at the license plates. I knew where it was from. The floodlight from the back porch shone inside the car, a sleek Cadillac, and inside the back seat I could see a well-worn spot where a dog had spent a great deal of time. Dog hair and mud were smattered on the dark leather and nose prints dotted the window.

Fuming, I stomped back inside and slammed the door behind me. I took the stairs two at a time, and marched down the hall leading to the master bedroom just as I heard the sound of frantic rummaging coming from behind the closed door.

The dog barked again. Someone shushed him with a hiss.

I didn't bother to knock. Pressing my ear against the wood, I distinctly heard the sounds of someone scrambling around inside the bedroom. The click of high heels on the hardwood floor let me know that the person inside was definitely a woman.

The click-clack of heels came to an abrupt halt behind the door. She was hoping to hide behind it and surprise me.

That was her second mistake.

Her first mistake was being there in the first place, because I was not in the mood for this.

Slowly, quietly, I turned the doorknob until the catch released. Then I put my shoulder against the wood and shoved as hard as I could.

Virginia Gable squealed when the heavy oak door crashed into her.

She yelped with alarm and struggled to push it back but I had her pinned and I wasn't about to let her go.

Saint Christopher, her Welsh corgi, barked and nipped at my ankles, trying to herd me away from his mistress.

"Easy, boy," I said.

He darted back and forth, barking and nipping at my feet, but I knew he wouldn't bite me. Saint Christopher and I went way back. I was a better friend with him, by far, than I was with his owner.

"Hello, Virginia."

"Marley, you're crushing me!"

A perfectly manicured hand slid around the edge of the door and I could see her pushing with all her might. But I'd spent my entire young adult life bucking hay bales and slinging saddle tack, and even though I was only average in size, Virginia was no match for me in strength.

"Toss out the wrench, or the hammer, or whatever weapon you happen to have," I told her.

"I don't have any weapon," she said.

My response to that was to shove even harder on the door.

"Alright! Alright," she said.

I eased up on the door just enough to give her room for one arm.

To my astonishment, something that looked like a hot pink electric shaver clattered to the floor and bounced a few feet away. I squinted to get a closer look and realized it wasn't a shaver at all.

"Is that a Taser, Virginia?" I asked.

"Do you have any idea the sort of people who are after me?" she asked.

I gave the door one last shove for good measure before stepping back and letting her out. "Yeah, I think I have a pretty good idea."

She was rubbing her wrist with one hand when she came out and trudged over to the bed. She plopped down on the mattress and gave me a sullen look. Saint Christopher immediately sat at her feet, both ears plastered down and head bent.

She absently scratched him, looking almost as dejected.

"So how long have you been hiding out here at Paul's?" I scooped up the Taser and shoved it in my back pocket.

"You should be careful with that thing," she said. "I practiced shooting it at my sofa and accidentally lit it on fire."

"Have you accidentally lit anything else on fire today?" I asked.

She glanced up, her face pinched. "What are you talking about?"

"Someone burned down my house. Leif's house. Our house."

Her eyes bulged with what appeared to be genuine astonishment. "They did? Marley, that's terrible."

I studied her expression. She looked shocked, and sympathetic. Which immediately made me suspicious. "Terrible. Right."

Virginia sat up straight and her lips curled back. "Why are you looking at me like that? You don't think I had anything to do with it?"

"I'd never dream of it." Mock sincerity dripped in my tone.

She glared at me for a full minute before standing up and smoothing the front of her white pencil skirt. She wore a red silk top and her heels perfectly matched the shade of the blouse. Probably, she dyed the shoes to match. She straightened her gleaming white blazer and gave me a look of disdain.

"It's after Labor Day," I told her.

She glanced down at her white outfit. "I had to leave Chicago in a hurry, alright?"

"I know." My voice was heavy with meaning.

She looked over the top of her nose condescendingly. "What do you mean, you know? How could you possibly know that?"

"Because your loan sharks came to see me at the house today." My face was heating up.

Instead of growing pale with worry or fear, Virginia frowned and her eyes narrowed to slits. "What did they look like?"

"One was big and fat, the other just big. They both had a lot of gold jewelry and the fat man called the big man Bobby."

"Bobby and Gino. What did you say to them?"

"Gino? You borrowed money from a guy named Gino?"

She gave a snort. "I borrowed money from Mr. Theo Thompson. Give me a break, would you? And what did you say to them?"

"I told them you weren't home. I told them you were out shopping," I said.

"Marley, that was an incredibly stupid thing to do. Now they think I am here in Killdeer." Her eyes were flashing.

"And exactly how else was I supposed to get them out of my living room?" I asked.

She clamped her mouth shut and smoothed a stray strand of perfectly bleached blonde hair back into place.

Since it looked like she was doing the best she could to compose herself and control her temper, it seemed like the appropriate time for me to do the same. I eased myself wearily down on a desk chair and took a calming breath. The matching desk was tastefully decorated with a lovely stained glass lamp, and I tossed the Taser beside it. Of course Virginia would buy a weapon that was pink.

Virginia eased down on the bed and neatly folded her hands in her lap. "So, where is Leif right now?"

I rubbed my temples, trying to fight off the burgeoning headache. "On his way back as we speak."

She looked slightly relieved by this, and I let my forehead fall into my hand while I tried to quell my urge to choke her.

"You know, it's not going to take them very long to figure out what happened to you," I said.

Virginia and I had never gotten along. I'd known her for a little over five years, but I'd always known her as Leif's wife. Now that I was Leif's wife, and she was officially the ex–Mrs. Gable, I was having difficulty coming to terms with the situation.

Virginia had always struck me as haughty, aloof and cold. But as I sat across from her looking at the way she forced herself to sit beauty-pageant straight with one eye on the door and the other on me, I could see that she was a shell of the woman I had once known.

One hand shook slightly, and her usually perfect makeup was smudged. Even the tailored clothes she wore hung on her like she was a coatrack. She'd recently lost several pounds and she looked hollow. Her bluster was all cover.

Virginia wasn't the barracuda I'd once known. Now she looked more like the worm on the hook.

I stood up and handed her Taser back. She blinked with surprised, but she took it and reached for an ample designer handbag on the nightstand. She slid the pink Taser inside wordlessly, not looking at me.

"Virginia," I said. "How long have you been here? It's sort of important."

Defeated, she allowed herself a moment of weakness and rubbed the back of her neck. "Three days."

"The house looks great," I said, feeling ridiculous the moment I said it.

"There was nothing else to do but tidy the place up," she confessed. "No TV. No Internet. I don't even have my cell phone."

"Why not?"

"I was afraid that if I had it, someone might be able to use it to find me," she said.

"So why are you dressed like you are going to a job interview?" I asked.

Her face was rigid with stress but her outfit was chic, as usual.

She pouted a bit, but after hesitating for only a moment she shrugged. "I knew that Leif was going to be in Billings tonight. I was going to leave earlier to try and catch him, but that's when you showed up. I had to hide up here instead."

"You aren't in touch with Scott, are you?" I asked.

Scott was Virginia's son, and Leif's stepson. The kid worried about Virginia like a parent.

"No. I called the attorney Leif uses in Billings, and he let it slip. I thought that if I could just have a minute to talk to him alone maybe I could get some advice."

"And perhaps some cash," I said.

She had the decency not to protest. "I'm in a lot of trouble."

"How much trouble? You could sell that nice Cadillac in the back yard," I suggested.

"I'm in a lot more trouble than one lousy car can dig me out of," she said.

Saint Christopher had curled at Virginia's feet and his tired eyes were starting to droop. Suddenly his ears perked up and he bounced to his feet.

Before either of us could slow him down, the corgi dashed down the stairs barking.

I followed him at a sprint and saw Virginia dash after me, digging frantically inside her handbag.

When I got to the bottom of the stairs Saint Christopher had both paws up on the front door and was barking excitedly. Cautiously I peered through the window, and saw, to my immense relief, that Leif was standing on the front porch peering back. He smiled when he saw me.

The moment I opened the front door and he saw the corgi his face registered stunned amazement.

It took him about half a second to process what he was seeing. He came inside and set his briefcase down carefully, and rubbed his forehead with a grimace. "Where is she?"

I jerked my head towards the top of the stairs.

Saint Christopher was bouncing at his feet wildly. The corgi was so happy to see Leif again that he was impossible to ignore. "Yes, yes," Leif said, bending to pet the wiggling dog. "I see you."

Saint Christopher rolled on his back and gratefully accepted a deep scratching.

Virginia came gliding down the stairs in a choreographed sweeping entrance.

She stopped beside Leif and gave him a winning smile, then bent forward and pecked his cheek before he could take a step back.

"It's good to see you," she said.

I felt my jaw muscles tighten seeing her cozy up to him with so much familiarity.

Leif took one look at my tight expression and pivoted away to close the front door. "Ginni. We need to have a talk."

His pet name for her had always been Ginni.

He shot me an apologetic look. "Let's all sit down first," he said, cringing as the three of us made our way to the living room.

He was obviously not very happy to see her.

I pulled the long drop cloth from the sofa and sat beside Leif.

Virginia removed a cloth from one of the leather chairs. The three of us sat down, like grown-ups, to discuss the problem.

As she eased herself onto the chair gracefully, I glanced down at my appearance and felt my confidence wane considerably.

I was still dressed in the same filthy rags I'd worn to clean the house that morning, and every inch of me was stained with soot and I looked like a true ragamuffin.

Virginia, on the other hand, was the picture of perfect. I couldn't help but think about the contrast between the two of us.

Virginia cast a forlorn look at Leif as she sat primly in the chair.

It took all my strength not to knock her to the floor and put my foot on her neck.

"Ginni," Leif began with obvious strain. He was looking at her with an expression of utter disappointment. "You have managed to make a true mess of things this time."

"Listen, I can explain," she said hastily.

He held up a hand and stopped her. "No, you can't. I am not interested in hearing it in any case. Your irresponsible behavior has cost me dearly, and I was greatly tempted to let you swing in the wind."

She dropped her chin and if I didn't know better, I would have sworn she was suppressing tears.

He sighed and shook his head as if to clear it. "But for the sake of Scott, I've agreed to make this right. The telephone number you gave to my attorney turned out to be legitimate, and I've offered Mr. Thompson an amount I believe he will be agreeable to accepting."

She stood up and made a move to hug him, but he lifted one hand. "Don't be grateful. The next time there is a problem like this, you will be on your own. I am not going to be available to dig you out of any more holes."

She slumped into the chair. "I understand."

It was like watching a father scold a teenage daughter who had snuck out of the house.

Realization dawned on me, and in a flash I understood deeply why it was that Leif had been attracted to me.

I suddenly didn't feel so self-conscious about my appearance. Virginia may have been adept at matching blouses to shoes, but when it came to day-to-day living, she was a mess.

"These next few days are going to be critical," Leif said. "And you coming to Killdeer has made this much, much more complicated. Ginni, I dearly wish you would have gone to D.C. instead but there is nothing I can do about that now. Since you had the poor judgment to come here, I don't have any other choice but to take immediate action."

"I didn't know what else to do," Virginia said, crestfallen.

Leif's jaw hardened. "So you decided to bring your troubles here and in so doing endanger Marley with your selfish actions? You had to know that coming back to Killdeer would lead anyone who was looking for you straight to my home."

"It used to be our home. I thought it was so far out of the way nobody would be able to find me." Her lower lip actually quivered.

He pinched the ridge of his nose with two fingers, looking exhausted. "In any case, it is my problem to deal with now, and I realize the solution I have will not be very agreeable to everyone, but we don't have any other choice."

I put a reassuring hand on his arm and gave it a squeeze. "Whatever you decide to do, I will back you up one hundred percent."

He gave me a faint, grateful smile.

Virginia watched the gesture and her lips tightened noticeably.

"We have all had a very long day," Leif said, getting to his feet. "I need to leave in three days to meet with Mr. Thompson and tomorrow we need to decide what we will do in the meantime."

"Three days?" Virginia asked.

"These things take time." Leif's piercing blue eyes practically shot sparks, and I could tell he was almost at the end of his patience.

She shrugged one shoulder. "Just transfer him the money. It can't be that difficult."

His mouth tightened. "In order to make this payment I will be required to fling money across two continents and an island. It is complex."

"I don't understand why you can't write him a check," she said.

"Virginia, please try not to be an idiot for one second," I said.

She sniffed, her face galloping from anger to resentment. "Fine."

Leif's eyes looked more exhausted than I had ever seen them. He stood up and turned towards me, and for a moment I thought he might lose his balance. He wobbled for a moment and leaned the backs of his knees against the sofa to steady himself.

"Are you alright?" I asked, putting a hand on his shoulder.

He offered a weary smile. "Just good and tired."

"We can make some decisions in the morning," I said. "I'll go get your laptop from the car."

He looked at me with an overwhelming expression of relief. "I don't suppose there is anything to eat?"

"You won't believe the junk my father piled into the shopping cart," I told him. "It's a teenager's dream come true in the freezer. Ice cream, pizza and cinnamon rolls in a tube."

Virginia moped past us as she went upstairs wordlessly.

Saint Christopher glanced between her and Leif for a moment, and then bounded after her. When she had gone into the far bedroom at the end of the hall and closed the door, lugging a suitcase, Leif wrapped one arm around my shoulders and crushed me to him.

"I am so sorry, sweetheart. This didn't have to happen. I blame myself."

I squeezed him back and leaned my head against his chest gratefully. "It's not your fault. Honestly, you have managed to handle this a lot better than me. When I caught her hiding here in the house I pinned her behind the door in the bedroom and almost broke her wrist."

He leaned back and gave me a look of admiration. "Remind me never to sneak up on you."

He retrieved his briefcase and headed for the kitchen while I went outside and dug his laptop out of the SUV.

We spent the next hour brainstorming, eating cookies and talking logistics. After careful deliberation, the two of us decided not to make any concrete plans until morning. We were both too tired and mentally strained to think clearly.

The linens were a bit dusty, but otherwise the bedroom was made up like a five-star hotel.

We went to bed early, gratefully pulling back the sheets on the king-sized four-poster, and the second Leif put his head on the pillow he was asleep.

It took me over an hour before I started to drift off. The day had been so chaotic it felt like it wasn't quite real.

But the worst part of it was the fact that Leif's ex-wife was sleeping less than fifty feet away.

My mind kept replaying the scowl she had shot Leif before she'd left the living room.

Once he had agreed to help her, all pretense of apologetic behavior had vanished.

I was starting to think that giving her back that hot pink Taser had been a bad idea.

CHAPTER 6

Saint Christopher barked me awake with frantic doggie alarm sounds and in a flash I was out of the bed and racing down the stairs before I realized where I was. The corgi spun circles at the front door, barking angrily. Whoever was on the other side, he didn't know them.

It was chilly in the house and the cool air snapped me fully awake. The sun was up, so it had to be at least six, but still too dark to be much later. It was a bit early for visitors.

A loud knock on the front door startled me, but Saint Christopher's barking had already alerted whoever it was that someone was home.

I had the good sense to stop myself before opening the door. "Who is it?"

"Hey? When did you get a dog?"

I blinked with surprise. The voice was intimately familiar. "Allen?"

When I pulled open the door, my ex-husband stood on the porch, both thumbs looped through his belt. He craned his neck through the opening until he spotted the corgi. "Hey, boy. What's your name?"

Saint Christopher shot through the door. He recognized a dog person when he saw one.

I watched with morbid fascination as my ex-husband bent down to scratch the ears of Leif's ex-wife's dog. Saint Christopher was wary at first, but Allen's childlike adoration of dogs quickly won the corgi over, and soon the two of them were practically wrestling like teenage boys.

"Allen, what are you doing here?" I was standing in the doorway in my pajamas.

"Told you," he said, still scratching the dog playfully. "I need to talk to you."

"Look, I'm sorry I hung up on you. But things are not exactly normal for me right now. Whatever it is you need to say, now isn't the best time."

He stood up, the broad grin on his face relaxing into a more businesslike expression. He was dressed in his Fish and Wildlife shirt and wore his gun belt, so he was apparently on duty. Allen was a game warden from Missoula, but for some reason he had driven all the way down to Killdeer just to see me.

Allen leaned a hand on the door frame. "We came to talk to you in person because, like I said, it's not something that should be said on the phone. Your dad told us you would be up here. Sorry about your house, by the way."

"We?" For one terrible moment I thought he meant Caitlyn, his girlfriend. This scene was on the verge of turning into a soap opera. Had Allen brought his new girlfriend over to meet me for some odd reason? My head was spinning from trying to keep track of all the exes.

"We drove down to Livingston last night and came the rest of the way this morning." He jerked his chin towards the driveway.

Parked beside my SUV was Allen's Montana Fish and Wildlife truck. Sitting in the passenger seat was someone I had never expected to see again for as long as I lived.

"Bruce." My knees nearly buckled at the sight.

My mouth went completely dry and I had to clutch the door handle to keep from wobbling over.

Allen beckoned to the man sitting in his game warden truck, and to my astonishment, my former coworker climbed from the vehicle and walked slowly up the front steps. He stopped a few feet away and tipped his black Stetson. "Marley. It's good to see you."

He looked exactly how he had more than two years ago when I'd walked out of his office for the last time. Still wearing the same scuffed and battered Tony Lama kangaroo boots, the plain white shirt, and the same black jeans that I had always joked made him look like a waiter. The man standing on my front porch was Bruce Duvekot. He had been the criminal investigator at my former job, and he had been my friend.

Until it all went horribly wrong, that is.

I had worked as a manager in the little branch office of the Montana Fish and Wildlife service in Helena for nine years. I'd been fired, blamed for ruining an investigation that had imploded, and my last day on the job had been dramatic, to say the least

Bruce and I had stepped over the lines of propriety time and time again during my tenure there, but not in any sexual way. He and I had never been anything more than friends, in spite of what Allen had believed. No, the lines we crossed had all been professional. Bruce had confided in me when it came to the cases he was investigating. We'd sat for hours discussing logistics, timelines, motives and opportunities of the people Bruce was hoping to bust. To say that he had broken protocol was an understatement. To say that I had been privy to information I legally shouldn't have been was like saying holding up a gas station was a smidgen inappropriate. Bruce had practically told me everything he was working on, when he was working on it.

When a poacher Bruce was close to arresting suddenly left town, hid or destroyed all of the evidence that had been on his property, and vanished without a trace, my friendship with Bruce suddenly came under intense scrutiny. Our office consisted of only five people. We'd all become close, and the regional office management decided Bruce and I had become too close. Particularly in light of the fact that someone

Bruce had been investigating for months had suddenly disappeared right before being arrested. It was obvious someone in our tiny office had tipped him off. Or made a tragic mistake. Either way, there would be no happy ending.

One of us had to go.

Since Bruce had a wife and two kids to support, when word of an internal investigation of our office hit the newswire, I'd submitted a letter of resignation. It took me five minutes that afternoon to clean out my desk, and empty out nine years' worth of memories into a big cardboard box and escort myself off the Fish and Wildlife property. To say that things had ended badly would be kind.

It had been a disaster. My reputation had been shot. I'd slunk back home to Killdeer and accepted charity from my father, and I'd been forced to take a job I hated to make ends meet. It haunted me to this day.

And here was the man who was indirectly responsible for one of the worst chapters in my life, standing on my porch with a face that looked like he had just slammed his hand in a car door.

Bruce stared at me imploringly.

"Want some coffee?" Really, what else could I say?

An obvious wave of relief washed over his face as he gratefully stepped through the open door, black Stetson in hand.

I led them to the kitchen, Saint Christopher padding after us, excited by all the sudden activity.

"When did you get a dog?" Allen asked again, nodding towards the corgi.

"He belongs to Leif's ex-wife," I said.

The two men exchanged a look, but wisely didn't comment.

We ended up standing around the kitchen table, and as I busied myself with the coffeepot the two of them sat down with grim expressions. They didn't say anything. I could see that they were trying to decide who would go first.

They were obviously not here on a social call. Nobody said a word as I started the coffee perking.

"Bruce, how have you been?" I asked conversationally. "The mustache looks good on you."

The investigator glanced up at me, his eyes darting to Allen with concern. "I've been better."

Bruce and I looked so much alike we had constantly been mistaken for brother and sister. We both had strawberry blond hair and green eyes, and we were the same height, almost to the centimeter.

Of course Bruce outweighed me by fifty pounds of muscle, but it had been a running joke around our office that the Fish and Wildlife service would only hire you if you could bring a sibling along.

"Where's your husband?" Allen asked.

At his question, Bruce's eyes widened. It was obviously news to him that I had gotten married.

"He's in bed." I reached for three cups and rummaged in the refrigerator for cream. "He had a rough day yesterday. I don't think he even heard the dog."

I slid coffee in front of Bruce and he wrapped his hands around the cup, looking consoled that he had someplace to put his attention other than on me.

Allen accepted his cup and gulped from it greedily.

"Alright." I eased into a chair. "What's so important that you had to drive all the way down here to say it in person? Did you hear about what happened and you wanted to come check on me or something?"

"You mean, your house burning down?" Allen asked. "We didn't know about that until your dad told us. We went to the ranch house first, looking for you. He told us you were here."

A warning bell went off in my head. Whatever it was they had come to say, neither of them seemed eager to explain. I felt tired all over again.

Honestly, bad news always seemed to travel in packs.

Bruce leaned back and folded his arms across his chest. "I think there are a few things that we need to clear up between us."

I took a sip from my mug. "Okay."

"Marley, I think I owe you an apology," Bruce said. "A big one."

That surprised me. I wasn't sure what to say next and decided the safe thing to do was stick with the classics. "Okay."

"You were not fired from the Fish and Wildlife office," Bruce said. "I told you a lie about that. Officially, as far as management is concerned, you resigned without giving notice."

It was like a tiny earthquake went off down the center of my spine. I looked at Bruce, then to Allen, and back to Bruce with my jaw hanging slack. "What did you say?"

Allen leaned forward and muscled his way into the conversation. "Do you remember back in August when you told me that I didn't know everything that had happened to you when you had gotten fired? And that maybe you wanted to keep that information to yourself so that you wouldn't hurt someone else?"

My cheeks colored at the memory. The conversation with Allen had been a weak moment for me, and I'd been full of self-pity. As usual, Allen and I had been in the middle of a fight, and the phrase had popped out of my mouth before I could stop myself. "I remember."

"I couldn't let that go," Allen said bluntly. "So I went and saw Bruce and asked him what the hell had really happened when you left the office."

"You did what?"

Bruce cut in, lifting a hand between us to stop the argument before it could get started. "No, it was the right thing for him to do."

"How do you figure?" I asked.

Losing my job with the Fish and Wildlife office had been a serious blow to my self-esteem and confidence.

It was still a painful episode from my past and now I was reliving it all over again.

Bruce squared his shoulders and plunged in. "Right after the poacher I was investigating disappeared, you submitted a letter of resignation, and you signed it and gave it to me to give to the main office. Remember? Well, your letter never made it to the main office."

"What are you saying?" I asked.

"I wrote a second letter saying that you were resigning, that your father had recently suffered some debilitating health problems, and you were quitting effective immediately so that you could go back to Killdeer to take care of him. I just told you that I would deliver your letter to the regional supervisor. I didn't. When I took you into my office that day and said that you had been fired, I wasn't exactly being honest."

Bruce froze in his chair when he saw my face. He swallowed hard and leaned back slowly.

My hands clenched into fists. "Since when has my father ever suffered from debilitating health problems?"

My eyes must have shot flames because even Allen held up one hand and spoke softly to me. "Babe, take a breath. Let him finish."

I was so angry I could have chewed nails and spit bullets. "Allen, you gave up the right to call me Babe when you slept with Caitlyn."

"Marley," Bruce said quickly. "I was protecting you."

My voice pitched up an octave. "Protecting me? I was the one protecting you."

"From what?" Bruce demanded. "What did you think you were doing by writing that letter?"

"I thought I was saving your job." My hands were still clenched.

"I thought I was saving you from a criminal investigation," Bruce said, his hands pressed on the tabletop like he was trying to keep it from floating into orbit.

We stared at each other for a moment, both of us breathing like we had just run a three-legged race.

Allen sat up straight, cautiously, and patted the air with his hands. "Now, everyone just calm down."

My teeth made an involuntary grinding noise. "I am calm."

Allen sighed. "We went over this in the truck on the way down here. Bruce, you thought Marley had tipped the poacher off, or that she had maybe inadvertently said something that led to the guy fleeing town and blowing the investigation."

Bruce looked down at his hands and nodded. "I should have known better, but I thought she may have screwed up. I was doing what I could to make it look like she had to leave the job, not like she was running away."

"Marley," Allen said, before I could speak. "You thought that Bruce had made a mess of things, and you were covering up for him and taking the blame."

"Of course I was."

Allen looked back and forth between the two of us. "And it never occurred to you to actually sit down and, oh, I don't know, talk about it?"

We looked away from each other, embarrassed. At least, I felt embarrassed. I had no idea what Bruce was feeling.

I rubbed my eyes. "It was my fault that he confided in me about his cases and I felt plenty guilty about it. I was always hounding him to talk about things that stumped him, to try and work them out between the two of us. You both know I can't leave things well enough alone and I'm always sticking my nose in where it doesn't belong."

"I thought that she would be safe from an investigation if she went back to Killdeer and never showed up in Helena again," Bruce said, looking at Allen with a plaintive expression. "That's why I told her she had been fired. So she would stay away."

Allen shook his head. "You two are pathetic."

Bruce winced, but I wasn't surprised by the remark. Allen never had leaned towards the diplomatic.

"Both of you, just shut up and sit there and listen, alright?" Allen said. "You both screwed up, but good. Only now you've got a real chance to fix it."

A sharp comment sprang to mind, but before I could voice it, Allen pulled a small digital tape recorder out of his shirt pocket and set it on the table between us.

He pointed at me. "Just hit the play button and stop being so damn argumentative."

Reluctantly, I punched the button with my thumb and rotated the volume dial up to full.

A woman's voice, obviously speaking on a cell phone with miserable reception, squawked from the speaker, and I had to strain to understand what she was saying.

Her voice was raspy, like she smoked a pack of cigarettes for lunch every day. She sounded frantic.

Her words came out in a rush. "John Hill went and got his self killed because he couldn't keep his big fat mouth shut."

I sat up instantly.

Allen's eyes flicked from me to the tape recorder but he didn't utter a sound. He'd obviously already heard it and was gauging my reaction.

The woman rasped out a cough. "I thought he was screwing around on me. I put one of those Cheating Husband GPS phones in his saddlebags right before he went out for that three-day thing with the Cottons. Well, John turned up missing. Right? Guess who went over to John's and cleaned out his garage right after that. His partner, that's who. The son of a bitch killed him. I know it."

Sounds of rummaging paper rattled over the tinny speaker.

Her voice continued, shaken. "And why in hell would John's partner go and pour a new slab of concrete out back of that garage two days after he went missing? Huh? It don't make any goddamned sense. He killed John and stuck him under that slab, I'm tellin' ya."

She coughed again, ragged and sharp. A half sob rattled the speaker. "Just . . . just check it out. The phone said 46-03-56 and 110-15-43. That's the numbers it showed when I got the last place it sent from. It went dead after that. That's where John . . . oh God! That son of a bitch killed him up there, I just know it."

The line went dead.

I sat in utter silence, staring at the tape recorder. Both men watched me, waiting.

Finally I looked over at Allen. "Where did you get this?"

"It was left on the poaching tip line at your office."

All of my old inquisitive instincts were going off like a Klaxon. "Why am I just hearing about it now?"

Bruce blushed deep crimson. "Because, ah . . . well. It got lost in the chaos after you quit. You were the one in charge of archiving the tapes from the tip line calls, but the new gal they brought in didn't actually give the recordings to me to screen, she archived them. She thought they had all been gone through, and honestly, the first week after you left, things were wonky."

Allen shrugged. "After you told me you were protecting someone, I went and saw Bruce, and asked if I could have access to all the info concerning John Hill. Since, well, I knew he was the guy you and Bruce were looking at for poaching, right when you quit the office."

"Right after I got supposedly fired," I said.

Bruce shot me an apologetic look. "Sorry."

"Anyway," Allen said impatiently, "that's when this tape turned up."

"But you have no idea who she is?" I asked.

"Not an inkling," Bruce admitted. "Can you place her?"

I shook my head, trying to sift through my tattered memories. "I'll admit, her voice sounds familiar. But I can't put a name to it."

Allen took the recorder and shoved it back in his pocket.

He stared at me pointedly. "So, it looks like your boy Hill didn't pull up stakes and disappear because he thought Bruce was about to punch his ticket. He disappeared because the, and I quote, son of a bitch, killed him."

"Why is this woman leaving something this important on the poaching tip line?" I asked.

"I'm assuming that she is talking about her cheating boyfriend, John Hill," Allen said. "At least, she thought he was cheating. If I was gonna speculate, I'd say she packed his bag with one of those GPS tracking phones that sends out its location every fifteen minutes and downloads it automatically to your e-mail. So he vanishes, right? And those were the last coordinates sent from the phone. Then her boyfriend's partner pours a fresh slab of concrete behind his garage for some odd reason."

"And she guesses that her boyfriend is murdered and buried under that slab," I said.

Bruce continued the narrative. "So she wants to point someone in the right direction, but if this partner of John Hill's is willing to kill him over antler velvet, he'd be willing to kill a woman if she ratted him out. She called the tip line because she knew it would be anonymous."

"Do you realize what this means?" I asked.

Allen laughed bitterly. "You two were so hell-bent on covering up for each other, you didn't do your damn jobs?"

The full weight of my own stupidity pressed down and I felt sick.

"You know what the worst part is?" Allen asked. "Instead of working out what really happened, you two tried to cover up for each other. The solution was staring you right in the face and didn't even see it."

"Well," Bruce said, sounding dejected. "We sure see it now."

CHAPTER 7

Allen let Bruce and me wallow in our self-pity for a full minute before speaking again. Finally he spun his coffee cup around and slid the handle away with nervous energy.

His voice sounded determined. "Fischer Lake."

"What's at Fischer Lake?" I asked.

"Apparently, that's the place John Hill was murdered," he said.

"Is that what she was talking about on the recording?" I asked.

"Yep. The numbers she rattled off were GPS coordinates. The lake is in the high country on the Cotton Ranch in the Cross Fell Range."

I tumbled through my geographical knowledge of the state of Montana and couldn't place it in my head. "Okay, where is it?"

Allen reached behind him and snagged a paper napkin off of the kitchen counter. He opened it and laid it flat in the center of the table.

"We are here, in Killdeer," he said, dipping his finger in his coffee cup and putting a wet dot on the south central section of the napkin. He put another dot higher in the central section of the napkin. "Fischer Lake is here."

I squinted at it. "That's a big mountain range, isn't it? Looks like it's north of the Crazies."

Allen nodded. "It is due north of the Crazies, in Sweet Grass County. There is a lot of territory up there."

The Crazy Mountains were a sprawling stretch of post-card beautiful Montana wildlands that hadn't changed much since Bat Masterson and Wyatt Earp had been kicking around the West. If the Cross Fell Mountains were close to it, then they would be rugged, and untamed. And isolated.

"Is it private land?" I asked.

"It's Forest Service land," Allen said. "There is a grazing lease on the place that is held by Nash and Stephanie Cotton. But it's not going to be theirs for much longer."

"Are they selling the ranch?" I asked, confused.

"Nash Cotton died two summers ago. His widow, Stephanie? She can't keep up with it, from what the local warden told me," Allen said, filling me in. "Stephanie is sixty, and she's tired of it. She is letting the federal grazing lease retire, taking her big fat check from the government, and moving to Scottsdale."

"So, the place where John Hill may have been killed is a working cattle ranch," I said.

Allen grumbled. "If you can call it that. Since Nash died it's been a mess. Bills not paid. Equipment starting to fall apart. Word is the ranch is crumbling slowly and Stephanie is letting it die. The point is, according to the tip from John Hill's girlfriend, whoever she is, we may be looking at the location where he was murdered."

"But you said the partner poured concrete by the garage two days after Hill disappeared," I pointed out.

"Likely, Hill was killed on the mountain, and hidden beneath that slab," Allen said, nodding definitively.

"That's a long way to go just to hide a body," I said.

Allen shook his head. "Not if you have a pack horse."

"What did he do? Smuggle the body out while he was on a guided hunting trip?" I asked.

"More like, I think he was moonlighting," Allen said cautiously.

Bruce and Allen exchanged glances. They could see I was trying to sort it out in my mind. There was still something they weren't telling me, and I could sense their hesitation.

"How could a guy access private land with a horse and a pack mule, and nobody notices him?" I asked.

"Drawing a paycheck," Allen said. "We think he was working for the Cottons. Remember what the woman said? That 'three-day thing with the Cottons'? He was working as a hired hand for the ranch."

"Maybe, moving livestock?" I asked.

"The Cottons' spring cattle drive," Bruce told me.

Allen crumpled the napkin and set it aside. "It was May when John Hill vanished. The Cottons do a spring cattle drive first week of May, every year, like clockwork, and they are in the habit of hiring a string of outside hands, from all walks and stations of life, to work the drive because it's a big job."

Bruce rubbed his chin. It made a rasping sound as his hands played across the stubble. "We think this cattle drive was an excuse to take John Hill out in the middle of nowhere to murder him where nobody would notice the sound of a gunshot and there would be no blood splatter in a living room to worry about. Then the killer rode off the mountain with a pack horse loaded down with a couple hundred pounds of deadweight."

"John Hill was only 5' 9" and was slender," I said, recalling the photos and description of him from his file. "He couldn't have weighed more than one-fifty. He wouldn't be too hard for a big man to wrap up in a tarp and haul up on a mule. Guys do that all the time with field-dressed carcasses, and buck mule deer weigh one-forty, easy."

"I called Stephanie Cotton and found out a few things," Allen said.

"Did you ask Stephanie to give you a list of all their workers who were there in May two years ago?" I asked.

"You gonna let me finish?" Allen snapped.

Bruce dropped his eyes to the table.

I noticed he had been a bit more quiet than usual.

Apparently he and Allen had already come up with some scheme and he was letting Allen do most of the talking.

Allen continued, impatient. "So, as I was saying. Since Nash died two years ago, Stephanie hired a bookkeeper to manage the payroll and such, and all of the old records were dumped. Nash was the only one who knew everybody he hired, and sometimes it was all on a handshake and paid in cash anyway. Stephanie has no idea who her husband had working up there that spring. So that means unless someone goes up there and actually talks to the old hands who were there two years ago, we might not be able to find out the identity of John Hill's partner."

"Well, that's just great," I said.

Allen went on. "So, I made some more calls. The Cottons started their final fall roundup yesterday. They are shorthanded."

Allen's eyes rested on me. His expression was hopeful.

"That so?" I asked. "Imagine the coincidence. The Cotton Ranch is shorthanded and you and Bruce need to find an excuse to go up there and poke around."

"We, ah, we need somebody to go up there and poke around, on our behalf," Bruce said quietly.

Now we were getting to it.

My eyes pivoted between them. "You want me to go up there and work as a hired hand, don't you?"

Allen charged ahead, undaunted. "It wasn't that hard to convince them to hire you. Nobody wants to work the Cross Fell Mountains because of the bears."

"Bears?" I felt a flip-flop in my gut.

One thing Killdeer had plenty of, it was bears. But seeing them from the safety of an automobile all the time didn't necessarily mean you got used to it. A bear getting into your garbage cans was one thing, but having one snuffle around outside a flimsy tent while you cringe inside your sleeping bag was another.

"And you want me to hire on part-time and go up to Fischer Lake to see if I can find who was working the drive when John Hill vanished," I said.

Allen gave a half-smile. "That's the idea."

"Why can't the two of you go up there and work cattle for a few days?" I asked.

"Marley, think about it," Bruce said. "Do you know how busy it's about to get with hunting season coming? I am in the middle of two cases that simply cannot wait. You think I could get permission to go search an area where a murder, may, or may not have been, committed? It's not possible."

"Don't you want to see if my theory is right?" Allen asked.

"It's not a very good idea to have a former employee working an investigation," I pointed out.

Allen tilted his head back and forth. "Not an investigation. More like a fact-finding mission."

"John Hill is probably buried underneath the concrete outside his old garage back in Helena," Bruce said. "I am working on getting a warrant, and in a week or so we will have found his body. But it would be helpful if we could find some evidence of the location where the murder was committed, and that tip on the hotline sounded credible to me. But it's a long shot and I know that. Probably, you won't find a damn thing. However, if we could get a list of names of the cowboys who were up there two years ago, we could start running background checks and try to determine who Hill's partner was. That will be some valuable information for us to have."

It all made sense, in a depressing sort of way.

I thought about the two men who had stalked into my house the day before and then burned it to the ground just to send a message. I thought about the pained look on Leif's face when he had come home and been forced to deal with Virginia's problems, knowing I had been at risk because of her. And I thought about the strain it was putting on him, wondering what would happen next. Wondering if I would be safe or if I would be caught in the cross fire between him and his ex-wife.

"I'll do it." The words popped out before I could stop myself.

Both men stared at me.

I looked up, determined. "I'll do it. How hard can it be?"

Allen heaved a relieved sigh. "This will help us, Marley. It might give us the name we need. All you have to do is take a look around the lake. If there is anything that stands out, you can mark the spot and we can come back to it later. Because, really, what are the chances that you will find anything?"

Bruce reiterated. "You search the area around Fischer Lake. Note anything important, and then you get out. While you are there, ask around and write down the names of the men who worked the drive two years ago."

"You won't be alone," Allen told me. "Todd Ramsey is already signed up to meet you there."

I swiveled my head towards Allen with confusion. "Todd Ramsey, the brand inspector? How in the world did you get him to volunteer?"

Allen looked smug. "He wants to get appointed to the Livestock Loss Board, and he will do anything to make himself look like he cares about ranchers. Since Stephanie is letting her grazing lease expire I told him it would look good on his résumé if he was up there for the last roundup on the Cotton Ranch."

"Does he have any idea why you really want him to go up there?" I asked, suspicious.

Allen flapped a hand impatiently. "He is also a Search and Rescue volunteer. And yeah, of course he knows. I wouldn't send him into a situation without details. Todd is six-two and could kill a bull elephant with a slingshot and a Twinkie. I'm not worried about it."

Todd Ramsey was a legend in Killdeer Valley. He was so strong he'd never been in a fistfight in his entire life. Even stupid people weren't stupid enough to tangle with Todd.

"I could just ask him to pick up the corner of the mountain and then I could look underneath it for shotgun shells," I said.

Bruce chuckled. "I was against sending you up there when Allen first suggested it. But when I found out who would be going with you, I changed my mind. Anyone would be comfortable sending his wife on the mountain if Ramsey is looking out for her."

"Ex-wife, unless there is something Marley needs to tell me," said Leif quietly. He stood in the hallway behind us with a slightly amused expression.

I clambered to my feet. "Did we wake you?"

Leif shook his head. "No, no. The dog managed to get inside the bedroom and hopped up on the bed. He was my own personal four-legged alarm clock. Now, maybe while I have some coffee you could explain to me why you three are discussing sending you someplace."

As Leif pulled open three cabinet doors searching for cups, I lifted the coffeepot and held it ready. When he finally managed to locate the dishes in the unfamiliar kitchen, I poured him a cup from what was left in the pot and explained everything that Allen had revealed to us.

Leif took it all in, nodding, not interrupting. I told him the details carefully, and halfway through the explanation it occurred to me that I hadn't bothered to introduce Leif to Allen and Bruce. Well, they'd figure it out.

I wondered what they made of my new husband. I had always thought Leif resembled Yul Brynner, in a suit. Finally, after I had explained it all, he slowly set his cup on the counter and crossed his arms over his chest. "How long would this cattle drive take?"

Bruce started to protest, but Allen waved him into silence. "Three or four days."

"And it's something you feel comfortable doing?" Leif asked, holding me with his steel blue eyes.

I shrugged one shoulder casually. "I've done four cattle drives in the past. There is nothing to them. To tell you the truth, they can be mind-numbingly boring."

"This drive is taking place in a remote area? Difficult to find?" Leif asked.

"Way off the map," Allen said.

"It might help solve our more immediate problem," Leif said, giving me a knowing look.

"I suggested that I go," I said quickly.

"You would have to take Ginni," he told me.

My face fell. I'd forgotten all about Virginia.

"Ginni," Bruce said, glancing between Leif and me.

"My ex-wife has come to stay with us for a few days," Leif explained wearily. "She might enjoy some fresh air."

Allen and Bruce looked at each other, daring the other to ask the obvious question.

I cut in before either one of them could blurt out something tactless. "Can she ride?"

"She has experience with English saddles only, but she is capable," Leif said.

"I'm not sure how the foreman will react to having a second person show up, unannounced, but as hard as it's been to hire good hands I would bet he'll be grateful," Allen said.

Bruce looked slightly doubtful, but didn't say anything.

"As long as Marley has no objection, I'm in favor of it," Leif said.

I wanted to find some reason not to take her, but seeing the tired look in Leif's eyes stopped me from arguing.

I gave him an encouraging smile. "It will be fine."

At that moment Virginia walked down the hallway trailing her Welsh corgi, and stopped when she saw the four of us crowding the kitchen.

Allen took one look at her standing there with her perfect blonde hair disheveled artfully, a pair of fluffy slippers on her feet, wearing a wisp of a silk nightie barely covering the important bits, and immediately let his mouth have full rein.

"Geez, Gable. What are you, Mormon or something?"

I kicked at him underneath the table as hard as I could. But my bare foot managed to miss Allen's ankle entirely and landed squarely on the chair leg instead.

Leif barley registered a smirk at the comment, choosing instead to ignore it.

"Nobody ever needs to remind me why I divorced you, Allen," I said.

Virginia glared at the lot of us for a moment. Then she shrugged and padded to the coffeepot, which had the dregs of a half-cup left. She poured what remained into a handy water glass and gulped it in two long swallows.

"Ginni, I'd like you to meet Marley's ex-husband. Allen . . . Hunter is it?" Leif began.

Allen leapt to his feet to extend his hand. Virginia sneered like it was slightly less repulsive than a dead snake. She did not bother to shake it.

Her tone was caustic. "It's a pleasure to make your acquaintance."

"I'm Bruce Duvekot," the investigator said, reaching up reflexively to tip a hat that he wasn't currently wearing.

Half-naked women seem to possess some sort of strange power over men. At least Leif appeared immune to Virginia's lack of clothing.

Then I recalled it was probably because he had seen it all already. I had to suppress my glare.

It was Leif who broke the spell. "Gentlemen, I need to get to work on a few things. But, before you leave, could you please see to it that I have all of your contact information, and could you let me have the phone numbers I will need to be in touch with the ranch where Ginni and Marley will be staying for the next few days?"

"I'll run to my truck and get all that," Allen said, casting one last forlorn look at Virginia and nearly walking into the wall as he tried to make it to the hallway.

I hated to admit it, but Virginia was beautiful. Too bad she was not busy being beautiful six or seven time zones away from Montana.

"Are you putting us up at a resort for the week?" Virginia asked, looking at Leif with doe-eyed sweetness.

"You are not going to a resort," he replied, a sharp note in his voice.

"Oh. Well, I'm sure it will be fine, whatever it is," she said.

"Marley, could I see you in my office?" he said, turning away from her and studying the hallway. "Ah, where, exactly is the office?"

I walked with him back to the living room and instead of turning towards the stairs I veered to the left and led Leif through a tall doorway. I'd seen the inside of the house, top to bottom, by now. The layout of the rooms was now clear in my mind.

It wasn't as large as Leif's former office had been, but it was well lit with large windows looking out towards tall pine trees. The desk was ridiculously ornate. Oak, with multiple drawers and slots, a rolltop cover and carved trim. His old desk had been practical. This one was striking.

Leif eased himself down on a brown corduroy love seat and rubbed his forehead with one hand. It took him a moment to speak, and he seemed to be thinking about what he wanted to say. When his tired eyes met mine, I was surprised at just how exhausted he still looked. Well, the day before had been a terrible experience for both of us, after all.

"Yesterday was a bit of a disaster," he said. "I think you need an explanation. No doubt, the men who came to see you wanted to make sure I got the message about Ginni. I feel terrible that this happened, and I'm sorry."

I sat beside him and scooped up his hand in both of mine. "Don't apologize. It wasn't your fault. And look. I saved my wedding ring."

I held up my left hand to show him that I was still wearing the beautiful platinum band he'd given me.

He gave me a bright smile and kissed my knuckles. "You are forever the optimist."

"I'm more the type to see the world for what it is, not the way I want it to be. Getting upset isn't going to help you, and all it will do is make me miserable. We've got a problem. Let's look at how to solve it."

The look he gave me nearly broke my heart. He seemed so relieved, and grateful.

"This changes things. Sending you to a remote location in the mountains is a very good idea." He squeezed my hand tight. "I'm confident the two of you will be impossible to find where you are going, and it will allow me to resolve this money issue without worry. I will go to Chicago today and try to get this over with as quickly as I am able. Can you handle getting Ginni ready for this trip by yourself? She can be difficult sometimes, and I wouldn't normally ask this of you, but we seem to have been handed an opportunity to take you both out of harm's way while I work out a resolution."

It stuck in my throat, but I managed to say the words. "I can handle it. We will need to get her some real clothes and a useful pair of boots. But, if it's like every other cattle drive I've ever been on, the food is provided."

"Marley, after all of this is over you won't ever have to worry about dealing with an issue like this again. But, for the time being, let's just concentrate on getting through this next week and after I am home we will set down some rules for how to put up some barriers between us and Ginni."

"I couldn't agree with you more. But right now, don't worry about Virginia or me. She will be a pain in the neck but I'd bet that she will find a way to make the best of it."

She would, or I'd wring her neck.

A shadow of concern crossed his face and he draped one arm around my shoulders. "This situation with your vanished poacher won't be something I will need to be worried about, will it?"

My intuition said otherwise, but my pride took over before my brain could engage. "You won't need to worry."

"Because if this really is a homicide, my better judgment would be that you avoid it," he said.

I wanted to be truthful, but I also wanted to get to the bottom of what had happened to John Hill, and in the process, finally put the rumors about my incompetence to rest once and for all. But more than that, I couldn't stand the thought someone might have been killed and the death had gone unnoticed because of a blatant mistake on my part. This was an opportunity for me to right a terrible wrong. I wasn't about to miss it.

My smile was a bit forced, but I wanted to say what I thought would sound reassuring. "Honestly, the chances that I will find anything up on that mountain are remote. It's probably pointless for me to even be looking around at this lake in the first place. You don't need to worry. The guy disappeared well over two years ago, and most likely he is buried underneath that concrete slab up in Helena. And besides, I'll be surrounded by a dozen men on horses with guns, and in a situation like that you'd have to be crazy to make trouble."

"If you are sure, then," he said.

I gave him a kiss on the cheek and squeezed his hand. "What's the worst that could happen?"

The look he shot me said it all.

CHAPTER 8

"We're lost."

I shot a piercing glare at Virginia, but decided to keep my mouth shut.

The sun was dipping alarmingly low behind the rugged mountain range, painting long shadows over the dirt road and casting the pine trees in a pale gold glow.

A jackrabbit sped across the road and I tapped the brakes once to give him a chance to make it to the safety of the thick sagebrush.

Virginia and I had been driving for several hours, and her sour attitude was wearing me down. The isolation and tough terrain weren't making the trip any easier.

Allen's hand-drawn map sat in my lap, and we bounced across a long stretch of washboard road so rough it rattled my teeth, and I nearly dropped it.

I snatched the map with my left hand before it could slide underneath the seat and steered the battered truck back to the center of the road.

"You have no idea where we are." Virginia looked at me over the top of her movie-star sunglasses.

"We took I-90 east and we just got off 191 at the junction," I said. "We are not lost."

"Can't this thing go any faster?" she asked, her pout extending from me to include the old pickup truck I was struggling to drive.

"It can, but then we would both need to have our kidneys replaced," I replied, wishing that she would focus on something other than how bad everything was.

"Where did you get this piece of junk, anyway?"

My patience was almost gone. "It's my father's old truck. Remember? It was your idea that we use a car other than your Cadillac. So we wouldn't draw attention to ourselves."

I looked down at her outfit.

Virginia caught me looking at her. "What?"

"Where did you get those boots, anyway?" I asked.

"They're Coach."

"They're useless," I said.

"They cost over four hundred dollars," she snapped.

"And they might last ten minutes on a cattle drive."

She made a point of using her middle finger to shove her sunglasses back up on the bridge of her nose and turned away to stare out the passenger window. Her straw cowboy hat was an expensive Stetson, but since it was late September and we were going to be at an altitude of around six or seven thousand feet, it wouldn't do much good. She should have gotten a snow hat with big fuzzy ear covers instead.

"How much longer until we get to the ranch?" Virginia asked.

"We aren't going to the ranch. We are meeting them at the base camp," I explained.

"What if I need to use the restroom?"

I waved a hand around, indicating the landscape that was so isolated even the coyotes needed a GPS. "Find a bush. It's not like anybody is going to see you."

At least I'd been able to talk her into buying a decent heavy coat and a couple pairs of blue jeans. The fuzzy sweater she was wearing had to be angora. It was pearl white.

She leaned an arm on the backrest and glanced in the bed of the pickup. "Saint Christopher needs to stop so I can give him a drink."

I had no idea what the foreman of the cattle drive would say about having a Welsh corgi show up without permission, but I figured that was Virginia's problem.

All I knew was that Todd Ramsey, the skyscraper-tall brand inspector from Killdeer, was supposed to be there and that he was expecting Allen to send someone up to the base camp to meet him with instructions. Allen had filled me in on the few details he had given to Todd, and the operative word was few. The only information the big brand inspector had was he might be searching for a missing person, but he should keep the information to himself and not share it with anyone on the ranch crew. A sharp feeling of dread washed over me when I thought about what Virginia and I were really supposed to be doing up on the rugged mountain, but the fact that Todd would be there, and would be on our side, gave me comfort.

"There will be a creek at the base camp," I told Virginia. "Saint Christopher can get a drink then."

"It's almost dark. Are you sure you know where you are going?" she asked.

I reached down and pulled the knob that lit up the headlights and didn't bother to reply.

According to Allen's map, the base camp would be about a half-hour drive from the third cattle guard, and we had crossed the third cattle guard twenty minutes ago. I had to put up with complaints from my passenger for another ten minutes and then I would get a merciful break. I wondered idly if Saint Christopher would like to ride in the cab while I put Virginia in the truck bed.

"Listen," I said, turning to look at Virginia so she could see I was deadly serious. "We cannot talk about the real reason we are here."

"Well, really Marley. It's a little embarrassing for me. It's not like I will be blabbing about it to a bunch of strangers," she said defensively.

"I'm not talking about Bobby and Gino and your money problems," I said. "You cannot talk about the fact that we will be searching for evidence of a crime while we are at Fischer Lake."

She blinked at me a few times with no expression, and I wondered if she ever bothered to register the problems suffered by the little people.

"If anybody asks, I will just say I'm your cousin," she said, repeating the story we had agreed upon. "From Denver."

I looked at her French manicured fingernails and pearl earrings and it was all I could do to keep from groaning. "Yeah, they'll believe you are from Denver."

I slowed the truck as we nosed over the crest of a sharp hill. As we rolled down the other side of the steep road I caught sight of what I'd been hoping to see. A brightly burning campfire sparked and flickered through the dim twilight with at least a half dozen shadows circled around. For one brief terrible flash I was reminded of the wall of flames that had chased me down the stairs when my house had burned down only thirty hours ago. I shook off the memory and concentrated on slowing down my father's battered pickup truck. A short row of vehicles was parked side by side well away from the campfire, and I pulled up beside the last truck, parked and killed the engine.

As soon as I slammed the door Saint Christopher was clamoring at the sides of the truck bed to be let out. He had never been allowed to ride in the back of a truck before, and he'd been so excited about the trip we had tied him in so he wouldn't get carried away and jump out. He wiggled with glee when I started to undo the rope, positively bursting with happiness at being included in the adventure.

Well, at least one of us was having a good time.

Virginia shouldered me aside. "Let me do it."

I bent to retrieve our sleeping bags and the huge duffle containing our gear.

I hefted the huge duffle and both arms strained. "What the heck did you put in here?" It had to weigh almost seventy pounds.

"Just the essentials," she said.

Saint Christopher was free. He tore out of the truck and hit the ground running.

I had noticed a portable corral not very far away from the campfire, but I hadn't seen any cows in it yet so I figured it was safe for him to have a run around and explore the place.

"You must be Allen," said an unfamiliar voice.

When I spun around in the fading light, a young man, a very young man, was staring back.

He balked when he saw me. "You are not Allen at all."

His thick yellow hair made him look like an Iowa farm boy, and in the last wisp of light I saw that his teeth glinted with silver. He was wearing a set of top and bottom dental braces.

I wiped my hand on my jeans and held it out. "I'm Marley."

"Samuel." He shook my hand with surprising strength. "Allen said he would be here to meet up with the crew, but, that must have changed?"

"Allen said he would be here?" I began. "Uh, yeah. That's changed. It's not going to be possible for him to make it."

Samuel was obviously disappointed, which confused me, because I'd been under the impression the only person who had been in contact with Allen was Todd Ramsey. Who was this kid and how did he know about Allen? Something wasn't right.

"Has the brand inspector gotten here yet?" I asked.

Samuel cleared his throat. "Todd sent me instead."

We stared at each other for a moment while the weight of the situation started to sink in.

"Instead?" I said.

Samuel laughed, but it wasn't the sort of laugh that inspired a lot of confidence in me. "He couldn't make it either."

Virginia stepped forward with a gleaming smile. "Hi."

Samuel looked at her, and his eyes rotated back towards me. "Are you kidding me? Come on. Where is Allen?"

Virginia stood next to the kid with her hand held out. When it became clear he wasn't going to shake it, she let it drop to her side and proceeded to ignore him.

"You are not getting Allen," I told him again. "It's just me and her. So, why isn't Todd Ramsey here?"

Samuel quirked half a smile. "He got kicked by a steer. Broke his tibia. Or, fibula, or something."

I dropped my sleeping bags on the ground, feeling a wave of dread wash over me. "Did he tell you anything about this trip? Anything, oh, I don't know, helpful?"

Samuel squinted at me. "He said that Allen would tell me everything I needed to know."

Barks and squeals of terror shattered the stillness and a beige shape ran towards us. Saint Christopher burst out of the clearing and tore past as he sprinted to the truck.

The tailgate was still down and in one herculean leap the corgi lunged. He jumped inside the truck, slid across the bed and hid behind the spare tire as best he could. He looked absolutely terrified.

Virginia let out a squeal and my first thought was that a bear had lumbered into camp and we were under attack.

Almost without thinking I started to reach for the crowbar in the bed of the truck when I heard a low growl.

"Leave it," Samuel said with one firm command, uttering the order with a low voice.

Then I saw the other dog. He had run the corgi down and was tucking his hind legs underneath him to make the leap for the back of the truck.

The dog, plain brown with a black muzzle and swishing tail, looked like a small German shepherd with short hair. The moment Samuel spoke the command the dog halted his pursuit and sat down obediently.

"What," said Virginia with a snarl, "is that thing?" She looked back and forth between Samuel and the dog with murder in her eyes. "And why was that thing chasing my Saint Christopher?"

"That's just Gus," the kid said. "Now let me get this straight. Allen sent you two up here to meet me?"

"That is a Belgian Malinois," Virginia told us. She poked Samuel on the shoulder with two fingers. "What is a child like you doing with a Malinois?"

Samuel gave her a hurt look. "I'm twenty-four."

"Those dogs have a reputation for aggressiveness," Virginia said with a haughty tone. "They need a firm hand."

Samuel stared at her with a deadpan expression. "He's just a mutt I got from the pound."

"That animal is no mutt," she said. "Saint Christopher is a registered Pembroke. I know an expensive working dog when I see one."

"Can we decide who is going to win best in show at Westminster later?" I asked.

Samuel shoved his hands into his cargo pants pockets. "We've got about a minute before Mr. Lamb comes over here to see what is taking so long."

"Is Mr. Lamb the foreman?" I asked.

"He is the foreman, the drill sergeant, and the angry Catholic nun all rolled up into one man," Samuel said. "And he thinks you are supposed to be one guy, not two women and a short dog."

"Allen is my ex-husband. I'm doing him a really big favor," I said.

"Your ex-husband? You might want to say you are married. I think that will go over better with the crew."

"I am married," I said, feeling testy.

"Fine, I really don't care. But what I do want to know is, why Allen couldn't be here?" Samuel asked.

"It's almost full-swing hunting season."

Normally that phrase would explain everything to someone familiar with the schedule of a game warden.

Samuel just blinked at me.

"Okay, so he's busy. Who's she?" he asked.

"My cousin," I said.

He frowned at me. "Your cousin?"

"From Denver," Virginia added.

Samuel looked at her boots. "Uh-huh."

"All you need to know about this situation is that—"

"Dammit, Sam. What are you doing over here? Building a hotel?" asked a raspy voice.

The light had almost faded to nothing, but I was able to make out the shape of a stringy cowboy with legs so bowed a yearling calf could have run between them.

He shuffled over to us and stopped when he saw me. "Who's this, now?"

Samuel recovered in a hurry and cut me off before I could answer. "'Member that fella Allen I was telling you about, Mr. Lamb? Well, he couldn't make it. But this here is his wife—"

"Marley," I said quickly, stepping forward and giving him a nod. "And my cousin. Virginia."

"From Denver," Virginia said, trying to be helpful.

Mr. Lamb, his face lined and tanned like a piece of beef jerky, swiveled his head around and actually took a step back when he saw Virginia.

"Good God," he said. "I wasn't expecting this."

103

"I've worked four drives in my time, Mr. Lamb," I said, feeling like I was in the middle of a job interview. "I'm sorry my husband couldn't be here. He . . . he had some business to attend to."

I held my breath. We were really winging it, and if Mr. Lamb didn't like the look of us, he could send Virginia and me packing without a single word of explanation. Whatever the ranch foreman said was written in stone.

For once, Virginia kept her mouth shut and tried her best to look polite.

Mr. Lamb gave me a stern once-over with deep-set eyes, his lips furiously working a wad of chewing tobacco. After what looked like serious internal deliberation, he sighed. "Well, we need the help. Since Jimmy quit we are short a hand anyway. Unpack yer gear. We'll see how you work out tomorrow."

He shuffled back towards the camp, shaking his head noticeably. This was not the best way to get started. I could see already that Virginia and I were one mistake away from getting fired.

Samuel bent to retrieve my duffle bag. "What's in this thing? A set of horseshoes or did you put the whole horse inside?"

"Dog food," Virginia said.

He dropped it to the ground at once. "Your dog. Your problem."

Samuel's dog, Gus, waited for his master with endless patience and sat perfectly still, until the kid gave a short chirp of a whistle. Gus was on his feet in an instant and ready to go.

Samuel snatched up both sleeping bags and hefted one under each arm. Since Virginia couldn't even begin to lift the duffle, I lugged it as best I could, trailing after the kid through the camp as he led us to a canvas tent set up close to the fire.

As we walked past the brightly glowing fire, the ring of surprised cowboys turned as one to watch us. Two of them actually stood up, and I swore I heard someone say "tar-nation" as Virginia brought up the rear.

Samuel tossed the sleeping bags onto a couple of cots set up inside the sturdy wall tent. He switched on a battery-powered lantern that sat on the ground between the cots, and as he stood up, he made sure to catch my eye.

"Until we get a chance to talk, not a word to anyone," he cautioned.

"That goes for you, too," I said.

He didn't look any happier about the situation than I felt. But, until we had a chance to talk someplace out of earshot of the rest of the crew, the best plan was to say nothing at all.

He left the tent and Virginia stumbled inside, staring at the ground with irritation. "I can't see a thing. My contacts are all gritty."

Saint Christopher slunk in at her heels, keeping a wary eye out for the brown monster that had attacked him. But Gus had vanished, probably out in the trees bringing down a deer or chasing a mountain lion. The Malinois was not as big as a German shepherd, but he vibrated with potential energy like a stick of dynamite.

Virginia fell onto the closest cot and let out a sigh. "Thank God we are here."

Her corgi jumped up on the bunk, seeking reassurance.

"Virginia, get him down. Now," I said quickly.

"Why would I do that?"

"Because dogs do not go on the cots at a drive," I said. "If Mr. Lamb sees it he will go ballistic. Dogs stay on the ground."

I could see there were a great many unspoken rules about working a cattle drive that Virginia simply didn't know about. For the first day I would have to watch her every move to make sure she didn't make a mistake and put us both on the bad side of the foreman.

I gave Virginia a hard look.

Reluctantly, she snapped her fingers and pointed the corgi down. His ears were already plastered back as far as they would go, and her admonition made him look even more wretched. His adventure had turned into a nightmare in the blink of an eye. As I peeked outside the tent at the ring of curious, rugged, and unknown faces illuminated by the campfire, I knew exactly how he felt.

CHAPTER 9

Voices, movement and the sounds of a waking camp brought me out of a sound sleep. I sat up in total darkness and fumbled for the lantern on the ground. My stiff fingers finally managed to switch it on. Yawning, I rubbed my eyes and pulled on my jeans, my teeth chattering the moment I was outside my warm sleeping bag. The camp was probably close to seven thousand feet above sea level, and although it was cold now, I knew it would warm up to at least sixty degrees by the afternoon. Until then, numb fingers would be the status quo.

As I was lacing on my boots I saw Saint Christopher curled at Virginia's feet on top of her cot. This was going to be harder than I'd originally thought.

"Time to get up," I said.

She didn't move a muscle, and I marveled that someone could sleep through the noise coming from outside the tent. Virginia didn't seem to notice.

I kicked her cot.

She snorted once and sat up with a start. "What time is it?"

"Four-thirty. Let's go. Time to work."

"Four-thirty." She turned slowly to look at me. "In the morning?"

Virginia was pushing fifty, but in the light of day she looked thirty-five due to an extensive and determined campaign waged with expensive cosmetics and discreet plastic surgery.

Her makeup was always tasteful and perfect and her hair done with care. This morning, however, she looked every day her true age, and even I felt a little bit sorry for her at seeing the state she was in.

I felt a little sorry for myself at this point too. My nerves were frayed, my temper was at the breaking point, and considering the hellacious week I'd had so far, it was a miracle I hadn't suffered a complete nervous breakdown. Then I reminded myself there simply wasn't time for that now. I'd have a nervous breakdown later.

"Get dressed fast. Breakfast will go by in a hurry, and then we have to catch the horses." I pulled on my coat and headed outside.

I wasn't surprised by the lack of greeting from the cowboys circling the fire. I counted ten men, and mentally the number of cattle we would be rounding up ticked up a few notches. With Virginia and me, it would be an even dozen riders. That meant we had at least five hundred head to gather, maybe more.

Wordlessly, I got in line and helped myself to bacon, biscuits and coffee, noticing from the corner of my eye the curious glances from the men.

The bacon was thick and salty. The coffee tasted like smoke.

Mr. Lamb came to stand in the glow of the firelight and nodded at the crew, tipping his battered black felt cowboy hat up on his forehead to get everyone's attention. It was a classic hat. A bullet-sized hole pierced the brim, and the band circling the ancient felt was made from rattlesnake.

A tan line below his forehead made his face look like a brown mask, but above the hat line his skin was ghost white.

As the grumpy foreman surveyed his crew, he looked irritated.

The low whispers ceased at once and the foreman had everyone's undivided attention.

He nodded in my general direction. "This here is Mrs. Hunter. She's riding with us, on account of her husband couldn't make it."

I gave a nod to the circle of men. "You can call me Marley."

Not in my wildest dreams would I ever correct a ranch foreman. In any case, it didn't matter if these men thought I was Mrs. Hunter or not.

To a man, they sized me up, their faces betraying a bit of disappointment from the announcement that I was someone's wife already.

Mr. Lamb continued. "The other lady is her cousin."

"Virginia," I added helpfully.

"She want us to call her Mrs. . . . ?" asked one of the bolder cowboys.

I cleared my throat. "You can just call her Virginia."

Let them figure it out on their own.

"I can't speak to her experience," Mr. Lamb admitted.

Stone silence met Mr. Lamb's words. The crew was practically bursting with curiosity, and it was so painfully obvious even I could sense it.

The foreman gave a long sigh. "The cousin is from Denver, so you-all try to be understanding."

Murmurs of "Oh, Denver" drifted through the camp. Apparently, being from Denver explained any eccentricities one displayed.

"Yesterday was a mess. I can't tell you how sorry a sight it was to see a crew this size fail to set up a portable corral in under an hour, and I don't want to hear about the busted wagon wheel. It's no excuse," Mr. Lamb said, his tone hot as a branding iron.

Nobody spoke. One didn't dare speak to the foreman during an ass chewing, even if it was to apologize.

"I want two men to finish digging that latrine this morning. No more damned excuses. There's a couple shovels in the tack wagon."

Virginia wouldn't be very happy to discover we didn't have porta-potties in the camp.

"Today we need to make up for lost time. We've got three days of hard riding ahead of us." Mr. Lamb rested his angry eye on each man in turn.

I'd forgotten how stern a ranch foreman could be. But, knowing what I knew about cowboys, it was understandable. They could be a handful, and to keep them in line took a foreman with a steel spine and a wicked streak of pragmatic suspicion. I knew from what Allen had told me that these men were a ragtag bunch of stragglers who hadn't worked together before, but you wouldn't know it by looking at them. Oh, they were ragtag, alright. But each man was obviously experienced, and even though they didn't know each other, they knew the job.

Mr. Lamb inserted his first wad of Copenhagen chewing tobacco between his lower lip and teeth, spat on the ground once and wiped a hand on his faded chaps. "We've got six hundred fifty head of steers and heifers to round up by the twenty-fifth. Mrs. Cotton instructed me to tell you all there will be trucks coming on the morning of the twenty-sixth, that's Wednesday for those o' you who can't count, and if anybody wants to stay on that extra day to help load, she'd throw in a full day's pay for it, even if it only takes a few hours."

Nods of agreement went around the circle of men. It didn't look like Mrs. Cotton would have any trouble finding hands to load the stock when the time came.

"Since Mrs. Hunter doesn't know the territory, we need someone to take her and her cousin up for the first day," Mr. Lamb said cautiously.

Six hands shot in the air.

"I know the trail best," said one eager cowboy.

He was immediately shoved aside by another man, and Mr. Lamb heaved a weary sigh.

It was Samuel who finally broke through the chaos and tugged at the foreman's shirtsleeve. "I'll do it."

Mr. Lamb gave Samuel a relieved nod. "Right. Mr. Weller here will ride with the ladies."

Sounds of disappointment reverberated through the camp.

"We've got six radios. Burris, you and Wat take one each. Ira, you and Dan take one, I'll take another and Sam here will take the last," Mr. Lamb told the crew.

There was no way I would be able to keep the names straight.

I tried to put faces to the responses of 'yes sir' as Mr. Lamb spoke, but things were moving too fast for me to sort the men out.

Not that it mattered. I wasn't here to make any friends after all. My real mission had nothing whatsoever to do with cows, but until I could figure out who had been employed by the Cottons on this drive two years ago, I had to work the roundup like I meant it. As long as I kept my mouth shut and my head down, the rest would take care of itself.

"Finish breakfast and saddle up," Mr. Lamb said. "Anson, you and Patrick got morning cleanup and when yer done you can finish up digging that latrine."

Two men groaned and started the arduous task of buttoning up the camp. It would be a thankless chore and I wondered what those two particular men had done to get on Mr. Lamb's bad side.

The crew hustled to do his bidding, and Virginia finally stumbled from the tent with a blurry-eyed look on her face, and a wary Saint Christopher trailing behind her like a baby duck. The corgi had learned his lesson about running off willy-nilly and wasn't taking any more chances. He didn't move more than a foot away from her ankles.

"Marley," said a voice behind me. "That's a funny name for a girl. How did you get dragged all the way up here from Denver?"

I turned and gave the man standing behind me a faint smile. My mind nearly jammed while I fumbled with my rehearsed response. "Oh, I'm not from Denver. My cousin is. It wasn't that far for me to come."

He held out a hand, uncharacteristic for a cowboy, and I noticed he wore hiking boots and a brand-new blaze red North Face polar down jacket. Not a true cowboy then, that was for certain. This man was more like a backpacker or a hunter. I shook his hand and he grinned at me with a gleam in his eye.

"You know that all these guys are licking their chops over the two of you." He shook his head with mock disgust. "You will have to sleep with one eye open."

His tone was light and jovial, and his smile seemed genuine.

I couldn't help but chuckle. "My .357 sleeps with one eye open for me. I'll be fine."

His face lit up with amusement at my remark, and he tilted his head to one side, appraising me. "I'm Dan. And I'd like to apologize in advance for anything ungentlemanly these bandits might say or do while you two are riding with us. They were all raised by wolves, from what I can tell."

"I was raised by wolverines, so we should get along fine," I said flippantly.

He smiled faintly and finished the last of the breakfast from his stainless steel plate. He turned away to toss the plate in the dish bucket and cocked a grin at me over his shoulder. "I was going to tell you that if any of these characters gave you grief, to let me know. But I see you can take care of yourself."

"And then some," I said.

Dan tugged on a pair of heavy gloves and pointed vaguely off to the right of the camp. "The corral is over there. Watch your step going to get your mount. We've had bears."

All my bluster was gone in a flash. "Bears?"

He watched me for a moment, thoughtful. "Just one. So far."

My eyes involuntarily scanned the darkness frantically. It wasn't that I didn't like bears, not at all. I loved them. But I loved them more when there was something immovable and solid between them and myself.

"You don't like bears?" Dan asked.

"As long as they are doing whatever it is they do all day someplace far away from me, I am fine with them."

Being terrified of bears didn't make me weak. It made me sensible.

Honestly, I couldn't understand why anyone wouldn't be afraid of an animal that could decapitate you with a swat.

Dan watched me nervously searching the darkness and smiled. He pointed to his chest, and pulled aside his red coat. "My antibear device."

Strapped to his heavy belt was a long holster, and I almost gasped when I saw his pistol. "Good God. What is that?"

Dan looked at the pistol he wore appreciatively. "This is my Smith and Wesson .500 Magnum. Because I don't negotiate with grizzlies."

He gave me a wink and walked away into the darkness. How he managed to navigate was beyond me. I could hardly see my own feet in the dim light.

Mr. Lamb appeared at my side and looked at my half-finished breakfast disapprovingly. "You a fair rider?"

"Average. I can handle a pasture pony better than a cutting horse," I admitted.

"Get with Ezra. He's got the beard with the white streak in it. He'll set you up with a horse. And, your cousin? She a decent rider?"

"I guess we'll find out," I said.

Mr. Lamb didn't look pleased. Like all foremen, he liked to know everything about everyone who was working for him. Having a mysterious woman on his crew wasn't an exotic adventure for the foreman. It was a monumental inconvenience.

"Just tell Ezra to put her on Buck," the weary cowboy told me.

"Buck?" I asked, not entirely sure I had heard him correctly.

Mr. Lamb spat on the ground. "Buck for his color, not what he likes to do."

With that, the foreman walked away.

Virginia was on the opposite side of the fading fire feeding a strip of bacon to her corgi. I groaned inwardly. Another thing we would need to talk about. One did not feed people food to dogs on a roundup.

I waved her around the campfire and she reluctantly trudged to where I stood.

"Do you have a canteen?" I asked. "We'll be out for several hours, and you'll need water."

She looked at me like I had just spoken in Swahili. "We'll be out where?"

"Virginia, you have to ride with me. I can't leave you alone in the camp. And anyway, nobody just sits in camp."

"Are you seriously going to tell me that I have to go riding out there and look for cows?" she asked.

Strangling her came to mind. But instead, I pasted on a bright smile and took away her plate. She managed to snatch the last piece of bacon from it before I tossed it in the dish bucket where is sat on a tree stump.

"Get a canteen out of the duffle bag, and a flashlight. Start walking that way," I pointed, "and when you see horses, stop and wait for me."

I left her, hoping against hope that she would at least be smart enough to bring gloves.

Walking with more confidence than I actually felt, I stomped away from the fire into the pitch darkness and managed to get several yards before stumbling and nearly falling on my face. Wisely, I slowed down and let my anger seethe on the inside, but not bubble up to the outside. It was going to be a long day and I needed all my strength, and I needed to not break my neck.

As I walked in the general direction I hoped the horses were corralled, an eerie feeling crept over my skin.

What was it that Dan had said about bears? That there had only been one in camp so far?

My paced quickened and by the time I could hear the snuffling of horses and the shuffling of hooves, I was practically jogging. Being alone in the darkness was a lot creepier when you knew that something out there might want to have you for breakfast.

Faint starlight illuminated the landscape just enough that at least I wasn't blindly wandering around in a big circle, and in my haste to reach the horses I nearly ran into an ancient wooden corral.

There was enough light to see the outline of the rails, and as my eyes adjusted more I finally saw a couple lanterns set up on the opposite side of the corral. Movement told me that the horses were being saddled there, and I started to work my way around to the other side when I heard a growl.

Straining my eyes and feeling my heart skip, I looked ahead of me and jumped back a step when I saw a man watching me from the darkness. It hadn't been a growl; he'd cleared his throat to get my attention. He didn't utter a word and stood there motionless.

I couldn't see his face. It was unnerving. "Ah, are you Ezra?"

He hardly moved when he spoke. "I am."

A few moments passed. It seemed I was the one who would have to get the conversation rolling. "Mr. Lamb wants you to saddle Buck for Virginia."

He turned and walked back the direction he had come without giving me any response.

My mouth had gone dry and I tried to swallow. "Well, he sure is friendly."

By the time I managed to work my way to the other side of the corral, the lanterns were finally within range and I could see a half dozen men milling around, hauling saddles and fighting with the tangled reins from a pile of bridles that had been haphazardly dumped on the ground. This roundup was a mess, compared to the others I'd worked before. No self-respecting foreman would allow his men to treat tack like so much dirty laundry and leave it in a heap. This wasn't going to be an easy job. Mr. Lamb was a tough boss, but it was clear the crew was lacking in enthusiasm.

"G-eesus, it's cold! Ezra, don't give me Possum. I hate that damn palomino. Give him to Dan," said a lean cowboy hopping from foot to foot.

The horse wrangler turned to look at the cowboy with an expression like a glacier. "Possum's got great action."

"Yeah, but he spooks at two things," said the cowboy.

"What two things?" asked Ezra.

"Everything that moves, and everything that doesn't move," the cowboy said.

"I'll take him," said someone from the darkness.

I recognized Dan's voice, even though the long shadows from the lantern made seeing faces difficult.

A hand fell on my shoulder and I flinched nearly a foot off the ground.

"Sorry," said Samuel. "Didn't mean to startle you."

"Make some noise, would you?" I told him.

Samuel led me towards the mound of bridles on the ground and the two of us bent to untangle the mess. His dog, Gus, sat a few paces away, watching the whole scene like he understood every word being said.

When I stood up, Ezra was looking at me with eyes like glass. It probably took the guy six or seven years to blink once.

"I'm giving you Jericho," he said, staring at me.

"Um. Thanks?" I said hesitantly.

Samuel didn't address the wrangler directly, and looked at his bridle when he spoke. "How about Sugar Beet for me, Ezra?"

"Fine. You catch him."

Samuel groaned a bit, but he shimmied over the top rail of the corral and waded into the herd of milling horses fearlessly.

In the dim light from the lanterns I finally got my first good look at the face of the quiet wrangler called Ezra.

Before I could stop myself my mouth fell open and I looked away before he could catch me gaping at him so shamelessly.

Ezra's black beard did have a white streak cutting through it on the left side of his jaw, exactly as Mr. Lamb had said. It looked like someone had taken a paintbrush full of whitewash and drawn a straight line down through the man's beard. But that hadn't been what I'd found myself staring at. Ezra's eyelashes on his left side were white too, but only on the left side.

The white streak didn't stop there. A shock of pure white hair ran in a straight line through the center of his eyebrow, and continued right up through his black hair to the top of his head.

It looked like a bolt of lightning had hit him squarely on top of the head and traveled down to the bottom of his jaw, leaving a white streak in its wake.

I had never seen anything like it, and immediately I cast my eyes down so that I wouldn't be tempted to ogle.

Luckily I saw a Bobbyng flashlight coming towards the corral through the darkness and I turned my attention away from the strange wrangler.

A squeal and a yip, accompanied by the flashlight Bobbyng wildly, told me that Virginia had arrived and had just run into the corral and managed to step on Saint Christopher at the same time.

She swore a blue streak and the flashlight started to slowly make its way around the rails. She stumbled to my side and Saint Christopher took one look at Gus and ducked behind Virginia's knees in a flash.

The brown dog appraised the corgi once, gave a yawn and proceeded to ignore him. Samuel had commanded that he leave the corgi alone yesterday, and to my amazement, that was exactly what Gus was doing.

Two cowboys behind Ezra glanced at the corgi sideways, but kept their opinions to themselves as they led their horses through the old gate and tied them to the rails.

It took the crew about an hour to inspect gear, clean hooves, check that each horse had good shoes and that none of the animals were limping or looked sore in any way. The handheld radios were tested. Some of the men worked with a lasso, practicing on the top rung of the corral posts, and I wasn't surprised to see that they all looked like they could hit a match head with a rope. A couple of the men smoked, but they kept a wary eye out while they did. Apparently the foreman disapproved of smoking because the men who smoked kept palms cupped over the glowing embers at the ends of their cigarettes, and cast worried glances around as they indulged.

False dawn was just beginning to show when Mr. Lamb arrived and surveyed his crew with a hard look. All the cigarettes had been stubbed out and the men stood more or less at attention.

The foreman glanced at one of the cowboys. "Patrick, I don't want you riding Dash today. He was acting sketchy. I'll take him. Why don't you saddle up Hot Damn?"

I marveled that these men had only been working with this string of horses for twenty-four hours, and already they were on a first-name basis with each animal, and knew the foibles of the troublemakers to boot.

There was hardly enough light to see by, but almost on cue the cowboys started to mount up.

Virginia tugged the sleeve of my coat. She bobbed up and down, trying to keep warm. "What time is lunch?"

All I could do was shake my head. It was going to be a long day.

CHAPTER 10

Jericho turned out to be a smaller horse than the other long-legged monsters that Ezra had saddled for the men. He was black, head to tail.

It wasn't until the sun was above the trees and melting the frozen dew from the fall leaves that I noticed the spots. A smattering of white dots peppered Jericho's rump, like a checkerboard had been painted on his dark hide.

The little black gelding was an Appaloosa, not a quarter horse as I'd originally thought.

Virginia and I rode up the steep slope of the mountain, trailing behind Samuel as best we could.

Sugar Beet, the tall red mare Samuel rode, climbed like a mountaineer and showed no sign of tiring.

The dog Gus, ran back and forth between Samuel and the tree line with excitement, hoping to scare up a rabbit or a squirrel.

After a half hour of hard riding, Samuel finally eased his pace and came to a stop in the middle of what passed as a sheep trail.

I eased Jericho to a standstill beside him and we both sat and watched as Virginia lingered a good distance behind us, kicking her unhappy mount impatiently.

Her horse had both ears plastered flat, and he chewed the bit with his head down. From the way Virginia was reeling in the saddle I wasn't surprised. The horse obviously had a lot more experience than she did.

Saint Christopher panted to a stop beside me and collapsed on the ground.

Samuel sucked through his teeth when Virginia finally managed to reach us, looking at her with a sneer.

"Get your heels down and your toes pointed out," he said with disgust. "You look like a goddamn dude."

She looked down at her expensive riding boots. "What's wrong with my heels?"

"Never mind," he said, turning to look directly at me. "Let's get this over with. Who the heck are you and what are we really doing up here?"

I'd mulled this impending conversation over in my head on the ride up the mountain, and had managed to reduce the explanation to a couple sentences.

"Allen Hunter is my ex-husband. He thinks someone may have died up at Fischer Lake and he wants us to take a look. If we find anything, we are just supposed to mark the spot and next spring he will come back up to investigate."

I wasn't about to tell him that Virginia and I were really after a list of names, not a corpse. The less information I shared with the crew, including him, the better.

"Why are you doing this for him?" Samuel asked.

"I owe him a favor," I lied.

The kid worked his lips while he thought about what I'd said, looking like he wasn't quite sure he believed me.

His eyes fell on Virginia. "Okay, then what's she doing up here?"

His teeth glinted in the sunlight, and it seemed ridiculous that someone young enough to wear braces was interrogating us like a seasoned cop.

"I'm babysitting," I replied.

"That I believe," he told me, not bothering to hide his disdain. "So, this is sort of a missing persons gig?"

I stopped myself before answering. "What did Allen tell you?"

Samuel appraised me. "You mean, what did he tell Todd Ramsey?"

My cheeks flushed a bit. "That's what I meant."

"Just that he needed someone who could help out."

Up till now I'd been on the defensive so much with Samuel all I'd managed to do was scramble to keep up with him. But that was about to change.

"And how," I said with a stern look, "will you manage that?"

He took a long drink from his canteen. "I'm useful."

"Define useful."

He darted a look at me, and his eyebrow lift told me he'd gotten the message that I wasn't kidding around anymore.

His face fell. "Look, I know Todd. Alright? I'm a friend. He and I do Search and Rescue together and I've got a lot of experience in the high country. I grew up around here and I know these mountains."

"You don't look like you've got a lot of experience. What are you, a graduate student or something?"

"I just got out of the service," he said defensively.

"What branch?" I asked.

Virginia bobbed up and down in her stirrups. "I have to pee."

Samuel almost looked relieved at the interruption.

I waved a hand at the tree line. "You don't need to wait for the hostess to seat you. It's self-service out here. Just don't get lost."

She eased herself out of the saddle and wobbled away, squinting at me over her shoulder.

Saint Christopher didn't budge and stayed where he was in a heap, still trying to catch his breath.

I turned back to the kid. "What branch of the military?"

Samuel heaved a sigh. "The army. I did two years counting toilet paper in warehouses, alright? I just got out and I'm taking a couple months off while I figure out what I want to do next."

We stared at each other.

I didn't believe him, and he clearly didn't believe me either. But we were in it up to our necks, and neither one of us had much choice. Whether or not we liked it, Samuel and I would need to rely on each other until this was over.

"And anyway," he said with a wave at the landscape, "it gives me a chance to come up here and enjoy the great outdoors."

"Me too," I said.

He laughed. "What did you say it was you did for a living again?"

I let my eyes drift downslope, making sure no bears were snuffling through the forest headed in our direction. "I didn't say. But if you have to know, I'm a librarian."

"Right," he muttered, noticing the way I held my reins. "A librarian."

He looked like he believed that about as much as I believed he'd spent two years counting toilet paper for the army.

Virginia finally stumbled out of the trees and managed to climb back in the saddle after hopping up and down on one leg several times with her left foot caught in the stirrup.

At least she mounted up on the correct side.

Buck heaved a sigh when she dropped into the saddle. Both ears folded back as if to say, "Oh, it's you again."

When she was finally sitting upright, Samuel took a long look around the area. "Pay attention because here's the gist of this terrain. We are on the east slope of the Cross Fell Mountains. This place is sort of shaped like a half-bowl, and it's got two streams running through it. The streams follow the contour of two cliffs that divide the bowl into three separate forks so you can't ride straight across, because the going is too steep. Each one of these forks has to be checked for cattle, one at a time. Starting from the bottom."

Virginia rolled a tube of lip gloss over her pout. "Can't we use a helicopter, or something?"

I closed my eyes with embarrassment. "Sorry. She didn't mean that."

"Yeah, I think she really did," Samuel said with amazement. "The important thing to know is that if you get separated from the others and you don't have a radio, 'cause God knows why Mr. Lamb would give you two a radio in the first place, it's beyond me—"

"Just tell us what to do if we get lost," I said.

"Ride straight down and eventually you will come out on the valley floor and you should see the camp. You almost cannot get lost. The bowl will take you back out the way you came no matter what, so if you are not sure where you are, and want to get back to camp, just point your horse's nose downhill and he should be able to do the rest. Mrs. Cotton's horses have worked up here many times and if you give them their head they will find the way home."

"How is it that you know so much about this place?" Virginia asked.

I pivoted in the saddle, the leather creaking underneath me. "That's actually a really good question."

"Like I said, I grew up around here," he told us.

"You don't exactly remind me of a ranch kid," I said, taking in his hiking boots and backpacker jacket.

"It's not like anyone around here would remember me," he replied testily. "My dad worked for the Forest Service during the summers here. But that was a long time ago. I was lucky enough to be able to tag along and I sort of got to know the place."

"What about Fischer Lake?" I asked.

"What about it?" he asked.

"How long will it take us to search the area? I am not sure how big it is," I said. "And I don't know where it is."

"Don't worry about the searching part. I'll take care of that," he told me. "And Fischer Lake is up in the northern area of this bowl. It's the third fork. It's not easy to reach, and we sort of might have a bit of a problem justifying going up there."

"Sort of might?" I asked.

"Well, Mr. Lamb won't send any of the greenhorns up there if he can help it," he said.

Then he gave me an exaggerated grin. "So let's just concentrate on getting through today."

I suppressed a grumble and let it go.

Maybe he was right, but I hated to admit it.

"What about the rest of the crew?" I asked. "What can you tell me about the men who are up here?"

Samuel rubbed the back of his neck with one hand. "I don't know that much about them. Mr. Lamb? He used to be the foreman for Nash Cotton years ago, but he retired. He came back for this job after Stephanie begged him to head up her last roundup. You know her lease is expiring and she's moving to Arizona?"

"Allen mentioned it," I said.

"The rest of them are unfamiliar to me. You probably know about as much as I do when it comes to this crew."

That was not what I wanted to hear.

My face must have clouded over with worry.

"Hey, it's not like they are escaped convicts or anything," Samuel said quickly. "They are just guys who need the work."

"You don't know if any of them has ever worked for the Cottons on this range before?" I asked.

His face twisted with confusion as he considered the question. "I suppose it's possible some of them could be rehires. Why? Is that important or something?"

"Maybe," I said cryptically.

Samuel stared at me with a skeptical expression.

"While you are trying to decide how much you are willing to share with me, maybe we ought to actually get to work?"

"Fine by me," I said. "Black Angus or Red?"

"Red. Oh, and watch out for the bulls. Stephanie has six bulls with her herd and one of them is a Brangus."

"I've never even heard of a Brangus," Virginia said. "Are you making that up?"

Samuel grimaced. "Wish I was. It's a cross between an Angus and a Brahma. Crazy mean."

"How will I know which one is a bull?" Virginia asked.

Samuel started to say something that would most likely be incredibly inappropriate.

I cut him off. "Yeah, don't go there, kid."

He closed his mouth, disappointed.

"Bulls are big, much bigger than the cows," I told Virginia. "Just stay in the saddle and you will be fine."

Samuel suddenly stared back down the mountain. "Looks like we are not alone."

Two horses popped into view downslope of us, and their riders, when they spotted us parked on the trail in a cluster, gave a wave and headed up.

"Samuel," I said suddenly. "I think we should agree not to talk to anyone else about what we are really doing up here. Alright?"

He cocked his head sideways at me. "You aren't hiding from the cops, are you?"

"Not exactly the cops," Virginia said quietly.

"I would like it a whole lot better if you didn't argue with me about this." I gave him a hard stare.

My sharp tone threw him off, and he actually looked chastened.

He glanced towards the two cowboys, and after a moment, reluctantly shrugged. "It might not be a bad idea."

Gus, Samuel's sharp-eyed mutt, had probably been watching the two approaching cowboys the entire time we had been sitting in a circle talking. The Malinois didn't look a bit surprised by their presence. But as they rode closer the corgi jerked out of his coma and sat up with ears pricked. Saint Christopher whined once with concern, and to my surprise, Gus padded over and gave the corgi a quick nuzzle of reassurance.

Even Samuel looked shocked. "I've never seen him do that before."

"We need to get going," I told him. "Let's at least try to look like we know what we are doing."

I turned my Appaloosa downhill, but before I was two feet away, Samuel turned to Virginia with a quizzical expression on his face.

He leaned towards her in the saddle. "What did you mean by, 'Not exactly the cops'?"

Virginia mimicked his gesture and leaned towards him with a sweet smile. "Mind your own business, Junior."

It was a good thing we would only be working this job for three or four days. Any longer than that, and I was already convinced we'd have a second homicide to deal with.

CHAPTER 11

As my father would have said, it was rough sledding.

Jericho was smaller than the other horses and therefore more nimble, so I had the task of riding into the little cracks and crevices along the cliff face where the cows were likely to be taking shelter. The cows were crafty, suspicious and mean, and when they weren't hiding, mock-charging the horses, or refusing to budge an inch, they were running away at top speed. In spite of the fact that it was steadily getting colder each night and winter was fast approaching, they didn't want to be caught.

Our first problem was teaching Virginia which way to point her horse. Much to the chagrin of her big buckskin, named Buck, appropriately enough, she had no idea how to herd cows. After several failed attempts to scoot two heifers out of a tangle of chokecherry bushes, Buck simply gave up and stopped in his tracks. One ear was cocked back, the other tilted forward, and his head was lifted up as high as it would go in the universal horse sign of oh brother.

I was struggling to reach her and give her a short lesson in cattle wrangling, when Ezra, one of the cowboys who had ridden up to meet us, clicked his tongue and trotted his mount to Virginia's side. I was sure he was going to chew her up one side and down the other, but to my astonishment, Ezra simply explained to her the mechanics of herding.

"First off," he said, "you don't hold the reins like that. Take your left hand, no, your other left hand, and put the right rein under your first finger and the left one under your second finger."

"Why?" she asked. But she wasn't being snotty, as I'd anticipated. She really wanted to understand the process.

Ezra held up his left hand to demonstrate. "It lets you control the length of each rein. See? You can make each one longer or shorter, depending on what you want to do. And it is easier on the horse's bit. You don't need to choke up so much, give him a little breathing room."

Virginia relaxed her grip, and Buck blew out a sigh that sounded like relief to me.

"When you want a cow to move, don't go right at them," Ezra explained. "They panic and end up runnin' every which way. If you want a cow to head downhill, come at her from above and push her down. Buck ain't no racehorse. If she runs up, don't try and cut her off. Let her go a few yards, then ride up above her and push her back down. Chasing after them just gets them riled up. We don't do that unless we have to."

Maybe it was the shocking streak of white that sliced through Ezra's beard and hair, or maybe it was his tone, but either way he seemed to have gotten her attention. Virginia didn't complain or argue. Her look shifted from desperate to determined. She stood up high in her stirrups and searched the trees.

Two dodgy red heifers eyed her from the bushes, lifting their noses and sniffing the air. One of the heifers was tossing her head, looking like trouble, and her pink tongue flicked out as the heifer used it to clean her own nostril.

Virginia looked sickened. "That's the most disgusting thing I have ever seen."

"Guess you've never seen a water-belly steer," Ezra said, looking almost amused.

"What's a water-belly steer?" she asked.

"A steer with a calcium stone lodged in his urethra. Most of the time you have to cut off the penis and pull it out through a flap in the skin on his stomach so he can—"

"Oh God!" Virginia said. "I really don't want to know."

She shook her head, probably trying to get the image out of her mind, and with a determined expression she went after the two heifers.

When she pointed the two excited cows downhill and followed Ezra's patient instructions, they scrambled away from her obediently.

In a flash the heifers were trotting down the mountain towards another group we had just rounded up and soon our little herd had grown by two.

Virginia turned to Ezra and flashed a million-dollar smile. "I did it!"

"Good job," he said. "Only six hundred forty-three to go."

She urged Buck after the seven cows we had rounded up and pulled her straw hat down over her eyes. "Bring 'em on."

Against my will, I actually smiled.

More than likely it was the first thing that had gone right for her in a very long time. I could understand feeling satisfaction from a new accomplishment, even if it was small.

Samuel turned in his saddle and looked back at me with his mouth hanging open and his eyes popping. "Did you see that? She actually did it."

"Miracles do occur," I said.

The four of us rode on, stopping every hour to let the horses breathe and rest their legs. Since the riding was so steep it was much harder on the animals than a flatland roundup. I could feel the aches and pains already starting in my hips and back. I knew that by the end of the day my legs would be shot.

After two hours of diligent searching we had managed to round up twenty-three cows.

Their glossy red hides gleamed in the sun, and I marveled that animals such an unnatural color could hide so successfully in the thick brush and trees. Green, gold and red leaves splashed patches of fall color all around us, and as I studied the landscape I realized the Red Angus were the same color as the bright huckleberry bushes. No wonder they were so difficult to spot.

On more than one occasion I breezed right past a little cluster of three or four cows and didn't even see them, only to have Wat, the lean cowboy who obviously had a lot of experience, ride into the same patch of brush and come out with a small cluster of cows.

All I could do was shake my head and vow to do better next time.

The day stretched on, and I couldn't help but be amazed at the transformation gradually taking place.

Slowly but surely, Virginia was turning into a cowpuncher before my very eyes.

She attacked the mountain. She prowled the bushes, bending down and riding Buck under the boughs of low trees. She pushed her way into shady clearings and rode across wide streams fearlessly in her quest to find livestock.

She seemed to have forgotten all about her personal troubles. Her total focus was on finding cows and rounding them up.

She was relentless.

Some primal instinct seemed to have taken over. She emerged from a stand of willows with a scratch across her cheek, oblivious to it. Saint Christopher had abandoned her after she had forded the wide stream for the fifth time, choosing instead to flank Ezra, who seemed to more closely resemble a sane human being. The little corgi watched every move Ezra made, as though he was studying the technique of herding, too.

Before long, his instinct took over as well, and on more than one occasion the little corgi managed to cut off a flighty heifer bolting back up the mountain, and herd her back towards the others. He would always turn to Ezra and watch the wrangler's reaction, trying to see if he had done the correct thing. Ezra would quietly give praise now and then, or shake his head with disapproval and utter a curt reprimand, just to keep the corgi on the straight and narrow. It seemed to be working.

I managed to hold my own thanks to my Appaloosa. Jericho was so nimble he could scramble up into tight places the other horses couldn't go, and so the unspoken rule was that I would search the small cracks in the area along the cliff that loomed in the north, while the others focused on the brushy areas.

Samuel wasn't as keen to ride into places obscured by vegetation, and ended up taking the growing herd as his responsibility. Instead of pounding the bushes, Samuel and Gus stood sentinel at the herd, discouraging stragglers from wandering back into the thick trees while the rest of us added cows to the milling gang after flushing them out.

Gus seemed at a loss for how to deal with cows. He studied them from a safe distance, whining and hesitating, his black eyes staring at the sea of legs warily. It was clear he had never seen so many cows before and he didn't have any idea what to do with them. Once a feisty mother and her calf actually trotted after him, their noses bent to the ground with curiosity, and Gus fled with his tail tucked. Samuel looked mortified, but luckily I was the only one who had seen it. Had Wat witnessed Samuel's dog fleeing from a curious cow, he'd have never heard the end of it.

When the sun had reached its zenith Ezra stopped in a clearing and dismounted. The rest of us slowly gathered around him, and to my immense relief he heaved a saddlebag to the ground and pulled out lunch for everyone.

Well, lunch was a charitable term. Beef jerky, peanuts with raisins, a couple handfuls of dried fruit and some sort of oatmeal bar were all we got. But I was grateful for the break.

Virginia didn't bother to sit down and she ate everything Ezra handed to her standing up, munching wordlessly, her eyes scanning the trees for movement.

She wasn't exactly obsessed, but there was a real danger of that happening.

The radio hanging from Wat's belt squawked to life.

The voice was Mr. Lamb's, and he didn't sound happy. "What's your head count?"

Wat keyed the radio. "Fifty-one, Mr. Lamb."

There was a long pause, during which the five of us shared a wary look.

Finally Mr. Lamb's voice came back.

"We've got twelve," he said. "It's gonna take us two days to finish out this first fork if you don't pick up the pace."

The radio went silent and Wat simply stared at it. "Twelve?"

"That's not so good," Ezra remarked.

Virginia pointed towards a tall stand of aspen. "Hey, I think there's a cow in there." She was totally oblivious to the radio call, and eagerly watched the trees.

"Well, what are you waitin' for girl?" said Wat. "Go git 'em!"

Virginia hardly hesitated for a second before leaping back into the saddle and charging in.

"Thanks a lot," I said to Ezra with a lopsided grin on my face. "You'll get her all wound up on sugar and chasing cows, and then how in the world am I going to get her put down for her nap?"

Samuel laughed outright at that, and wiped the crumbs from his oatmeal bar on his pant leg. He glanced up at the trees where Virginia had vanished. "It sounds like she found it."

A series of loud crashes erupted from the foliage. A loud hoot of excitement told us that, yes, she had indeed found it.

The bad news was, it turned out not to be a cow at all.

Branches broke and leaves flew as something surged from the undergrowth.

Ezra stood up with his eyes locked on the trees. "Holy Mary mother of—"

Everything happened at once.

Samuel moved with lightning speed and dove for his saddle. Ezra took two huge steps backwards and fell in a heap when he tripped over his own legs trying to retreat.

Gus barked and jumped to his feet.

Whatever was coming, it was big.

And it was quick.

I turned and rose off the ground, my heart practically locked up with dread.

Convinced I was about to come face-to-face with a huge grizzly bear, a wave of panic seized my legs and I simply couldn't move.

A horrid crash and the sounds of breaking branches told us that something big was about to come charging from the trees.

And Virginia was hot on its tail.

"Run!"

It was Ezra yelling. I couldn't have obeyed him even if I had tried.

My body was paralyzed.

A brown shape lurched through the aspens, sending a spray of leaves and an explosion of branches in all directions.

A huge head burst through the golden leaves and all I could do was gape.

"Marley!" Samuel lunged for me and snagged my shoulder, pulled me behind Jericho and forced me to stumble out of the path of the charging animal.

It wasn't a bear at all, but something nearly as dangerous.

I almost collapsed when Samuel hauled me out of the way as an angry yearling moose calf sprinted right through the center of our clearing and ran for the stream at full speed.

"Move, move." Samuel pushed me for the cover of the trees.

Wat and Ezra were already running, and as Samuel shoved me through the first stand of aspens the mother moose exploded from the trees in mad pursuit of her calf.

She was a mature cow, and so tall she could step over the back of one of our Angus steers. Her great brown head swiveled back and forth as she tried to identify the threat to her calf. Her wide eyes rotated towards Samuel and me and locked on us. She belted out an angry snort, lowered her head and took a run for Samuel at full speed.

Gus appeared from nowhere, snarling and biting at the mother moose with ferocious determination. He planted in front of her and stood his ground, refusing to let her get close to Samuel.

The mother moose slid to a halt, not sure about the snarling creature before her.

Samuel grabbed my wrist and pulled me towards the trees. "Gus heel!"

The moose must have caught her calf's smell and as quick as she had made up her mind to charge, she changed it again, and trotted away from Gus with her long nose held high, taking huge strides towards the creek. The Malinois refused to give way and stayed where he was, barking with everything he had.

But the moose had abandoned the fight. She lumbered into the stream just as Virginia rode out of the trees with her cowboy hat crammed on her head sideways and her terrified horse quivering with shock.

Buck's nose had just come to the edge of the trees when he spotted what Virginia had forced him to chase. He locked up all four legs and slid to a halt.

It seemed like it happened in slow motion.

Virginia's mouth opened up in a surprised Oh as she sailed over the saddle and flipped a perfect somersault in midair before landing flat on her back. The only sound she made was an involuntary "woof" as the air blasted out of her lungs.

She lay still for a moment, unmoving.

Finally she managed to draw a ragged breath and, from her prone position on the ground, she yelled out. "Did I get it?"

Wat stared at her, furious. "Yeah, you got it."

We gathered around Virginia, a circle of concerned and irritated faces looking down at her.

"Are you alright?" I asked.

She blinked up at me, her mouth still open. "Of course I'm alright."

I gave her a hand and helped ease her into a sitting position. "Did you break anything?"

"How should I know?" she asked. "What are you all standing around for? You should be getting that cow before she gets away."

Wat gaped at Virginia, and shot a look in the direction the moose had fled. He seemed unable to understand what had just happened. "She does know it wasn't an Angus, don't she?"

"Where's my horse?" Virginia squawked.

"I'll get him." I sprinted after Buck, who was busy running for his life through the trees.

Sugar Beet and Jericho were still tied up where we'd left them. They wheeled around their reins in tight circles. The two horses rolled their eyes, snorting excitedly.

I managed to catch Buck before he ran all the way to Canada, and led him back to the clearing with his head low. He was momentarily winded and that was probably the only reason I'd been able to catch him.

Ezra was squatting on his heels beside Virginia when I got back, patiently explaining to her the difference between a moose and a cow.

"First off, they are brown," he said.

"And don't look anything like a cow," Wat said with a snarl.

Samuel was sitting beside Gus quite a distance from the others, talking to the dog, and trying to calm down. I could see at a glance that Samuel was upset but he was doing what he could to comfort Gus.

Gus whined and refused to let down his guard. It was clear he was still in full-on attack mode, and I gave the two of them a wide berth. They both looked like they were shaking from the shock of what had just happened.

The mother moose and her calf had vanished, moving downstream at a quick pace. The horses were tossing their heads, but otherwise didn't look any worse for wear. Jericho seemed to be more interested in trying to reach a tuft of grass than dwelling on the incident. As horses go, he struck me as levelheaded.

The only one missing was Saint Christopher. I looked around the clearing and finally spotted the little corgi sitting placidly by himself next to the saddlebags. He perked his ears at me when I called him and trotted to my side as if nothing at all out of the ordinary had occurred.

I gave him a scratch on the head and he wagged what passed for his tail at me. The corgi didn't look very concerned, and I assumed it was from exhaustion more than anything.

"That's enough excitement for one day," said Wat. He gathered up his horse's reins and climbed back in the saddle.

I did the same, and as Wat and Ezra rode off in opposite directions to get back to work, Virginia had managed to amble back into the clearing and climbed back on Buck with a whimper and a groan. I knew from personal experience that after a fall like that, she would be incredibly sore the next day.

We all dispersed to renew our search for cattle, and as I rode back towards the thick brush I glanced back to see if Samuel and Gus were up and moving. When I saw them both still sitting on the ground, I was a little concerned.

Gus had calmed down somewhat. I could see that. But Samuel's face was pale as snow and he looked like he was on the verge of tears. He cradled something in his arms, practically rocking back and forth around it, seemingly gathering comfort from the object. I had to squint to see what it was, and when I made out the shape of a black semiautomatic pistol clutched in his hands I turned away quickly before he saw me staring at him.

The moose had given us all a jolt, no question. But from what I could see, it had absolutely terrified Gus and Samuel. They still hadn't gotten themselves together. Gus was still frantic because it was clear his master was barely managing to cope with the stress of what had just happened.

The kid was an absolute mess.

Without a word I rode away quickly to give him some privacy. I doubted very much he would want me to see him weeping on the ground in a heap of nerves.

After seeing his reaction to the surprise of what had just occurred, I was fairly sure Samuel had been telling me the truth when he'd said he'd spent time in the army.

But now I was positive that he had been doing a lot more than working in a warehouse counting toilet paper.

CHAPTER 12

Sunset forced us off the mountain and back to camp.

After a full day of hard riding we had managed to round up only sixty-seven head of cattle and both Ezra and Wat looked sheepish at the small total. We should have gotten at least a hundred, but maybe the others had done better and we would have our goal of two hundred head for the day.

Virginia was still in the saddle by the time we dismounted at the corral, but only by the virtue of gravity holding her there. She was so exhausted she looked like she should have fallen to the ground hours ago. Saint Christopher wasn't in much better shape, and he had developed a nasty limp that seemed to hamper his every step.

I staggered back to the campfire beside Virginia after we had pulled the saddles from our horses, both of us dropping onto a huge log next to the fire that doubled as a chair and a table. Straddling the log I found to my immense relief that I could balance my plate of hot food on my knees with the wood supporting me, and my trembling legs wouldn't rattle the dish onto the ground.

Virginia leaned down close to my ear.

"Um, I have to go to the ladies," she said.

"Latrine is just past the tree line." Samuel pointed with his fork around the supply wagon, across the sloped field. "Straight on. Can't miss it."

"Latrine? I'm in hell." She looked incredibly unhappy as she minced off across the dry grass.

I tried to imagine the look on her face when she saw the outdoor version of a bathroom. Most likely it wasn't much more than a hole in the ground with a stout pine tree close by to hold on to for balance.

When she came back her cheeks were flushed. "That was disgusting."

She sneered down at me as if it was my fault.

"Didn't have a tree to hold on to?" I asked.

"It's this gaping hole with two boards lying over the top of it and someone nailed a round piece of wood on top of them. It's supposed to be a toilet seat. You should see it."

"A seat? Positively first-class," I told her.

She scowled as she frantically washed her hands with a bottle of water.

Mr. Lamb prowled the camp with irritation. Everyone was deathly quiet, and from the bits and snatches of conversation I could pick up, it came out that we had only managed to bring in a hundred and fifty-seven cows total. Not nearly good enough if we wanted to have them all rounded up by the time the semitrucks started rolling in.

The portable corral the crew had set up looked ridiculously huge with the meager number of Red Angus milling around inside. It was hard not to feel a sense of disappointment. And the six bulls, plus the one Brangus cross that Samuel had warned us about, were not inside the corral. So that meant we still needed to deal with them. All and all, it was turning out to be a miserable day.

The mood in camp was solemn, and not very many conversations could be heard over the crackle of the fire.

Virginia had eased herself to the ground and was using the log as a backrest. Saint Christopher was sleeping a few feet away from her, looking sullen and in pain.

As dinner wound down and darkness engulfed us, Ezra settled on the ground at the end of the log and patted his thigh, giving the corgi a come-here signal.

It obviously hurt him, but Saint Christopher padded to Ezra's side and flopped to the ground next to the wrangler's legs. Ezra ran his hand over the corgi's head a few times and then gingerly inspected each paw.

"Just footsore," he said. "One of his pads is raw. I've got some Bag Balm we can put on it."

Virginia was too tired to complain about someone else touching her precious corgi. But since it was Ezra, she probably wouldn't have spoken a word against it in any case. The man with the streak of white hair obviously had done something to earn her respect. He soothed a generous dollop of greasy-looking goo over the corgi's tired feet and not once did the little dog pull away.

"Don't lick it," Ezra scolded when the corgi sniffed his paw curiously, and at once Saint Christopher obeyed.

Ezra's white streak of hair and beard didn't look quite so sinister to me, now that I'd gotten to know the quiet wrangler better. But it was still a curiosity.

He caught me staring at him and gave a slight smile. "Electrical burn."

"Pardon?" I asked, embarrassed he had busted me looking.

"I was four. An extension cord shorted out. I was lying on it at the time."

"You were laying on an extension cord?" I asked.

"It was attached to a heated blanket we'd got from the Goodwill. We were sort of poor when I was little. Didn't have heat in the house sometimes."

I wasn't sure what to say. "That's sort of sad, Ezra."

"Not really," he told me, still scratching the corgi. "I don't have any memory of it."

Virginia groaned and tried to stretch her arms. "It's worse than Pilates." She fell back against the log with a deep sigh. She looked like she'd been pulled backwards through a keyhole. I was glad there wasn't a mirror close by that would show her how awful she looked. She'd want to leave immediately and find a day spa.

I was worn out, and felt like Virginia looked. But I still had enough left in me to do my own dishes and settle back against the fat pine log and enjoy the fire a bit.

For the first time since we had arrived, I finally got a chance to really look around the circle of faces surrounding the campfire. Mr. Lamb hardly counted as a hired hand, he was more like the Speaker of the House. Still, I counted him as one of the guys, and tallied up a few names to some faces as I studied them. All told, ten men sat in various stages of tired in a loose circle.

Dan, the guy I had started to think of as Mr. North Face, gave me a faint smile when his eyes met mine. Since he wasn't a regular cowboy, he probably knew how it felt to not quite fit in with the others.

I knew Ezra now, strong and silent. And Wat, the lean and mean roping machine. And of course, Samuel, who seemed to have recovered from the afternoon encounter, and looked like his old self once again.

I'd heard the names Burris, Patrick and Albert somebody—last name Ebersole? But I wasn't sure which man went with which name. I figured that information would sink in gradually.

I was fairly certain that Anson was the pale blond cowboy who had shoulders as broad as a defensive tackle. His stout frame looked chiseled.

As I studied the group of men, a nagging feeling of uncertainty gnawed at me.

Who were they, and where did they come from? I really had no idea. Some of them could have been here before, and maybe two or three of them had. Somehow that thought worried me. But they had no way of knowing who I really was, or what I was doing on this roundup, except for Samuel, of course. And he came recommended by Todd Ramsey.

My concern was probably unfounded.

I was certain beyond a shadow of a doubt that I had never seen one of these men before in my life. I'd worked hard the first night to identify anyone I recognized.

Beards, gray hair, different clothing or an unfamiliar context could always make a person more difficult to recognize. But after careful study I was certain that no one sitting around the fire with me was someone I knew. So, the chances that any one of them knew me were remote.

Still, it wouldn't make a lot of sense to broadcast my true purpose, so I decided to keep it quiet. It was the smart thing to do.

Mr. Lamb had since abandoned the campfire and gone to bed, disgusted with our performance as a group.

The crew was quiet, and the lined and rugged faces of the men looked even more drawn with the shadows from the fire.

Wat broke the silence by recounting Virginia's encounter with the moose, and to her utter astonishment everyone gave her a joking round of applause that she had done a somersault over the head of her horse and lived to tell the tale.

The mood brightened, and Anson, the big-shouldered blond guy, told a joke about a rodeo clown and an attorney that was so racy even I blushed.

Gus had been sleeping while we finished off the last of the hot water, a few of the men unapologetically swilling full cups of coffee only an hour before bed. Sometimes the tired went so deep even coffee wouldn't dent it. But as the last of the campfire died down to mere embers, Gus sat up quickly and pricked his ears towards the corrals. He paused, his head still as a stone and his nose working hard.

The men watched the Malinois, and as one they fell silent and turned their heads in the same direction.

I strained to hear what Gus was hearing, but all I could make out were the occasional snorts and grunts from the herd off in the distance.

The silence was eerie. At last, Gus lowered his head and lay back down beside Samuel, apparently satisfied that whatever it was he had heard was not his problem, or wasn't something that needed to be worried about.

But the damage was already done.

The men had hushed their conversation and the deep glow of the orange embers from the fire cast a supernatural aura over camp.

Even Virginia hugged her knees to her chest and looked more awake than I'd seen her all evening.

She gave a nervous laugh and wrapped her coat tight. "Doesn't somebody have a harmonica or something?"

Ezra looked at her askance. "That's just a myth, that cowboys play harmonicas at night to keep the cows settled down. Truth is, it scares the hell out of them. Any ruckus can send a herd into a stampede if they feel like it."

She looked irritated that she had been shown again to be ignorant. "What do they really do then?" she asked petulantly.

Ezra tucked his hands inside his wool vest. "They talk to them."

"They tell ghost stories," Dan said mischievously.

"I don't believe in ghosts," Virginia said quickly, looking at Dan with defiance.

After a long pause that seemed to thicken the very air around us, Ezra turned towards Virginia slowly, his white streak of hair giving him a supernatural appearance. "The Blackfoot believe in ghosts."

"Blackfoot Indians?" she asked.

"They have a story about these mountains," Ezra began, a soft breeze tossing a lock of his hair.

Wind moved through the night, and the thick pine trees surrounding us whispered to each other.

Wat eased a cigarette out of a hidden pocket and lit the end by holding it close to the fire. He leaned back and blew a cloud of smoke. "This is Blackfoot country. At least it used to be. They were here long before the white man even knew this place existed."

"The Blackfoot tell a story about a place called the Camp of Ghosts, and they say that it is here, in these mountains," Ezra said, his voice pitched low.

Even the dogs looked like they were listening to him.

"Long ago there was a man who loved his wife very much," Ezra said. He let his eyes fall on the embers of the fire and he seemed to drift away. When he spoke again, it was softly.

"His wife had given birth to a son. But she became very ill, and in a few days she died. The man was so sad that she was gone he took his son to live with his grandmother. The man told the grandmother that he was too sad to live without his wife, and that he was going to the spirit world to find her. He left the camp and traveled many days and nights, until he came to these mountains. He had almost given up hope, when he came to the lodge of a very old woman. He told the old woman that he was looking for his dead wife, and wondered if she could help him. The old woman said that she had seen the man's wife as she traveled into the Camp of Ghosts, and she also said that if he waited for her, she would go into the camp and try to find the man's relatives who had already crossed over to the ghost camp, and if she did, they would be able to take him there to see his wife again."

Ezra paused and not a soul breathed.

Everyone watched him in silence.

"The old woman did find one of the man's relatives. She took the man to him, and told the man that he could travel into the Camp of Ghosts, but that he had to follow her instructions or he would fail. She told the man that when he traveled to the ghost camp, he must keep his eyes closed and never open them. She said that the man's dead relative would guide him, but that if he opened his eyes even once, for any reason, he would never leave the ghost camp and would die there. She warned him that the other ghosts would make terrible sounds, make loud, unearthly noises, and try to frighten him into opening his eyes, but that he could not ever do so, no matter how afraid he was. She said that he would have to stay in the ghost camp for four nights without giving in to his fear, and on the fourth night if he had kept his promise and not opened his eyes, then his wife would be brought to him and they would be allowed to leave together."

Another breeze blew, momentarily fanning the embers of the fire and turning them from deep orange to yellow.

A few sparks lifted up in the breeze, looking like tiny shooting stars against the darkness.

"The man agreed to follow the old woman's instructions. He went with his relative into the ghost camp and kept his eyes closed tight. The other ghosts made terrible, loud noises and tried to frighten him into looking at them. But he kept his promise and for four nights he sat still and didn't open his eyes or run away. On the fourth night the ghosts could see that he would never give up, and they returned his wife to him and allowed them to leave the camp. But as his relation led them out of the ghost camp, he warned the man that from that day forward he must never be cruel to his wife, or punish her or strike her with his fists, or she would disappear and he would never see her again."

Ezra kept his eyes focused on the fire, and seemed oblivious to the rest of us.

"The man took his wife out of the camp and returned with her to his village. For many years they were happy together, but one day he told her to do something and she did not obey him quickly enough, and he raised his fist to strike her as punishment, and in that instant she disappeared in a flash and he never saw her again."

His words were so heavy, and his face looked so sad, it was possible to imagine him as the man who had lost his wife.

It was possible to imagine that it was actually Ezra who had made the mistake of mistreating the woman he loved, and she had gone away from him, and he had never seen her again.

Everyone was still for a long time after the story was finished.

Not a man in the crew was a stranger to mistakes that had cost him dearly, that fact was plain from the look on all of their faces.

But it was true of me, too.

All of us could see ourselves in the story a little bit, and maybe some of us more than others.

"That's why there are so many bears in these mountains," Ezra said, breaking the silence.

"What bears?" asked Virginia.

"They guard the trail that leads to the Camp of Ghosts," he told her. "They keep foolish people from going places that they shouldn't go, and doing things that they shouldn't do. The bears are a warning to stay away. At least, that's the way Mr. Lamb told it to me."

A shiver ran down between my shoulder blades and didn't stop until it iced a path all the way to my toes.

Of course Mr. Lamb would know all of the spooky ghost stories about the Cross Fell Mountains.

Correction. Spooky *bear* stories.

"You know why I know that story's not true?" asked Virginia with a sneer. "Because a man actually got punished for doing something bad to a woman."

With that, she stood up, dusted off her butt with both hands and stalked inside our tent without looking back.

The men watched her go, their eyes wide with surprise.

Someone gave a low whistle, and I doubted very much that Virginia would be the target of any unwanted amorous attention anytime soon. She had radiated poisonous anger with her outburst.

Her anger and contempt riled me. I allowed myself a fierce sense of protectiveness for Leif. He had always been kind and generous to her. Leif had never treated anyone unfairly. How could she feel so much bitterness? It was her fault that they had gotten divorced, and her words seemed ungrateful and selfish to me.

It wasn't only that. She wasn't the one who had just had her house burned to the ground around her ears. I had to force myself to sit outside our tent for a long time before I was calm enough to turn in. When I finally ducked under the flap I'd given myself a good long while to cool off.

That, and I wanted to make absolutely certain beyond a shadow of a doubt that Gus wasn't hearing the sounds of a bear wandering just out of sight of the fire.

Even as tired as I was, it still took a long time to finally drift off to sleep. My thoughts were jammed together in a tangle of worry and doubt. The worry came from being surrounded by people I didn't know, being stuck in a situation I didn't have a whole hell of a lot of control over, and the uncertainty of the threat from whoever had been unwise enough to loan Virginia money that she had no hope of paying back. Because of her, my house had gone up in flames and I was hiding out in the wilderness while my new husband cleaned up her mess. Up until now I hadn't had a lot of time to deal with the shock of losing all my possessions, but somehow the hard work and pressing job of the roundup had soothed my nerves.

It was easier to think about cows than to face the emotional fallout from what had happened to my home.

And then there was the second task I'd volunteered for.

Snooping.

When I had been sitting at a warm kitchen table surrounded by familiar faces, the prospect of crawling all over an unfamiliar mountain in search of signs of a killing hadn't sounded all that daunting. But now? All I could think about were the consequences of anger and revenge, the sense of loss that drove people towards it, and the devastation of the aftermath. Maybe it was the darkness and the looming, impenetrable mountainside. Maybe it was the thought of hungry bears. Or maybe it was simply that a man had likely vanished somewhere in this lonely high country. Whatever the reason, I was feeling a sense of dread that hadn't been there before.

John Hill, the poacher who had disappeared over two years ago and was indirectly responsible for one of the most painful chapters of my life, might very well have been murdered not far from where I was laying my head down to sleep. As awful as it had been when I'd lost my job, I would gladly do it all over again for the knowledge that John Hill was alive and well, and hadn't been killed for someone else's selfish reasons. Hopefully, when I finally managed to make it up to Fischer Lake, there would be nothing at all to find. It was perfectly alright with me if I was going to all of this trouble for nothing.

It was far better than the alternative.

CHAPTER 13

"Tell me about Angus Finn." Virginia looked at me over the top of her peanut butter and jelly sandwich.

I couldn't have been more surprised if she'd asked me how old I was, how much I weighed and how much money I made.

"Pardon?" I asked, my mouth full of beef jerky.

Samuel, Virginia and I had stopped for an early lunch, and the three of us sat together on a huge flat rock in the center of a tough scrub of bushes in an alpine meadow.

A thick stand of dwarf willows flanked us, and most of the grasses were golden brown and dry. The air was so still the only sound we could hear was the horses munching grass.

Since our previous day's hunting had been so miserable, just as he had predicted, Mr. Lamb had sent the entire crew back up on the first fork to continue searching for lost cattle. It was the largest of the three areas we had to cover, but that was no excuse for our dismal performance the day before and Mr. Lamb made sure we knew it.

We had been beating the brush all morning and had the scratches to prove it.

"Angus Finn," Virginia said again. "Whatever happened between the two of you? The last time I was in Killdeer you were a hot item. Then the next thing I know you are shacking up with my husband and Finn has vanished into thin air."

Samuel stopped chewing his food and looked between the two of us like he wished suddenly he was anywhere else but where he was, like maybe on a sinking ferryboat in the middle of the Baltic Sea.

"Shacking up with your ex-husband," I said.

"Whatever," she replied. "So why did Finn just blow town, and not a peep about why he was leaving or where he was going?"

"How do you know about that?" I asked.

She shrugged, taking another bite of her sandwich. "I used to work at the real estate agency, remember? I know everything that went on in that rat-ass little town."

"Killdeer is not a rat-ass little town," I said defensively.

"Do you know how many zip codes there are in D.C. where I was living when Leif and I got married?" she asked.

"No."

"About twenty. And how many zip codes does Killdeer have?" she asked. Her blonde ponytail was draped over one shoulder and she played with it absently while she grilled me.

"Bigger isn't always better," I told her.

"Yeah, try living in a town that barely has one zip code after spending a decade in a place where you can actually buy a decent pair of shoes when you really want them," she said.

"Then maybe moving to Killdeer was a mistake and it's better that you left," I suggested with a sweet smile.

She glared at me. "Finn. What ever happened to him? He was a dish."

I took a big bite of jerky and chewed it slowly.

Samuel shifted his weight and eyed me sideways.

He still looked uncomfortable, but it was clear his curiosity was getting the better of him. "Angus Finn? That's a weird name."

Virginia finished the last of her sandwich and took a swig from her canteen. "He came to Killdeer about three years ago and was working as the security guy up at this new weather station above town. He was so quiet. Nobody knew anything about him. It took Marley six months dating the guy before she even found out his real first name."

"How do you know all of this?" I asked.

"What, he was some kind of a spy or something?" Samuel asked, suddenly intrigued.

"He wasn't a spy," I said.

"Not really. But he was a government man," Virginia said.

"And how did you come to that conclusion?" I asked, not at all happy about the conversation.

My relationship with Finn had been brief and complex, and had ended badly.

He couldn't bring himself to surrender to a committed relationship because of an unresolved trauma from his past, and I had made the mistake of thinking that I could have a normal relationship with someone who carried a gun for a living.

"I met a lot of government guys when I was married to Leif," she said. "I know one when I see one. And he wasn't even an American government guy."

"He was South African," I said, grumbling.

"So you dated a black guy?" Samuel asked with excitement. The conversation was actually starting to entertain him.

"He was a white South African," I said. "Can we talk about something else?"

"I just want to know what made him leave town so fast. Everyone at the office was talking about it," Virginia said.

"You still talk to the other real estate agents?"

"Of course. How else do you think I knew that Paul's house was sitting empty and where to find the hide-a-key?" Her tone suggested that she was speaking to a stupid person.

My eyes narrowed.

"So, what ever happened to him?" she went on, oblivious to my hard look.

"He left," I said.

"Well, obviously," she said.

"I don't know why he quit his job," I said.

Honestly, Finn's rapid departure had been worrisome at the time, and had frustrated me. My feelings for him had been torn between tentative friendship and regret that we hadn't been able to manage a real relationship. But that was all behind me now, and since marrying Leif Gable, I'd managed to put Finn entirely out of my mind.

Until now.

"You must know something," she said, needling me. "Why did he vanish into thin air so suddenly?"

I threw out my hands with frustration. "Look, Finn was odd, alright? There is no question about that. Who knows why he left? That's his business. I even went to the airport to say goodbye to him on the day he left and he flat refused to tell me anything."

"You went to the airport to say goodbye?" Samuel asked. "Your new husband know about that?"

"It wasn't a big deal. But, true to Finn, it just got strange," I said defensively.

"What do you mean, it got strange?" Virginia asked, pressing me.

"Right before his plane took off," I said, knowing at once it was a bad idea to tell it but not being able to stop myself, "he gave me a cell phone."

"Wait," Samuel said, sitting up straight and getting into the inquisition. "He gave you a cell phone? That is strange."

"Well? Did he ever call it? Did you ever call him?" she asked.

"It didn't even have any phone numbers programmed into it," I said. "It had one long number that didn't make any sense to me saved in the contacts."

"What kind of number?" Samuel asked. "How did it start?"

"A zero with two ones, then the number twenty-seven followed by a bunch of other numbers. It looked like a date, like November twenty-seven," I said.

"It sounds like an international area code," Samuel said. "Did he tell you anything when he gave it to you?"

"Geez, Marley, didn't you ever even look it up on the Internet?" Virginia asked.

"Why would I do that?"

"Come on, he had to have told you something when he gave you the phone," Samuel said, nagging me as badly as Virginia.

I rolled my eyes with the ridiculousness of it all. "Just I.C.E. That's all he said. Three letters."

"I don't get it. What does I-C-E stand for? Did you two communicate in Morse code or something?" Virginia asked.

"No, no. It stands for In Case of Emergency," Samuel told her.

I stared at him. "In Case of Emergency?"

"It sounds like he gave you a way to contact him if you really needed to get ahold of him," Samuel said.

I felt like a hammer had just hit me between the eyes.

I'd been accused of being smart before, but at the moment I felt like the person who'd said it had made a slight mistake.

"But you probably lost the phone in the fire, so now you won't ever be able to talk to him again." Virginia sounded for all the world like she was slightly disappointed on my behalf.

"The cell phone was in the glove box of the car. The car was in the middle of the road when the house caught on fire and wasn't damaged," I said.

I'd forgotten all about Finn's odd departure and the cell phone, and I'd made great progress towards forgetting all about Angus Finn, too. Now here was Leif's ex-wife, obviously doing what she could to stir up trouble.

"It doesn't matter to me at all if I ever talk to Finn again," I said. "Ancient history."

She regarded me suspiciously. "Right."

"Listen," I said, my cheeks feeling hot. "You may not be able to believe this, but Leif and I are very happy together. I don't have any interest in other men anymore. I've got a good marriage and I'm going to keep it that way."

"If you two are so damn happy together, why is Leif liquidating all his companies?" she asked.

A stone of worry dropped into the middle of my gut. I knew he had sold one business, but the rest of it he didn't talk about.

"What do you mean, selling off his companies?"

She sighed and stood up to retrieve a package of Skittles from the saddlebags. She tipped the candy into her mouth and chewed. "His companies are dissolved. Well, two of them, anyway. He sold them off and quit."

"I suppose the attorney friend of yours in Billings let that slip," I said, feeling irritated that she knew more about Leif's business life than I did.

"No, the one in Denver told me."

"How many attorneys does he have?" I asked.

"Four," she said instantly. "One in Boston, that's where his import/export company used to be. One in Denver, one in Billings and one in D.C. who handled all his foreign currency exchange matters."

"Currency exchange?" I asked.

"And our divorce." She laughed at me. "You really don't know about what he does for a living, do you?"

I was suddenly feeling out of the loop in my own marriage. "He doesn't talk about it."

"Because he doesn't want you to worry your pretty little head about it," Virginia said.

"Why is he selling his companies?" I asked.

"Beats me," she said, wiping a hand on her jeans. "Dave gave me some excuse about Leif wanting to retire, spend more time at home and quit traveling so much."

"You don't believe that?" I asked.

"Leif won't ever get out of the game. It would drive him bonkers. He's not the type of guy to ever retire. Why do you think he has his own airplane? So he can move around whenever he wants. The idea of Leif spending more time at home is laughable."

Her revelations were troubling. "So what do you think he is really doing?"

"You think I have any idea?" she asked.

Samuel started gathering up the remnants of lunch. He headed for the horses.

"If you were going to hazard a guess." I looked at Virginia with my lips pressed together so tight they were probably turning white.

She tilted her head from side to side. "Well, I'd say he is wrapping up his businesses because he is getting ready to move again. Or maybe start another company and he doesn't want to deal with the headache of having all that other responsibility hanging around."

I didn't know what to say, so I didn't say anything.

She looked a little disappointed when I headed for Jericho, my spry little Appaloosa, and proceeded to ignore her while I climbed back in the saddle.

She gathered up Buck's reins and shot me a sly look. "You could always call Finn and see how he is doing."

"Never gonna happen." I clicked my tongue and trotted Jericho the opposite direction.

I left her in the meadow and headed towards the cliff face, intent on forget the entire conversation had happened. It was time to concentrate on the job, not worry about my sordid past.

When I heard hoofbeats behind me I turned in the saddle abruptly, thinking it was Virginia coming back to hound me again.

But it was only Samuel.

"Whoa, take it easy," he said, holding up one hand. "I don't care what kind of tramp you were before you married what's-his-name."

"You need something?" My face must have been a mask of anger.

He stopped next to me and rested his hand on his saddle horn. "I'm kidding you. Boy. She sure knows how to push your buttons."

"Sorry," I said, getting my temper back under control. "So, have you figured out a way to get Mr. Lamb to let us go up to Fischer Lake?"

"Not yet," he confessed. "But I'm working on it. Listen, this deal is starting to bother me."

"You aren't thinking about chickening out on me, are you?"

He shook his head rapidly. "No, but I've been thinking about this whole situation and there is something that bugs me."

As if what I really needed at this point was more trouble. I pasted a smile on my face that was so artificial it had to have looked like I was mocking him. "Okay, what's on your mind?"

"Todd Ramsey told me that this was a Search and Rescue operation."

I tilted my head back and forth, trying to decide how much information to give him.

I shrugged evasively. "Sort of. More like a possible Search and Rescue operation."

Samuel gave me a stern look. "He said that we were looking for a missing person."

"That's mostly the story," I said, feeling concerned. How much of the truth had Todd told to this kid?

He smirked at me. "Yeah, it's a story alright. What are we really doing up here?"

"You don't believe Todd?" I asked.

"I believe that Todd got fed a line of bull." He looked at me with a flat expression.

"What makes you think that?" I asked, getting a little worried that I might have to cough up the truth.

"Because, Stephanie and Nash never allowed hunters access to this area," Samuel said.

I swallowed hard while I tried to think of a good answer. "What makes you think we are looking for a lost hunter?"

"We are looking for a lost person," he said. "And who else would come up here and disappear besides a hunter?"

"Alright. There may have been an incident."

He grimaced. "How about some details?"

"Honestly, Samuel. We don't know that much. And that's the truth. There could be a crime scene up at Fischer Lake, but probably not. That's all I really know."

He pointed a finger at me. "I know there can't be a lost hunter up here. The Cotton Ranch is the only way to reach this area, and they never let hunters cross their property. That is a fact. A long time ago they did allow hunting, but some jerk shot one of their cows by mistake and that was the end of public access. The only people who ever come up here work for the ranch. So you need to level with me."

It was plain that Samuel was perturbed. He didn't like being misled, and I could hardly blame him. He was also a lot smarter than I'd given him credit for. Although it was probably a terrible idea, I realized I was going to have to trust him or I'd be on my own.

He dropped his hand back on his saddle horn and waited.

"Okay, we are not looking for a lost hunter," I said.

He relaxed a little, and I could see he was ready to listen without interrupting me.

"A couple years ago I lost my job at the Fish and Wildlife branch office in Helena because of a botched investigation. I was just an office girl, but I was sort of privy to cases that our investigator handled. There was a poacher named John Hill selling elk horn velvet illegally, and probably a whole lot of other stuff too. Somehow he found out the investigator in our office was on the verge of arresting him, and he disappeared."

Samuel looked unhappy, but he was listening. "A poacher, huh? Okay."

"All the evidence in his garage had been destroyed. All the hard work put in by the investigator was for nothing, and there was a huge misunderstanding. I thought the investigator had made a mistake, and he thought that I had accidentally tipped the guy off somehow and he'd crossed state lines to escape. As it turns out, we were both wrong. He might not have run off to Alaska, after all."

"So, let me guess. We are looking for John Hill?" Samuel asked. "Or, what's left of him?"

"It's possible that someone John was working with, a partner of his, decided that he was too much of a liability," I told him.

"And why in the hell would you be looking this far north of the Crazies?" he asked.

"We got a tip," I said. "It might turn out to be total fiction, but it seemed reasonable to check it out. We think that Hill might have been killed up at Fischer Lake and I am supposed to go up there and see if I can find any evidence of that. It's practically impossible, I know, after two years have gone by. But that's what I'm really doing up here."

Samuel was quiet for a moment, but his mood had darkened noticeably. "Do you know how goddamn risky this is?"

"I'll admit, the plan sounded a lot better on paper," I said.

"You don't get what I am telling you, do you?" He was on the verge of pissed off.

"This is a wild goose chase," I said, hoping to reassure him. "The chances of locating a crime scene are next to impossible. Allen is convinced that John Hill's remains are in Helena, under a slab of concrete. Whatever happened up here is just a memory. I don't see why you think there could be anything about this little excursion that's risky."

"The hell you don't. Want to know something about the way killers think, Marley?"

The stone settled back in my stomach. I looked at Samuel with a growing sense of worry.

"I'll tell you," he said. "Killers use violence to solve problems because they don't have the will or the drive to solve them with social skills. They are lazy. Pure and simple. If I whacked a guy up here in the middle of hell's-half-acre, do you think for one second I'd be ambitious enough to pack the corpse out and go hide it someplace else? How could you possibly pick a better location to hide a body than this mountain?"

I swallowed. "But the slab of concrete was poured two days after the guy vanished."

"I don't give a damn if there is a tombstone with the name John Hill chiseled on the face sitting on top of that stupid slab," Samuel said. "Would you bother to remove a body when you had all of this territory to hide it?"

I shifted back and forth in the saddle.

165

"Of course you wouldn't," he said. "We are not looking for a crime scene, girl. We will be looking for a body."

"We don't have any reason to suspect that," I said.

"Because you've already got this all figured out, don't you?"

"I've got the important stuff figured out."

"Like the history of all these men who are working this job, right? And Mr. Lamb himself told me that he doesn't know one single thing about any of the men on this crew."

"You asked him about that?"

"Damn right I did. He retired five years ago. Any one of these guys could have worked here in the meantime, and he wouldn't know about it. After Nash Cotton died, the whole place started to go to hell in a hand basket, and Stephanie handed the authority for this last roundup over to Mr. Lamb. She is practically already loading stuff up in the moving van and doesn't give a rat's ass what's going on. She doesn't even know who Mr. Lamb hired for this job."

The feeling of dread I'd experienced earlier was starting to creep back. "So?"

"Didn't it ever occur to you that the guy who killed your poacher might be riding with us on this roundup?"

I choked out a laugh. "That's not very likely."

"More likely than you might think," he said. "What would you do if you found out the place you had stashed a body was suddenly up for grabs again?"

"But this land is Forest Service," I said. "And the grazing lease the Cottons had is being retired. It's going to be turned back into wildlife habitat and there won't be any cows up here anymore."

Samuel slapped dust from his leg with his gloves. "But there will be hunters again."

"Maybe, sure. That could happen," I said.

"And what do hunters do?" Samuel asked.

"They hunt for game animals," I said with a sarcastic tone.

"But to do that, they have to do something else first," he said.

"Buy a hunting license? I don't get what you are trying to tell me."

"They walk."

He pointed to the ground. "They walk around in the woods. They tramp all over the place looking for spots that will be good to explore for game."

The stone in my gut suddenly turned into a buzz saw. "Oh."

Samuel nodded at me. "Now you see why I am upset?"

"I hadn't thought of this before."

"Maybe you should have," he said. "This area will have public access again after Stephanie is gone. It hasn't been hunted for years and all the locals know it. Everybody and their dog will want to get in here. There will be men crawling all over the place."

I frowned. "And game wardens following them."

"And if you had hidden a body up here, and you knew you had one chance left to get it out before that happened, what would you do?" he asked.

The answer was so obvious.

I couldn't believe it hadn't occurred to me before.

I felt my heart squeeze with the realization. "I'd go get it."

Samuel looked grim. "Right. That's what I would do too."

CHAPTER 14

I was torn between telling Virginia what Samuel had said and keeping it to myself so I wouldn't worry her. Until I could be certain Samuel's fear was not simply paranoia, the best course of action seemed to be silence. I needed Virginia to keep her wits about her, and telling her we might be looking for a corpse would not help.

For the time being I vowed not to say anything.

Samuel and I came to an uneasy agreement that until we actually found a body hidden up at Fischer Lake we would hold off on deserting the crew and running back to civilization for backup. I was far more convinced than he that searching the area around the lake would prove a waste of time. But I had to admit some of his worry had rubbed off on me, and I didn't sit as easily in the saddle as we continued our ride.

Not for the first time since we had embarked on this adventure, I wondered how Leif was doing and what sort of headway he had achieved. Had he managed to settle up with Virginia's loan shark? I dearly hoped so.

The rest of the afternoon was uneventful aside from two occasions Ezra had ridden to

Virginia's side and given her a lecture about herding etiquette. She had tried to take over Wat's position on swing, or the side flank, and Ezra had instructed her in his quiet but firm way how rude it was to do something like that.

It was considered poor form to get in front of another rider's position. As punishment for her overzealous actions, Ezra made Virginia ride drag the rest of the way down the mountain. Drag, the position at the very back of the herd, was the least desirable place to be. The drag rider ate dust the whole way. Ezra rode point, and only occasionally looked back to make sure Virginia hadn't abandoned her post out of sheer belligerence.

To my astonishment, whatever Ezra told her to do, Virginia stuck with until it was finished.

We rested the herd at half-hour intervals on the way down to camp. No one spoke. The sun was dipping low, only a half hour away from winking out behind the jagged mountains, and even the horses hung their heads as we finally reached the flat plain of the valley.

The day came to a weary end and we rode into camp, sore, tired and driving a measly fifty head of cattle.

I worked left swing, chasing the squirrelly calves back to the larger group of cows. As we rode closer to camp, Dan saw us coming and ran to open the corral gate, his red coat easy to see even in the dim twilight. He unlatched the swinging steel gate and shoved it open in a hurry.

Two long and ancient lines of high wooden fence gradually angled in, leading towards the steel corral like a funnel. As the cattle ambled between the two wooden fences, they squeezed together until they were in a tight bunch. The two old fences acted like a chute in a way, forming an ever-tighter border until eventually the herd was snugged into a crushing mob that had no other choice but to go through the gate into the corral itself. Sometimes the cattle resisted being funneled into the corral, and the odd heifer would bolt back down the chute, but the tall fences kept them from escaping and it was an easy task to get them pointed in the right direction again.

Dan shoved the gate closed behind our mob and gave me a wave and a grin. "Not bad. But we got over a hundred today."

Wat eased his horse to a stop beside me and tipped back his filthy cowboy hat. "Let's do a head count before we lose the light."

Dan settled onto the top bar of the corral, Wat and I looped our reins around the fence, and the three of us sat side by side waiting for the herd to settle.

The new arrivals sniffed, butted and shouldered their way into the rest of the herd. It was several minutes before they ceased the hustling around and settled down.

Wat and Dan counted fast, using their fingers to keep their eyes focused on each red back. I counted them in groups of five, ticking off on my fingers each time I added another five to the pile. In the end our counts were very close.

"I've got two hundred twenty-seven," Dan said.

"I count two twenty-eight," I said.

Wat lowered his hand. "I count two twenty-eight also. Almost two hundred thirty rounded up, but it's already Saturday night. We are behind a lot more than I would have thought, it being this late in the game."

My foot rested on the bottom rung of fence, and suddenly it began to tingle slightly. A low thrum, like a vibration, reverberated up my heel. I frowned down at the ground, looked back up at Dan and swiveled sideways. It almost felt as if the ground was humming. "You feel that?"

Dan nodded. "Yeah. Like thunder?"

Wat spun around and climbed off the corral. He darted for his horse. "Everybody in the saddle."

Jericho was dancing sideways, his eyes rolling. He could hear something that I couldn't.

It wasn't until I looked past the nervous Appaloosa over the rise of the field that I saw what was causing the sound of thunder.

A line of cattle wider than the far end of the chute was coming towards us. They were moving fast.

Someone on the crew had located a huge percentage of the herd, and they were bringing them to us in a hurry.

I jumped into the saddle and reached over Jericho's neck to untie the rein as fast as I could. I barely had time to kick him to a gallop before the first cow's nose crossed the wooden fence.

Wat and I rode fast to the end of the chute to flank the incoming herd, managing between the two of us to push the stragglers back and get them all pointed towards the corral. Dan was pulling open the gate and almost got pinned between the steel and the wooden fence as the trotting cattle rushed by.

Dust choked the air. Dung and urine carpeted the chute and my eyes watered and stung.

"Heads up!" called a voice. "Them bulls is coming!"

Mr. Lamb and the cowboy I thought was named Albert appeared at the back of the herd, both men waving their hats and cutting off would-be escapees on horses lathered with sweat.

I frantically searched the red backs of the cattle, looking for off-colored animals. There, in the very center of the crush. Six huge bulls ambled along in the throng. Even in the dying light it was clear the bulls were more bronze than red, and taller at the shoulder than the rest of the herd. Not only taller, but wider too. They looked chiseled out of stone, their muscles rippled under smooth hides like boulders under a taut sheet.

I scanned them fast, counted six, and gave Wat a wave. "I see all six bulls!"

He nodded when I pointed the bulls out, reflexively pulling out his rope to give him extra advantage.

A skilled cowboy could kill a rattlesnake with a lasso. It wasn't necessarily where you hit, it was how hard. Wat was good with a lasso, no question. If one of the bulls charged, he would stand a better chance of living through it if he had a rope. One good strike on the nose and a bull would hesitate. It was the only vulnerable spot on it's body. From the looks of these six hulking animals, I started to wonder if even a good whap on the nose would slow them down. They moved like oil tankers.

As the cows and calves scrambled by, the bulls came closer and closer to me and Jericho and I tensed up with anticipation. Jericho crow-hopped beneath me with nervous energy and I almost pitched out of the saddle.

"Watch that one, there," Mr. Lamb called. "He's got horns on."

Five of the bulls lumbered past me and the sixth huge beast came into view, bringing up the rear of the pack. His hide was smooth and tan, like the others, but he sported a set of blunt horns where the other five bulls had rounded heads. They had been dehorned, but this one had not. His hardware gave him a mean confidence I didn't like the look of at all. A bold bull always had deadly potential.

As if he'd read my mind, the horned bull stopped and pivoted his great head in my direction. He rolled one lazy eye towards me, and he studied Jericho from only a few yards away. He snorted once, looking curious. Instead of moving on with the others, the bull continued to stare at me like he had something on his mind. Steam shot from his nose. Then he rolled both ears forward and sniffed the air, long and deep. He pawed the ground once, and lowered his massive head.

Mr. Lamb was already shouting.

I couldn't understand a word he was saying. All of my flight instincts fired at once and my heart felt like it stopped. Jericho's ears folded back and he shuffled in retreat but there was nowhere for us to go. We were penned in by the wooden fence and retreat was not an option. Jericho threw back his head and reared. I squeezed my legs together as hard as I could.

Both of us knew what was coming.

The horned bull flicked his tail once, tossed his head like he was playing a fun little game, and charged.

I felt the impact when the bull's head rammed straight into Jericho's chest. My feet jerked forward in the stirrups and it nearly knocked me to the ground, but somehow my hand managed to grab the saddle horn and I stayed on.

Jericho was lifted into the air. The bull flipped the Appaloosa sideways and it was like being on the most terrifying roller coaster imaginable. When he had all four legs back on the ground the little Appaloosa backed up until his flanks hit the wooden fence behind us. We were trapped. Jericho squealed in fear.

"Jump Marley!"

The bull backed up a pace and lowered his head again. He bellowed once, preparing to charge.

I reached for the top rung of the fence but it was sheer chaos beneath me. Jericho was gripped by total panic and spun wildly in a tight circle, and all I could do was hold on and hope we didn't go down. If I hit the ground at the feet of this monster he'd kill me in seconds.

More from instinct than anything else, I lifted my right leg from the stirrup and aimed a wild kick at the bull's broad nose. It landed with a satisfying crunch.

The bull let out a grunt of pain and shook his muzzle from side to side with both eyes squeezed shut. When he opened them again, he zeroed in on the thing that had just caused him pain. He rolled his eyes with anger and bellowed a challenge. Then he fixed on us with true revenge in his eyes.

He wasn't playing this time.

Jericho reared.

The bull lunged.

All I could do was close my eyes and brace for impact.

A split second after I tensed for the attack, a deafening crack rang out. The sound pierced the air like a bolt of lightning.

I forced my eyes open and saw the bull staggering. He swayed on his tree-trunk legs once, and then fell to the ground in a heap. The impact sent up a cloud of dust like a bomb had exploded, and Jericho danced sideways to escape the falling monster.

Dan stood on the second rung of the corral holding a smoking pistol in one hand. He lowered the barrel when the bull groaned his last, and as quick as it had happened, it was over.

Cows scattered away from the fallen bull, heads down, scampering with fear.

It wasn't until I got a good look at the bull that I figured out what an amazing shot it had been.

One of the horns was split in half. Dan had shot the lunging animal directly in the head. With one hand.

I stared at Dan. "Wow."

"Is it dead?" Mr. Lamb called.

Dan gave me a nod. "You alright?"

My legs were trembling and my mouth was so dry I could barely speak. "I'm fine. But I think Jericho needs a day off."

Dan looked down at the Brangus with regret. "Guess I owe Mrs. Cotton a few thousand bucks."

"I'll gladly write her a check," I said with relief.

The Appaloosa was still vibrating with fear beneath me. He blew through his nose and pulled at the reins frantically and I did what I could to soothe him.

Mr. Lamb was out of the saddle in a flash, moved to wave away two curious heifers and inspected the bull cautiously. Just as he bent down to nudge the massive animal, the bull gave a cough and drunkenly lifted up his massive head.

"Jeeeeesus," Mr. Lamb said, backing away fast and mounting up again. "Dan, I thought you killed it."

"So did I," Dan said, watching as the bull staggered to his feet.

The bull groaned and regained his footing, shaking his massive head from obvious pain. One eye was half closed and his head dipped down on the side with the split horn like he was trying to escape the agony.

"You knocked him out cold," I said, watching with amazement as the bull quietly and obediently went down the chute and into the corral without any more fuss.

As soon as the bulls were inside the corral I dismounted and immediately undid the cinch on Jericho's saddle.

I let the saddle fall to the ground and knelt down to run my hands over the little horse's ribs. Jericho pranced sideways and wouldn't hold still.

I was not a bit surprised to see Ezra walking towards us like he was going into battle.

When the somber wrangler reached us I handed him the reins wordlessly.

"Anything broken?" Ezra asked.

"I'm not sure," I said. "He seems to be breathing okay, but you should take him. I'll get the saddle."

Ezra gently led Jericho away from the corral, casting looks of pure hatred back at the big Brangus as he did.

The wrangler had seen the whole thing, and there wasn't a doubt in my mind if the bull had killed Jericho, Ezra would have butchered him.

I doubted that he would have had the same reaction had the bull killed me.

The sun finished setting, and in the dim pink glow that remained, Mr. Lamb and Dan locked up the gate and did a hasty head count.

I was too shaken up to help them.

I hefted my saddle up on one shoulder and made my way back to the tack wagon.

After dumping my saddle with the others, I finally went towards the campfire, searching for dinner.

Albert, the cowboy who had ridden in with Mr. Lamb, stopped beside me and handed me a plate of hot food. My hands shook as I shoveled barbequed pork in my mouth.

Someone, Burris maybe, produced a shot of whiskey and I gratefully drank it in one gulp. As I rule, I never touched liquor. But today I made an exception.

The fiery juice warmed my cold chest and helped put my feet more firmly back on the ground. No one spoke, but when Anson, the pale blond cowboy with broad shoulders and tree-trunk arms stood up after finishing his meal, I was a little astonished when he reached over and took my empty plate to wash along with his.

It was obvious everyone knew what had just happened. Camp was somber and still.

They were not long on words of comfort, but the cowboys' silent looks of concern helped me rejoin the land of the living.

I settled onto the log beside the fire at last, and Samuel slid to the ground beside me, a sympathetic look making him appear even younger than he was.

"Thought we had lost you there for a second," Samuel said, his voice a bit shaky.

"I thought we had lost me too," I confessed.

"Mr. Lamb said one inch to the right or left, and that bull would have been hamburger."

I managed to laugh. "Are you kidding? Prime rib. No way would that animal ever be downgraded to hamburger."

Samuel's expression fleetingly shifted to relief. He could see I still had a sense of humor about it, and that seemed to allow him to relax. His shoulders eased down from their tense hunch and he absently lifted a hand to scratch Gus on the head. The Malinois had settled beside Samuel on the ground, completely at ease.

Virginia and Saint Christopher were nowhere in sight, and I imagined they must have already gone into our tent for the night.

"We've got three hundred and twenty-two," Samuel said quietly. "Mr. Lamb and Albert went to the lower plateau at the bottom of the second fork today and rounded up quite a few cows."

I shot a look at him. My eyebrows lifted with concern.

Samuel gave me a knowing nod. "I know. Today might have been a good time for us to nip up to the lake. But tomorrow the whole crew is supposed to ride the second fork on one last search, so everyone will be up there together."

"Then how am I going to justify searching the third fork and get up to Fischer Lake?" I asked, keeping my voice low.

"How are we going to get up there, you mean." He gave Gus another good scratch, and the relaxed dog slumped over on his side and heaved a happy sigh.

"Fine. How are we going to get up there?"

"There is a way, but we will have to do some walking. You up for it?" Samuel asked.

"Have I got any other choice?"

He shook his head. "No. But it's a long way. Probably seven miles."

I felt every muscle in my entire body ache with dread. "Okay. I'm up for it."

"Tomorrow morning everyone except Ezra and Mr. Lamb are supposed to go all the way to the top of the second fork and do a concentrated search from top to bottom. You and I need to find a way to get all the way to the top of the slope before anyone else does, and then we need to find a place to hide the horses until we can get back."

"I'm assuming there is a cut at the top, but that it's too steep to ride over," I said.

"It's ah . . . on the verge of being a technical climb. You aren't afraid of heights, are you?" he asked.

"Do you have any good news?" I asked.

"There aren't any more bulls loose on the range that we have to worry about." His tone was chipper. "Pack food and a lot of water in your saddlebags tomorrow morning. It's going to be a long day."

With that, Samuel kipped to his feet effortlessly and disappeared inside the darkness of his tent with Gus at his heels. When I stood up my body made troublesome popping sounds and I moved with all the speed and grace of a box turtle.

I stood by the fire for some time, warming my hands and feeling my nerves begin to untangle. Dan and Wat were engaged in a furious card game that I didn't recognize. Burris and Anson sat with their boots off, drying out sweaty socks and airing their feet by the fire. Ezra appeared, his ghost-white streak of hair and beard lighting up orange in the firelight. The quiet wrangler took his mug from its usual place by the fire pit and swilled the last dregs of coffee from the charred pot.

I could place a name to each face by now, and I studied the group of men carefully. They really were a ragtag bunch. Albert had a nasty scar that cut a jagged path across his chin. Anson was missing the tip of his little finger on his left hand. Dan had somehow managed to get a faint black eye I'd only just noticed. When Mr. Lamb strode through camp on his way to his tent, he walked with a pronounced limp.

Not one of these men was a stranger to hardship. They all had the scars to prove it.

I thought long and hard about what Samuel had said to me. Could it really be possible that one of these cowboys was a killer? As I watched them settle into their evening routine, I just couldn't believe it was possible. They all seemed too straightforward, honest and simple. Not simple as in stupid, but simple as in not complex. What reason could any man here have for wanting to kill John Hill? Not one of them struck me as the type of man to take up partnership with a poacher.

But what a man looked like on the surface wasn't necessarily a reflection of the way he was inside. In my past experience, killers, on the surface, looked like ordinary people. You could sit next to a murderer on a public bus and never even know it.

Still, I didn't want to believe that. It didn't seem at all likely that any of these cowboys could be capable of killing a man who had been a business partner.

But, as my good friend Sheriff Loy Shucraft had pointed out to me on many occasions, I had been wrong before.

CHAPTER 15

I groaned awake at four-thirty, fumbled for my pants and managed to pull them on without falling over, but only by the slimmest of margins. Every muscle and every bone ached.

Virginia snored on the other cot with Saint Christopher curled snugly on top of her feet.

My boots were stiff with cold as I pulled them on, and my wooden fingers tied the laces haphazardly. The knots would come out soon, but after my hands warmed up I'd tie them again and do a better job.

Virginia rolled out of her cot when I flicked on the lantern, struggled to open her eyes and stared at me. "I hate this."

"I guess you shouldn't have borrowed a bunch of money you couldn't even dream of paying back," I told her.

She gave me a surly look and got dressed.

The campfire was blazing hot when I went out to join the others.

Mr. Lamb prowled through the camp like a hungry tiger, looking for any excuse to pounce. I could see at a glance he was in a foul mood, and I wondered what could have possibly set him off. Almost single-handedly, Mr. Lamb had managed to round up a quarter of the herd the day before. Why was he so cranky?

"Listen up," Mr. Lamb began.

The crew sensed his irritation and no one dared make a sound.

"Today I was plannin' on having everyone but me and Albert here go up the second fork. But I've got my suspicions that Wat and Ezra, and the greenhorns," he said, staring straight at me, "may have missed a few head up the first fork."

A few pairs of sympathetic eyes rolled towards me.

"To make up for it, I want Ezra and Wat to go back up there, with Burris and Dan, and clean out any of the leftovers."

"You want me and Patrick to go up the third fork?" asked Anson.

"Did I say I wanted you to go up the third fork?" Mr. Lamb snapped.

Anson fell silent and took a subservient step back.

Mr. Lamb glared around the circle of faces. "Now get to it. The greenhorns will ride with Samuel, Ira and Anson up the second fork. Me and Patrick will skirt that area around the bottom and catch anything they flush."

The crew exchanged confused looks but nobody said a word. It wasn't necessary for someone to stay behind and catch the first few cows that came off the mountain because someone was always riding point. Maybe Mr. Lamb needed an easy day. He was well into his sixties after all.

"What are you all standing around for?" Mr. Lamb asked.

Everyone scrambled at once. Bacon was shoveled into mouths, boots were located and pulled on, coffee was gulped.

Dan sidled up next to me and lowered his head. "What's got into him?"

I shrugged, eating a buttered biscuit as fast as I could. "You did shoot Mrs. Cotton's bull yesterday."

"Yeah, but he had it coming."

I choked back a laugh and finished eating quickly.

By the time I managed to stumble my way to the horse corral, my boots had come untied and I bent to relace them. When I stood up, Ezra was staring at me with a blank expression.

"You ride Possum today," he said.

The quiet wrangler spun on his heel and walked away.

As I recalled, Possum was the spooky palomino that shied from just about anything that moved, and even a few things that didn't.

"Great," I said, trudging to the tack wagon.

As I hefted my saddle and headed towards the palomino, Samuel snagged my elbow.

"What are you doing?" he asked. "You should take Sugar Beet."

"Ezra says I get Possum," I explained.

"That's a really bad idea," Samuel said.

"It's because I almost got Jericho killed yesterday. Ezra is teaching me a lesson."

Samuel grumbled and stomped over to the quiet wrangler. In a matter of moments the chill dawn air was filled with shouting.

"You questioning my judgment?" Ezra asked.

"She's not a good enough rider," Samuel said, his voice pitched up an octave.

Mr. Lamb appeared out of nowhere and stared the two of them into submission. "We got a problem?"

Ezra dropped his chin and closed his mouth.

Samuel took one look at Mr. Lamb's somber face and shook his head.

"No problem," Samuel said.

Every member of the crew was tensed for trouble. Even Gus had taken a stand beside Samuel, his ears back.

"I'll take it easy," I said to Samuel. "It's going to be a long ride. Possum'll be too tired to buck me off."

Samuel stormed away and threw his saddle on Sugar Beet, muttering. "She's going to get bucked off and I'll have to scoop up what's left of her."

Ezra glanced at me and looked back at the flighty palomino, undecided. "Maybe I ought to give you Rooster instead."

"It's his withers," Mr. Lamb said.

The grizzled foreman appeared at my side in the dim twilight. He wasn't looking at me, but he made a point to cast his eyes towards the twitchy palomino.

For a moment I didn't realize he was talking to me. "Pardon?"

Mr. Lamb spit on the ground. "Possum's ticklish. He ain't spooky, he just doesn't like to have his withers touched. Keep yer reins high and he'll be fine."

The grumpy boss marched off before I could thank him.

"How did he know that?" I asked.

Ezra shrugged. "He's the foreman."

I made a serious mental note not to even think about touching Possum on the withers.

Since I had a habit of resting my hands on my saddle horn, it was possible I would end up on my ass at some point during the course of the day.

The crew mounted up and started riding just as the first rays of sunlight bloomed across the field. Pink turned to gold, and the crisp dew began to melt off the fading huckleberry bushes.

Samuel and I rode side by side. Virginia and Saint Christopher brought up the rear, and Gus darted back and forth between us.

Both dogs were in high spirits, in spite of the dark mood all of the humans clearly felt.

Nobody said a word as the crew fanned out and started the long trek up the mountain.

It shouldn't have come as a surprise, but when Samuel took charge of our little trio, he had us evading the rest of the crew by riding like we'd just robbed a stagecoach and climbing a hidden deer track so fast even the dogs were having a hard time keeping up.

The kid was sharp; there was no doubt about it. And he really knew his way around the mountain. At the pace we were setting, there was no possibility that any of the others on the crew could have beaten us to the top.

Each time Virginia tried to strike up conversation, Samuel cut her off with a hard gesture. At last he pulled us to a steaming halt in a small clearing and we slid out of our saddles quietly. The foamed horses gasped from the sprint up the mountain.

Samuel gathered us in a tight circle and kept his voice down. He looked at Virginia intently. "We will be back in a few hours. If anyone sees you, don't tell them where Marley and I are and what we are doing."

"What am I supposed to say?" Virginia asked peevishly.

"I don't know, think of something," Samuel said. "Just don't tell them we are at the lake."

We tied the horses and Virginia settled on the ground with a pout.

I realized with surprise that she wasn't upset we were leaving her, she was upset because she couldn't round up any cattle until we returned.

Samuel shouldered his pack and Saint Christopher leapt up with excitement. He gave the corgi a hard look. "No. You stay here, Toots."

Saint Christopher lowered himself to the ground, bereft. There was no worse punishment for a dog than telling him he couldn't go for a walk.

Samuel led the way up the slope, Gus bouncing along the trail beside us, and after a half hour of hard walking nearly straight up, we came to the bottom of the cliff face and stopped to rest. He tossed his backpack to the ground and rummaged through it.

"Where is this cut you were telling me about?" I asked, surveying the cliff dubiously.

Samuel took a long drink from his canteen. "You just have to take my word for it."

I stepped back and cautiously scanned the smooth surface of the rock above us, searching for any sign of a handhold or a crevice that I could shimmy through without falling to my death. "Ah . . ."

"It's just up there." He pointed over my left shoulder.

I pivoted and searched the pebbly gray granite cliff. Then I saw a tiny shelf protruding from the rock close to forty feet off the ground.

"That?" I asked, incredulous.

"Don't worry, it looks harder than it really is."

"If you are a mountain goat," I said. "Are you sure about this?"

"Trust me."

We rested another ten minutes, my adrenaline pumping as hard as a fire hose. When it was time to start the climb, Samuel spent a solid minute scanning the area to see if anyone was close by. The trees obscured us nicely.

"I will go up first, then Gus and then you," he said.

"Gus is coming?"

"We can't do this without him," Samuel said with complete seriousness.

My palms were sweating with worry as Samuel pulled a long rope and harness from his pack. When I saw the harness I relaxed.

"Thank goodness."

The kid gave me a look. "It's not for you. It's for him," he said, pointing to Gus.

"So, I'm beginning to get the idea just exactly who is expendable on our team," I said.

Samuel didn't reply, but simply walked upslope a dozen yards or so and wiped his hands on his jeans. When his hands were completely dry, he stepped close to the rock and inserted his fingers inside a tiny crack I hadn't even noticed.

With amazingly smooth motions, Samuel pulled himself off the ground. Hand over hand, he inserted his clenched fingers inside the crack and began ascending the rock face like it was a flight of stairs.

I stood watching him with my mouth gaping open.

The further off the ground he got, the quieter I was. I even stopped breathing at one point, so afraid any noise would distract him that I didn't even dare inhale loudly.

In a matter of minutes he was straddling the small shelf that hovered at least forty feet above me.

"Move back," he called.

I hurried away from the cliff and he dropped the harness. The rope, bright orange and blue, unraveled and the red harness hit the ground with a thud.

"Okay, strap it on Gus," he said.

The harness was relatively simple, and Gus held stock-still as I wrapped it around his chest and stomach.

He barked once with excitement and Samuel admonished him softly.

The Malinois fell silent at once, his ears perked up and his eyes bright.

"Okay, Marley. Climb up."

I stood up straight and stared at Samuel. "I'm sorry, but are you out of your mind?"

"I can't pull Gus up here by myself. It's only tough the first ten yards, then the rock slopes back and you can use your feet."

"This is a bad idea. This is a really bad idea," I said to myself as I pulled out my gloves.

Samuel called down to me. "No. Don't use gloves. You won't be able to get your hands in the crack."

"I don't think I can do this," I said.

"Sure you can," he said cheerfully. "I've watched you. Your saddle weighs thirty-five pounds and you can pick it up with one hand. You can pull yourself up here, no problem."

"This is crazy," I said to myself.

Gus cocked one ear at me, panting gamely. He was having a blast.

I wished I were still asleep on my cot.

"Okay, here goes," I said.

"Use the rope to help you," Samuel called. "I've got a good hold on it. But don't put your full weight on the rope or you'll kill us both."

"Wonderful," I said.

It was painful and terrifying, but I managed to jam my hands inside the crack, the way I had seen Samuel do, and use the pressure of my fingers to hold my weight.

One hand, then the next, then the next. I didn't look down. My feet seemed to know what they were doing, because they moved up the rock behind me almost as if they had a mind of their own. It was excruciating. After seven reaches with my arms shaking, I scrabbled hard and almost lost my grip, but managed to snatch the rope and jam my foot inside the crack.

The crack grew wider the higher I went, and I used the rope for balance as I crammed my toes inside the crack. The cliff did slope back exactly as he had told me and I was able to use my legs to climb up the rock and only held on to the rope for balance.

Gus must have been holding perfectly still the entire time, because the rope didn't even twitch while I was holding on to it.

Samuel reached down and grabbed my arm as I made it to the top, and as I looked over the edge I relaxed. The cliff was a sharp drop directly below us, but to the north going up, it tapered into an easy incline that would be a steep, but doable, hike.

"Good job," he said, pulling me up. He gave me a broad grin and his braces flashed in the bright sunlight.

I grinned back. "I can't believe I just did that."

"Now for the fun part."

The two of us sat on the shelf looking down at Gus. It had been nerve-wracking, but from the angle we were at now, Samuel's assessment had been correct. It was only really tough going the first ten yards and then it did get a lot easier.

That's not how it had looked from the ground.

"Get behind me and plant someplace flat and secure," Samuel said. "Then take up the slack as I pull Gus up, and if you feel me start to lose the rope, give me a little help."

I did as he instructed, and found a solid place to sit while I wrapped the slack rope around my back.

Samuel started to heave Gus up, hand over hand, but he only had to pull the excited dog three-quarters of the way before the Malinois managed to get his claws working and started to help with the climb.

It was only a matter of moments before Gus was scrabbling up the rock beside me, licking my face happily.

"Gross dog spit," I said, pretending to shove Gus away. "You are a handful."

We left the rope and harness out of sight behind a boulder and began the steep walk the rest of the way to the top. It took another hour before we broke through the tree line and caught sight of Fischer Lake.

I stared at it. "You call that a lake? It's tiny."

When Allen had told me it was a lake, I'd expected something larger than six or seven acres. But it was hardly any bigger than a pool.

The entire thing couldn't have been more than a hundred feet across.

"It will take us less than an hour to search the shoreline," I said. "This won't be nearly as difficult as I thought."

"It'll take us a lot less time than that," Samuel said. "Gus. Sit."

The Malinois instantly squatted on his haunches, coiled like a taut spring.

Samuel pointed to the edge of the small lake, his tone all business. "Seek!"

Gus broke into a mad sprint and tore for the water's edge.

Nose to the ground, he systematically ran a grid pattern back and forth along the tree area around the lake.

"He's an experienced cadaver dog," Samuel said. "If there is a dead body up here, Gus will find it."

"A cadaver dog? But I really don't think there is a body up here."

"Maybe a finger. Or blood? Who knows. Whatever's left of your John Hill, Gus will be able to find it. Even if it's only a tiny piece."

"Surely he can't smell blood after two years," I said.

"Probably not blood," Samuel admitted. "But if there is a bone or a bit of tissue, he can find it."

"Wow," I said, looking back and forth between the two of them. "That's impressive."

"We are a pretty good team, Gus and me." He found a flat rock and eased himself down.

"How long have the two of you been working together?" I asked, sitting next to him and feeling my bones pop.

"Four years."

I nodded. "So, Gus was, what? Helping you count toilet paper in the warehouse while you were in the army?"

"Yep."

"And where was this warehouse, exactly? Afghanistan or Iraq?" I asked.

Samuel's face clouded over for a moment. "Nepal."

His voice broke slightly as he said the word.

I respectfully closed my mouth and refrained from making any more smart comments.

After a few minutes of watching Gus dart around the woods surrounding the lake, my curiosity got the better of me.

"How long can a cadaver dog detect human remains after they are buried?" I asked.

"Years and years, if they are not buried too deep. That's the only thing that will prevent a dog from finding them. If your lost poacher is underneath too much soil, Gus won't be able to smell him."

"I doubt whoever killed John Hill had very much time to dispose of the body," I said speculatively. "There would have been other riders on the mountain to worry about."

"How much time do you think he had?"

I rocked my head back and forth. "It's tough to say. If it was planned in advance, then the killer hauled the body off of the mountain and we won't find anything at all."

"That doesn't make any sense," Samuel said.

"Well, Mr. Smartypants, what would you have done instead?"

"I would have brought the guy up here alive and killed him about two feet away from where I was going to dispose of his body."

I blinked with surprise. "You would?"

"It's a lot easier than lugging around a corpse. You said that the murderer was a partner of his? Was an associate?"

"That's the tip we got," I told him.

Samuel waved his hands. "Then why go to all the trouble of bringing a dead guy up here when you can just convince him to walk up under his own power? Then, blam! Shoot him and in a couple hours the body is buried and our killer goes back to work with the rest of the cowboys like nothing happened."

"Maybe," I said. "I'm still not convinced it went down that way."

"Well, if it was an argument that sparked the murder, and it wasn't planned, I will bet you a million bucks the guy is buried here under about a foot of dirt. That's all the deeper the killer would have been able to dig if he was in a hurry."

The implications of that hit me like a slap to the face. I started to reply, but before I could get out any words I was cut off.

Gus had stopped somewhere beside the lake and he was barking.

He was barking like he had just treed a mountain lion.

CHAPTER 16

I expected Samuel to leap to his feet and sprint to Gus, but he simply shoved himself upright and ambled towards the excited dog at a normal pace, not in any hurry.

His reaction seemed odd, until I realized he and Gus had probably done this dozens of times, and finding something wasn't an event any longer.

When we reached the excited dog Samuel stopped beside him and scratched his head. "Good boy. Show me."

Gus spun a circle on the edge of the lake and barked.

Samuel frowned. "Where? Show me."

Again, Gus spun a circle, barking loudly.

"I don't get it. Here?" Samuel asked.

We stood on the shore of the tiny lake, but the soil was not so much dirt as it was boulders and rocks.

If there actually was a body hidden beneath us, it would take a backhoe, or a well-placed stick of dynamite, to find it.

"How could a guy bury a body on this spot, under all these rocks, in a couple hours?" I asked. "There can't be anything here."

"He's never done this before," Samuel said.

Gus's ears shot forward and he looked at the two of us expectantly. He barked again, whined and sat down.

"He's indicating," Samuel said. "This is the place. I just don't see how it's possible."

"Maybe there is something here that is small, like a tooth or a finger or something too small for us to see?" I asked.

"Let's take a look around," he suggested. "It could be a magpie or coyote dragged a fragment of the corpse over here and that's what he is hitting on."

We both headed for the trees and scanned the ground as we walked. Gus whined behind us and barked rapidly.

"I wish I spoke dog," I said.

"He's saying, 'no stupid, over here,'" Samuel told me. "But I can't understand why he thinks it's under the rocks. I just don't think someone who would be worried about being discovered by other members of his crew at any moment would take the time to shift that much stone to hide a body. There must be something close, though."

We searched the ground slowly, inching along, and occasionally I bent down to turn over a branch or pull back a clump of vegetation.

"Hey, I think it's here." Samuel toed the ground at his feet several yards away from where I stood.

When I crouched down beside him a telltale flash of white came into focus. I brushed aside a few stray bits of dead leaves, tossed a stick aside and a fragment of bone appeared. The bone was long and very slender, and flanked on either side by four other bones nearly the same size.

I could clearly see the remnants of what looked like a hand.

I brushed aside a scraggly juniper branch that hovered close by so I could see the bones better, and they looked unnaturally white against the black soil. I snapped the limb from the low juniper and tossed it aside to get a better look. The bones were quite long, and very finger-like in shape. But something about them made me suspicious.

"Call Gus, would you?" I asked.

"Gus. Come."

Instantly the Malinois darted to Samuel's side.

Samuel pointed down. "Seek."

Gus sniffed the bones once, promptly turned his back on them and went directly to the edge of the lake once more. He spun a circle and barked several times, looking at Samuel with growing exasperation.

Samuel looked aghast at the dog's reaction. "Did you just forget all of your training?"

"It's not human," I said.

He crouched down beside me and picked up one of the bones gingerly. "Are you sure?"

"I'm sure. Look." I dug to the end of the hand, where the fingernails would be, and lifted a long claw from the soil. A chill went down my spine and I felt a horrible itch between my shoulders, like something in the forest was watching.

"It's a bear," Samuel said. "No wonder he didn't hit on this. But I could have sworn it was a person."

"That's a common mistake," I said. "The game wardens and biologists I worked with at the Fish and Wildlife office would sometimes get phone calls about hunters finding dead bodies in the forest. Usually, it turned out to be the paws of a bear. If the animal is young when it dies, the bones in the paw can look remarkably like a human hand."

"Well, it fooled me," Samuel said.

"It didn't fool Gus. But he seems to think that something is here."

We both looked over at the frantic dog. Gus barked again.

I stood up and surveyed the lake carefully. "Hey, if you only had a short amount of time to hide a body up here, and you didn't have any big tools to help you dig a hole, where would you put it?"

Samuel and I stared at each other. We said it at the same time.

"In the lake."

We walked to Gus and stared into the water.

At last the excited dog sat down, satisfied he had finally gotten his point across.

"How deep do you think it is?" I asked.

"Not very. Look, it's dead water."

Mosquitoes bounced across the surface gamely. Not one ripple broke the surface, telling me that the lake didn't have enough oxygen to support fish.

It was not very clear, but clear enough to see maybe three feet deep.

"Is it possible for a cadaver dog to smell a body underwater?" I asked.

"Sure. To a dog, water is nothing more than thick air. If the body is still decomposing, gases and fragments of tissue will float to the surface and leave a scent."

"But John Hill disappeared more than two years ago. Could there still be enough left for Gus to detect?"

Samuel glanced down and gave the dog a good scratching. "That water can't be more than forty degrees. And it's not going to contribute to decomposition as much as salt water, or moving water. Maybe. It's possible."

"How are we going to find out if he's down there?" I said, asking the obvious.

Samuel coughed. "I can't swim."

"You can't?" I asked.

"Nope. Not a stroke. I vote we walk away, tell Allen that Gus hit on something that could be in the lake, and let him deal with it in the spring."

I wanted so much to agree with him, but something told me there was too much at stake to simply walk away.

More important, if someone had killed John Hill and hidden his body in the lake, I wanted to know about it now, before going back to the crew.

But there was another reason I was determined to finish the search. Unless someone actually saw the remains, what was to prevent the killer from simply coming up to the lake and relocating the bones before law enforcement could start an investigation?

No, we had to be certain.

"Turn around." I started to pull off my boots.

"Are you nuts?" Samuel asked.

I unzipped my jacket and set it carefully on a rock.

When I started to pull off my shirt Samuel spun around and put his back to me.

"You are going to get hypothermia," he said.

"You know how hard it is to move that much deadweight?" I asked, speculating out loud. "Even if you are a big strong man, dragging a corpse is hard work. But it's a lot easier to just roll it into the water, don't you think?"

I slid my pants off and piled them on top of my coat. I hesitated to take off my bra, but the thought of wearing it soaked with freezing water was all the motivation I needed. I piled it with the rest of my clothes.

There was no way I was giving up my underwear.

Samuel snuck a peek at me as my feet slapped in the freezing water, but he spun back around instantly. "This is going to go down as my all-time favorite Search and Rescue mission."

I yelped when the rocks dropped off sharply and I found myself up to my waist in frigid water.

It was cold. Bone chillingly cold. The rocks were smooth but also covered in slime and my feet slipped and slid around like I was on ice skates.

"There is a deeper pool here," I said.

"You don't have to get in the water all the way," Samuel told me. "Just feel around with your toes."

"Eww, that's a horrible thought."

"As opposed to getting in a lake with a dead body in the first place?" he asked.

I started to say something smart-alecky in reply and felt my left foot slip. My mouth was wide open when my legs shot out from underneath me. My head plunged under the water.

The cold on my legs was nothing compared to the shock that went through my scalp as the icy water engulfed me. I let out an involuntary cry and bubbles blew out.

I had about sixty seconds before I froze to death.

Somehow I struggled to the surface and managed to gulp a great gasp of air.

"Are you alright?" Samuel called.

"Yes," I choked out. "Give me one minute."

I took a huge breath, and though it was painful to do it, I ducked my head underneath the water and clumsily spun a circle, trying to see something. Trying to see anything. It was dreary, murky, and I couldn't see any further than the length of my own arm.

My lungs gave out and I had to surface. My fingers were already numb, and my face was stiff with cold.

"Marley, this isn't funny. Knock it off and get out of there," Samuel said. "That's four-minute water. Stay in there much longer and you'll go into shock."

"One more," I called.

I took another gulping breath and submerged. The pool deepened sharply towards the center of the lake, and the water was nearly opaque. Pushing myself down, I reached out with both hands, searching. My fingers brushed against something and I spun frantically towards it, trying to see what it was.

Some sort of cloth, or blanket, floated in the water before me. My first thought was that this had been a total waste of time and Gus had hit on someone's old horse blanket, but as my fingers grasped the fabric and shifted it around, I could feel that it was a sleeping bag.

Sleeping bags didn't normally drift upright in the water. Something at the base had it weighted down.

I managed to turn the bag enough so the opening for the face was in view. I peered inside.

Bubbles shot out of my lungs towards the surface when I cried out with shock.

Through the gloom I saw my worst nightmare staring back at me. Floating upright inside the dark blue sleeping bag, his feet pointing down and his head only three feet from the surface of the lake, I saw the decomposing skull of John Hill grinning back at me from his murky tomb.

One look told me all I needed to know.

A single bullet hole, round and perfect, pierced the center of his forehead, directly between his eyes.

I shot to the surface and clambered for the shore as fast as my frozen limbs would carry me. I didn't even care that Samuel was getting an eyeful, I had to get out of that lake and nothing was going to stop me.

To his credit, Samuel didn't even blink when I half-stumbled to his side and started reaching for my clothes.

"No, you'll get them wet. Dry off first," he said.

I was shivering with tiny earthquakes and my teeth clattered together so hard I thought they would chip.

Gus was by my side in an instant and instinctively I threw my arms around him and pulled him to me. His warm fuzz felt like the best thing in the world.

Samuel took off his jacket and draped it over my shoulders. He had the decency to keep his eyes averted as he stood beside me holding out my hair so it didn't drip all over his coat.

"I saw him," I said through chattering teeth. "He's there."

Samuel took a step back and stared at the pool. "Goddammit. Do you think it was an accident? Maybe he drowned."

"Ah . . . no. He was shot in the middle of the forehead."

"But how could one man lug a body all that way and have the strength to haul it into a lake?" Samuel asked.

"Easy. Drag it with his horse to the shore, tie a rope around a heavy boulder and shove it off the edge. There's a really sharp drop only a couple yards from the edge. Hell, I could have done it."

We both fell silent as the implications of that sunk in. As soon as I was dry enough to put my clothes back on without soaking them, Samuel started handing me shirt, shoes, and boots and urged me to hurry with each article of clothing.

"We need to bug out. Let's go, Marley. We need to move."

I was still pulling on my jacket when he tugged me to my feet and led me away from the lake. My feet were freezing and slow to react, but Samuel urged us to a trot and the blood started pumping again. It helped immensely that the day was sunny and warm for fall. But the mild weather didn't seem to give Samuel any comfort. He was on high alert, scanning the trees and reaching over to pull me along if I started to lag behind.

"Can't we rest?" I asked, feeling light-headed and nauseous.

"When we get back to where we left the horses. Keep moving."

He jogged ahead of me, turning every few paces to urge me on. It was all I could do to keep up.

By the time we reached the cliff face I was ready to collapse. Samuel harnessed Gus quickly and after I sat down to grip the rope, my head was swimming and stars shot across my vision. We lowered Gus to the ground, the last ten yards straining what was left of my strength as I helped Samuel hold the dog's weight.

When Gus was on the ground, Samuel turned back to me. "Ready?"

"Just push me over the side," I said.

Samuel knelt down and peered into my eyes. He put one hand on my neck and felt my pulse. "Take a few breaths, alright?"

He handed me water and I cautiously drank a few swallows. It was ridiculous, but I had a sudden and intense craving for M&M's.

As if on cue Samuel shoved a piece of beef jerky at me and ordered me to eat it. Then another swallow of water.

Then he was pulling me to my feet and wrapping my hands around the rope.

"One foot down, hand over hand, keep moving," he said.

I managed to jam my toes into the crack like I had done on the way up. It was slightly easier going down, but my arms were shaking by the time I was running out of purchase for my feet, and the crack grew too narrow to support my toes any longer.

It took all the strength I had left to hold on to the rope the last ten yards. When I was still six feet off the ground my hands simply gave out and slipped off the rope. I tried to catch myself but it was too much for my tired muscles to manage and I fell to the ground hard.

"Are you alright?" Samuel called. He was already tossing down the rope behind me and descending rapidly.

Stupidly, I watched him climb down, lying on the ground directly beneath him as he scaled backwards down the cliff. If he fell he would crush me.

At that point I really didn't care.

Gus sat beside me and gave me a sloppy lick on the side of the face. When Samuel's boots hit the ground beside me he started removing Gus's harness as fast as he could and coiling the rope inside his pack like his life depended on it.

When he zipped his pack closed, and all evidence of our adventure was safely tucked away inside, he relaxed enough to search the tree line for any signs of other people.

"Okay, on your feet. Let's go."

He didn't wait for me to move, and simply hauled me upright with a mighty pull.

At least we were going downhill now.

I was barely walking by the time we made it to the clearing where Virginia waited with the horses. She jumped with surprise when we stumbled through the trees. I practically fell on the ground, gasping for air.

"What took you so long?" she asked. "That man Patrick was here looking for us."

Samuel and I looked at each other with concern.

"When was he here?" Samuel asked.

"About an hour ago."

"I thought he was supposed to help Mr. Lamb pick up stragglers as they came down to the field?" Samuel asked.

"Mr. Lamb told Patrick to come and help us because he thought we would need adult supervision. Patrick wanted to know why you two weren't riding. I told him you were in the bushes screwing."

I sat bolt upright. "You did what?"

"Captain Wonder-Dummy didn't give me a better story," she said, giving Samuel a sour look. "It got rid of him, didn't it?"

"Everybody on your horse, now," Samuel said. "Marley, I don't care if you have to use a rock to get up there, I want you in the saddle."

It wasn't easy, but his urgency was clear to see, and I forced myself to my feet and managed to climb on Possum without falling over the other side.

The three of us rode out of the clearing, Samuel leading the way, and to my astonishment a small herd of ten or so heifers milled around just inside the tree line.

"Where did they come from?" I asked.

"You think I sat around and didn't do a damn thing while the two of you were out on your little field trip?" Virginia asked. "I was actually working."

The three of us drove the cattle down the mountain like we had been hard at it all morning, and did our best to look like that was all we had been doing.

Forcing myself to go into that lake had not been easy, but it had turned out to be essential. As I swayed in the saddle from fatigue, my brain sifted through the foggy mess of thoughts swirling in my head well enough to understand the implications of what we had found.

John Hill had been killed by his partner, here in the mountains, exactly as his girlfriend had feared. But unlike the theory put forward by Allen and Bruce, he wasn't buried underneath a slab of concrete after all.

He was still here.

And ten heavily armed men, any one of whom could be his murderer, waited for us back in the isolated camp, miles and miles from the nearest police station.

Suddenly, Samuel's paranoia didn't seem so silly after all.

CHAPTER 17

We broke for lunch well past one, and I found myself flanked on either side by both dogs as I sat in the dry grass of a small clearing. They seemed to know I was on my last legs and were doing what they could to provide sympathy.

Virginia sat with her back to me, and Samuel paced while he chewed from a plastic bag holding a summer sausage. He used a long hunting knife to slice off pieces of the sausage and talked while he ate.

"We should leave," he said.

"We can't leave," I told him.

Virginia tilted her head back and glared at me. "What's going on? Why are the two of you acting so odd?"

Samuel sheathed his knife on his belt and carefully wrapped his lunch. "Marley and I found a dead guy in the lake."

Virginia shot to her feet. "That is not funny."

"He's not joking," I told her.

"Then he's right," she said quickly. "We should go home. I need a shower and I'm sick of this place."

"We can't go home," I said. "Remember?"

Virginia snorted and sat back down. "And I suppose that's all my fault."

"As a matter of fact—"

"You two are hiding up here." Samuel looked back and forth between us. "You came up here to get away from something."

I finished chewing the last bite of my squashed sandwich. My saddlebag had flattened it, but I didn't care. Protein was protein.

"We are laying low for a few days while my husband clears up a financial misunderstanding with some of Virginia's creditors."

"You think it is safer up here with a murderer?" Samuel said.

Virginia bolted to her feet again. "The dead guy in the lake was murdered?"

"Everyone take a breath," I said.

"This is insane," Virginia said. "I say we leave right away."

I palmed the wrapper from my bologna sandwich and folded it inside my saddlebag. "If we go home now, before Leif has had a chance to clean up your mess, do you think your buddies Bobby and Gino will have just forgotten all about us? No hard feelings?"

She clamped her mouth shut and crossed her arms like a five-year-old. "I don't know. Probably not."

I rubbed my eyes and rested my forehead in my palm. "We have to figure out which one of them did it."

Samuel stopped his pacing and spun around to face me. "Seriously. That is not our job."

"You have a better idea?" I asked.

"I've told you my better idea."

Virginia mumbled something, but when I looked at her she turned away. She shook her head a few times and seemed to be on the verge of saying something. But when I gave her a questioning glance she waved me off and shut her mouth tight.

Virginia was holding something back, but she seemed determined not to share.

"What?" I prompted her.

"You think the person who killed the man in the lake is someone on the crew?" she asked.

"It doesn't do us a bit of good not to assume that," I said.

"How do you know all of this?" she asked. "Is that what you and your ex-husband were arguing about back in Killdeer?"

I didn't say anything, and her eyes narrowed to slits. "You knew about this the entire time."

"We had a tip," I admitted.

"What tip?" she demanded.

"The dead guy was partners with someone, and the dead guy had a girlfriend who left a message suggesting that her boyfriend's partner may have had something to do with his disappearance."

"May have had?" Samuel asked bitterly.

Virginia picked at a torn spot on her designer jeans. "But, even if he is here, he wouldn't be stupid enough to do anything to us, don't you think? Not with all of these other people around."

Samuel sat down, crossed his legs and propped his elbows on his knees. "I suppose that being with a group gives us a little bit of protection."

I felt my shoulders slump. "Maybe."

I sorted through our problem in my mind while Virginia sulked and Samuel worried. One thing that hadn't changed was the method we could use to figure out who killed John Hill. Finding John's body in Fischer Lake altered a great many things, but my original goal of figuring out who had worked the cattle drive two years ago was still valid.

"Listen," I said to both of them. "The smartest thing we can do now is figure out which one of the crew killed our lake man and stay as far away from him as possible until we can get the hell out of here."

They both reluctantly nodded.

Samuel stared at the ground and Virginia kept picking at the hole in her jeans like she wanted to say something, but couldn't quite bring herself to spit it out.

"Does everyone agree?" I asked.

"This isn't exactly how I pictured this trip going." Samuel's tone was sullen.

I rubbed the back of my neck. "Let's figure out what we already know and go from there."

"What do we know?" he asked. "Not a whole lot as far as I can see."

I took a moment to straighten out the thoughts that were sloshing around in my head. It wasn't easy.

"We know that John Hill was a poacher," I began.

"And he was in business with someone else, a partner, who was probably the guy who killed him," Samuel said.

"And we know that he was killed two years ago, in the spring."

"How does that help us?" Samuel asked.

"Just stay with me," I said. "Allen and Bruce and I came up with an idea while we were trying to figure this out, and there is one way we can solve it and figure out who killed John."

"Why are you so certain the dead guy in the lake was murdered?" Virginia asked.

"Because there is a bullet hole between his eyes," Samuel said bluntly.

She swallowed and looked away.

"We just have to think about the logistics," I said. "There is only one question we need to answer, and when we do, we will have figured out which one of the crew is our killer."

"What's the question?" Samuel asked.

"Since our guy was killed two years ago, we need to find out which one of the crew was here at that time, working the spring drive."

Virginia laughed with heavy sarcasm. "Oh is that all? We will sit down at supper tonight, get everyone's attention and make an announcement. Hey everybody. Which one of you stooges worked here that year the guy disappeared? Sure. Great idea."

"It's not that simple," Samuel said.

"Yes, it is," I told them both. "But we can't ask them directly. We have to be careful. There are nine men on this crew that we need to check out. I really don't think it was Mr. Lamb because he was already retired when John was killed. So that leaves us eight suspects."

Samuel shook his head back and forth. "We don't have a lot of time. Are you sure this will work?"

Both dogs jumped up and Gus barked a warning.

The three of us fell silent as the sounds of a rider clomping through heavy brush echoed through the clearing.

Hot Damn, the heavy-hooved gray gelding Patrick favored, lumbered into the clearing, and when he spotted us he jerked to a halt with a loud snort of alarm.

Patrick waved. "Hey, your calves are runnin' off."

Virginia shot from the ground, grabbed Buck's reins and was instantly in the saddle. She didn't say a word as she galloped from the clearing towards the trail where we had left the cattle.

I managed to get to my feet without stumbling and reluctantly headed for Possum. I was surprised that, even after all of the revelations I'd just delivered, Virginia still had her newly discovered, wild determination to round up the cows. If only she could muster as much enthusiasm for dealing with her personal problems . . .

Patrick shot Samuel a suggestive wink and gave a nod in my direction. "Giddy up, Pardner."

Samuel blushed crimson and looked so guilty anyone would have believed we'd had a torrid afternoon ripping each other's clothes off in the bushes. I was mortified for a moment, but on the bright side we didn't need to worry about coming up with a believable reason why we had both been absent for the entire morning.

Patrick kicked his gelding into a trot, and Samuel and I trailed after.

Samuel and I exchanged silent glances, knowing that the time for planning was over. There wasn't anything else for us to talk about. We both knew what we had to do. The kid looked less than happy, but at least he wasn't arguing about our course of action any longer.

The three of us tried to continue with the work as if nothing extraordinary at all had happened.

The afternoon was punctuated with successes and failures.

Patrick took up with our group, and the four of us hunted the hidden areas of the mountainside in a tight pack. We came across an ancient dirt-floor log cabin, mostly collapsed, with three stubborn steers squatting inside. They stared out at us from inside the old structure, tossing their heads defiantly.

Saint Christopher charged in and dutifully chased them out with vicious barks and snaps.

As the steers bolted through the tilted doorway, the corgi trotted behind them victoriously.

Everyone was laughing, watching the twenty-pound dog chase the eight-hundred-pound animals like he was a timber wolf.

As the day wore on I let down my guard and forgot Mr. Lamb's warning about Possum's ticklish spot.

We'd stopped for water and I rested my hand on the palomino's withers.

Without warning Possum exploded.

Instantly the world went sideways and I grabbed the saddle horn with both hands.

Possum bucked backwards and threw his head down. The reins jerked from my grasp and I squeezed my legs as hard as I could until the tornado beneath me died down.

Three heifers close by looked at us askance, sniffing the air and doing what they could to determine what had caused the palomino to go insane.

Finally their curiosity waned and they darted past, racing to join a gang of calves a short distance away.

"What'd you do to him?" Patrick gave the palomino a cautious look.

I held still for a moment, waiting for another burst of crazy, but Possum seemed to have settled down.

I shook my head, bemused. "Are all the horses on this ranch leftover rodeo stock? Where in the hell did Mrs. Cotton get this animal?"

Patrick shrugged. "I couldn't say. It's my first time working for her. I just moved here from Arizona six months ago."

My eyes shot to his face. He looked relaxed and I didn't see even a hint of evasiveness in his expression.

He trotted off to help Virginia and Samuel, and as I watched Patrick ride into the trees I shook my head at my own good fortune.

His answer had been genuine and spontaneous.

I felt pretty confident that Patrick was no longer on my short list of suspects.

"One down, seven to go," I said quietly.

I managed to reach forward and snag the reins without sending the palomino into another bucking frenzy.

By the time I caught up with the others, the cattle were pointed downhill and our herd had grown to twenty-nine head.

Not bad for half a day's work. For once I was grateful for Virginia's overzealous attitude.

As we descended into the valley and made our way to the corral, I could see the herd inside the portable steel circle had grown considerably since last I'd seen it.

Ezra, Dan and Ira were crouched on the top rung of the corral, counting cows.

Patrick whooped a warning to them that we were coming. The three men hustled to open the gate and we funneled our little band of misfits inside.

Burris was nowhere in sight, but the other three cowboys who had been told to ride up the first fork were there, and I assumed they had all gotten back with their cattle just before we had. If they had found any, that is.

I joined them on the fence and we watched the newcomers muscle their way through the group to get to the stock tank. Shoving and pushing rippled through the herd as the late arrivals vied for a shot at the water and it took a long time for everyone to settle down.

The six bulls placidly chewed cuds in the center of the herd, their tan hides rippling with the occasional skin-flinch to discourage pesky flies. Failing that, a well-placed swat from tails as stout as a bullwhip effectively set up a cloud of pests buzzing a fast retreat.

The horned bull rolled one dark eye towards me. He chewed, swallowed and turned away, not showing any desire to assert himself today. His left horn was split where the bullet had ricocheted off it. One eye was half-closed. He looked like he had a horrible headache.

After the milling cows settled into relative calm we started counting.

Ezra counted quickly and effortlessly. He finished long before I did, and Ira shot him a nasty look when he called out his count.

"Four eighty-six," Ezra said.

"Dammit, you made me lose track," Ira said.

I kept my concentration long enough to get to the end. "I got that too. How many does that leave?"

"One sixty-four still on the mountain," Ezra said. "We should be able to get them all by the end of tomorrow."

Dan lifted his legs over the back of the fence and dropped to the ground. "I'm starved."

Ezra watched Dan hustle to the campfire, seemingly waiting until the other man was out of earshot. Then he turned to look at me with an unreadable expression. "Did Possum buck you off?"

It had been close, but I'd managed to stay in the saddle.

I returned Ezra's blank look. "Nope."

His lip gave an almost imperceptible twitch. "Huh."

"How is Jericho doing?" I asked.

Ezra turned away. "Fine, but you can't ride him tomorrow."

"Why not?" I asked.

"Because trouble looks for you. I think Possum and you deserve each other."

With that he tossed his legs over the fence and stepped to the ground. He headed for the campfire without looking back, leaving me feeling sheepish and guilty.

Ezra was right.

Trouble did seem to look for me. And somehow, no matter how hard I tried to prevent it, it always managed to find me.

CHAPTER 18

The camp hummed with the noise of early evening, a soft pale glow of low sunlight bathed the field with pastel color and painted us all with rose hues.

Everyone was jovial and the reassuring sounds of clinking plates and rattling pots did a lot to chase away my demons.

It was a comfort to be settled into normal everyday actions like eating and washing up. I'd finally managed to warm my feet at last, stretching out my cold toes towards the fire with my boots and socks resting beside me. My hair was tied in a stringy ponytail and my scalped itched. Scratching it didn't help, so I did what I could to ignore it. It would be another two days before I could have a proper bath.

Across from my log chair, Wat and Anson sat beside each other on cut stumps of wood, the two of them arguing about who had rounded up more cattle today.

Mr. Lamb was busy in deep conversation with Ezra, the quiet wrangler's head bent low, listening.

I sat on my end of the log while

Virginia kneeled on the ground a few paces away. She was busy pulling a mass of burrs from

Saint Christopher's mangy hair, admonishing him gently about getting into the thick brush and ruining his coat.

The fire shot sparks high.

All at once Burris and Patrick made a mad dash around the camp, each one trying to rope the other's legs as they ran. It was a footrace, rodeo style, and the two men tossed loops at each other relentlessly.

Burris stumbled and fell into the dirty dishes bucket, sending steel plates and cups flying.

Mr. Lamb shouted a stern reprimand and they instantly ceased the chase.

But the two of them snickered as they tidied their lassos and only a hard look from Mr. Lamb prevented them from starting right back up again.

As I watched the two chastised cowboys settle down and sit on the ground by the fire, the difficulty of the task at hand weighed heavy.

In spite of Samuel's doubts, I'd already decided that at least one of these men wasn't guilty of murder. I'd eliminated Patrick as a suspect.

It was only one but it was a start.

Burris, his face shadowed with brown stubble, sat on the ground with his back propped against the wheel of the covered supply wagon.

Patrick had tipped his hat forward and looked like he was trying to nap.

Burris absently twirled his lasso with one hand and I couldn't help but note his skill.

He was lean and tough, like most cowboys, and not very tall but he carried himself like a bigger man. He expertly roped Patrick's feet with hardly any effort, and in retaliation Patrick threw a well-aimed clod of dirt that hit Burris in the chest.

"Where did you learn how to do that?" I asked.

Burris glanced up, looking like he wasn't entirely certain I was talking to him. When he saw me staring straight at him, he twirled his lasso again. "You know. Around."

"Burris rode the circuit," Wat replied. He looked delighted to shamelessly volunteer personal information about Burris.

"The circuit," I said. "You mean professional rodeo?"

Wat eased himself up from his stump-chair and ambled to Burris's side. "He and his partner could stretch a steer in six."

"Six seconds?" I asked.

Anson, the burly blond cowboy, let out a low whistle from where he sat by the fire. "What are you doing here if you can do that?"

Wat fished a flask from his hip and took a swig. "'Cause he was gone so much, his girlfriend started licking her chops every time the UPS guy came by to make a delivery."

I felt my eyebrows arch of their own accord, but I managed to keep my mouth shut.

Wat leaned down and stared at Burris. "He gave it up so's he could keep an eye on her. Leave it to a woman to ruin a good man."

"Shut up, Wat," Burris said. "I just got tired of it, s'all."

"How long ago were you a pro roper?" I asked.

Burris stared at the ground.

"He quit in January after he came in sixth in Las Vegas," Wat said, still staring at Burris. "'Cause he's a damn sandbagger."

"I hated all that moving around," Burris explained. "Vegas, Oklahoma City, Pocatello, and Rosemary gonna have a baby soon. What kind of life is that?"

"He was the best heeler in three states," Wat said, looking at me with a disgusted expression.

"So, is this your first time working a roundup?" I asked. "Or have you done this before and just came back to it?"

Burris coiled his rope carefully. "My first. This is just a job. I need the cash."

"You could have all the cash you wanted if you woulda' stuck with it," Wat told him.

"Lay off," Patrick said, giving Wat a cold eye.

I was finished poking into Burris's affairs, and mentally I scratched him off the list. It would be difficult to murder someone in the wilds of Montana while you were busy riding the rodeo circuit a thousand miles away.

That left six men to question, and we would have our killer. If they were all telling the truth, that is.

Saint Christopher sat up abruptly and sniffed the air.

Gus had stirred as well, and he padded to the edge of camp, his nose held up high and his ears standing at attention.

Samuel noticed his dog and strolled over to the Malinois, bending to scratch his head. "What's up, Gus? Huh, boy?"

Gus sniffed again, his nose working the air furiously.

Mr. Lamb watched the dogs carefully, his leathery face looking like old tree bark as the dimming sunlight glanced off it from low in the sky.

The horses, corralled a good distance away, pounded up a cloud of dust and milled in tight circles.

I got to my feet to see what they were upset about and noticed that the horses were vying for positions inside the herd. No one wanted to be standing on the outside. They skittered in circles inside the corral with nervous energy.

"Dan," Mr. Lamb said quietly. "Hand me over that pistol of yours."

"Why?" Dan asked.

"I don't want you thinking you're the Lone Ranger again."

Dan made an unhappy face, but when Mr. Lamb shot him a hard look, he reluctantly pulled his heavy pistol from his belt and handed it to the foreman.

The noise of camp died to a whisper, and Ezra watched the milling horses with a wary eye.

Both dogs were now on high alert, but it was Gus who barked first.

Saint Christopher barked too, but then he lowered his ears and took two steps back, reluctant to stay where he was. He located Virginia and whined softly.

Gus growled and tensed his back legs.

"Stay, boy," Samuel commanded. "Stay."

Gus wasn't barking any longer, he had lowered his head and the only sounds coming from the Malinois were deep, primal growls.

"Everyone get'cher eyes on them trees," Mr. Lamb said.

Everyone in camp was on their feet now, and a dozen pairs of eyes were trained on the distant corral.

"Marley put your boots back on," Dan said.

Both my feet were bare. I pulled on a sock and crammed my foot inside my boot.

My second boot was giving me trouble, and as I bent to pull it on, a frightening sound echoed from the corral.

221

The horses were running. Their hooves pounded up clouds of dirt and they all but vanished beneath the dust.

"They'll kill themselves getting out," Ezra said. The wrangler broke into a sprint and ran across the field.

"Dammit, Ezra," Mr. Lamb said. "Burris, you and Ira go with him."

The two cowboys looked back and forth between each other and Mr. Lamb, their eyes showing huge circles of white.

"Are you deaf?" Mr. Lamb asked them.

"I'll go," Patrick said. He started for the corral, and Burris instantly bounced to his feet and followed.

The two men were friends, and it was clear Burris wasn't about to let Patrick head into uncertainty without him.

Ira stayed with the rest of us, a look of relief spreading across his face.

Broad-shouldered Anson looked over at Virginia, glanced at the other two men as they trotted fast towards the horses, and hesitated, clearly torn between going with them and staying.

Anson had struck me as benevolently chauvinistic, and I could see from his expression he was reluctant to leave a woman alone while danger was present.

Mr. Lamb made the choice for him. "I'm going to see to it. If it's a bear, I don't want any of you yay-hoos going off half-cocked and shooting it. You understand? Bears aren't dangerous if you leave 'em be."

The surly foreman stalked away, still clutching Dan's heavy pistol.

"Bears aren't dangerous? That's easy for him to say. He's got the gun," I said quietly.

Ira kicked over one of the tree stump chairs and rolled it to the edge of camp. He stood it back upright and jumped on top, gaining another two feet in height.

He shaded his eyes from the last rays of sunlight and scanned the tree line slowly. "There's something spooking them horses. I don't see it yet, though."

The first day I helped on a cattle drive several years ago, I learned quickly that nobody was better at spotting tiny shapes at long distances than a working cowboy.

Whatever was upsetting the horses wouldn't be able to go unnoticed for very long.

I tugged on my second boot and started lacing it frantically when Anson and Samuel both went for their weapons.

Mr. Lamb was already a dozen yards from us but when he looked back and saw the two men reach for guns he stopped. "Keep yer guns put up. I don't want the two of you shooting me. If it's a bear we'll spook it out of camp."

Samuel looked flabbergasted. "But Mr. Lamb, there have been grizzlies sighted in this area."

"I don't give a good goddamn if there've been dragons sighted here," Mr. Lamb said. "No shooting. Got it?"

"Is he serious?" asked Virginia with disbelief.

Anson and Samuel slowly replaced their guns and watched as Mr. Lamb strode fearlessly across the field towards the corrals.

The old foreman held Dan's pistol casually in one hand, almost as afterthought. He apparently didn't think he would need it.

Virginia was on her feet now, looking pale and breathing hard. "What should we do?"

"I'm going for the truck," I said.

Samuel grabbed my arm and brought me up short. "No you're not. It's two hundred yards from here. A grizzly can outrun a horse."

I could feel my own panic. "I don't care. Let me go."

Samuel held on. "Not one more step. You stay here with the rest of us."

"Marley, a truck is just like a crunchy treat with a chewy center to a bear," Ira said. "A truck won't protect you."

Samuel glared at Ira. "Thanks a lot."

"Are there really grizzlies here?" Virginia asked. "Are they worse than the other kind?"

Ira snorted out a laugh. "Like the great white shark of the forest."

"That's not funny," Virginia said.

"I don't care what Mr. Lamb told you," I blurted. "Somebody, for godsakes get a rifle."

Pitiful, fear-laced pleading from a woman was all the motivation Anson needed, and he instantly jerked his rifle from its scabbard.

He checked it for shells and chambered a round.

"That a aught-six?" Wat asked him.

"It's a thirty-thirty," Anson said.

I swallowed down bile that was creeping up my throat. "Will a thirty-thirty stop a bear?"

"Oh, sure," Ira said. "It'll give him a nasty cold from the draft of all the little holes you poke in him. It should kill him in about a week, after he's done eating you."

"Jesus, Ira," Samuel said, giving me a worried look. "Will you shut the hell up?"

Virginia was probably keeping it together better than me. I could feel both my legs vibrating like a jackhammer.

A shout came from the horse corral, and I backed up with a start until I bumped into Dan so hard I almost knocked him over.

Dust flew in the air off in the distance and we could see the horses running in a tight circle inside the corral. Ezra was shouting, but the dim light wasn't enough to show us what was happening.

Samuel pulled his pistol from his pack and both dogs whined and paced.

Every one of us focused on the chaos coming from the corral. But the dust and dim light obscured everything and we couldn't see what was happening.

When Mr. Lamb let out a yell off in the distance, followed by furious whoops and angry calls, every man in camp moved like he'd been hit with a cattle prod.

Virginia and I were herded to the center of a circle of men so quickly I didn't have time to register what was happening.

Some primitive instinct took over and the men clustered around us, backs to the fire, looking like they were ready for anything.

"Did you hear that?" Ira asked, peering towards the wagon. "I heard something."

"Ira, I swear to Christ if you don't shut up—" Samuel began.

"No I'm not fooling around," Ira said. "Did the horses break out? Something's running behind us."

"Bear," Virginia said.

Her voice was so even and calm what she said refused to penetrate my skull.

"Bear," she said again, pointing.

A sandy-beige streak of fur tore through the field behind camp, veered behind the covered supply wagon and lumbered to a sudden stop on the other side. Even from the opposite side of the fire I could hear the animal's deep breathing.

Everyone stared straight at the wagon, but it hid the bear from view and we couldn't see the animal. But we could hear it pacing.

Someone starting whimpering pathetically, and I realized it was me.

Dan took a step forward and wrapped his hand over my mouth from behind.

No one made a sound. The crew looked like they had all been flash-frozen and nobody moved. Gus's hackles were raised so high he looked like he had gained twenty pounds, and the moment the bear stopped pacing, the Malinois started barking like it was the end of the world.

We waited for the charge.

Under the bed of the wagon I caught a glimpse of one hairy foot, black claws as long as my fingers digging into the dirt with each step, and my legs shook so violently Dan propped his knee against my thigh to keep me from buckling.

Anson slowly crouched down and peered underneath the wagon. His eyes shifted back and forth and he stood up, eased himself around the fire with two steps, and lifted his rifle.

Anson trained the barrel on the wagon and waited. He followed each pacing step back and forth, not sure which side the bear would rush from, and when a beige nose poked from the left side of the wagon he eased back the hammer.

Anson pulled the trigger just as the bear tore from behind the wagon. He missed.

The bear ran for the trees. A sandy-beige streak of fur and pumping legs bolted away madly. It moved with unimaginable speed.

Anson thumbed the hammer and raised his rifle, but just as he squeezed the trigger Mr. Lamb appeared from nowhere and grabbed the barrel with one hand.

The shot flew harmlessly into the air, sailing over the top of the bear into the trees.

"I said," Mr. Lamb growled, "no guns."

The foreman took Anson's rifle away with a stout jerk and watched as the bear disappeared into the thick trees.

Dan dropped his hand away from my mouth at last, and I almost fell to the ground the moment he let me go.

Everyone around me stared at the foreman with stunned disbelief.

"It weren't no griz," the foreman said, glaring at the cowboys, his shoulders heaving with anger.

"That wasn't a black bear, Mr. Lamb," Anson said quickly. "He was way too light."

"Cinnamon," Mr. Lamb said. "He's just cinnamon-colored. Not a grizzly. What did that animal ever do to you. Huh? What gives you the right to shoot him?"

Anson opened his mouth to argue, saw the look in Mr. Lamb's eye, thought better of it and stifled his words.

Ezra and Burris jogged into camp, panting from exertion.

Ezra stared after the bear. "We rousted him. He was in the corral. You should have shot him, Anson."

Mr. Lamb turned an angry eye on all the men. "Anyone shoots one of them bears and you'll have to deal with me. I don't want nobody, and I mean nobody, killing nothing on this drive except mosquitoes. You all hear me?"

Mumbles of "yessir" and shuffling of feet were his only reply.

"Far as I'm concerned," Mr. Lamb said. "They was here first. They'll be here long after we are all dead and gone. Leave 'em be. They got just as much right to be here as we do. Maybe more."

The foreman cast one more serious glare around the camp before heading back to the corrals. "Patrick, help me check them cattle. We don't want any of those steers getting out tonight 'cause of weak fencing."

No one said a word, but I could tell what everyone was thinking. They were thinking that Mr. Lamb had just made a terrible mistake. If the bear had decided our camp would be a source of food, I doubted very much even fear of humans would keep it at bay. As darkness fell, I wondered if I would even get an hour's worth of sleep. If I did, I knew exactly what would be in my nightmares. I'd already seen it.

CHAPTER 19

Morning came and I could feel the fog from lack of sleep clogging my head. As expected, I'd only managed a few hours of shut-eye, my head spinning with leftover adrenaline and fear. If we didn't quit this roundup soon, my hair would be streaked with white like Ezra's in no time.

Virginia silently rolled out of her cot and got dressed without complaint.

Her placid expression was a bit of a shock, and I felt a pang of pity for her. She had never been exposed to anything like this before as far as I knew, and from her gaunt expression I could see it was taking its toll. But somehow she was managing. I hated to admit it, but Virginia was tougher than I'd thought she would be.

Breakfast went by in a blur, and though it was a good hour and a half before we were all in the saddle and heading up the mountain, it felt like mere minutes to me.

Mr. Lamb gave stern instructions to the crew. He was determined to do a systematic search of each section of the mountain in turn, and everyone was instructed to ride the third fork all day.

Samuel and I shared a weary look, knowing we might have had the opportunity after all of getting to the lake without having to sneak around. But, even if we had, there was still the problem of all the other cowboys. And they would be curious about why I was skinny-dipping in the middle of a workday.

It was probably better that we had hiked up to the lake the day before and gotten it over with.

The horses lumbered up the hill slowly, and everyone complained of aches and pains from three days' worth of hard high-country riding.

The third fork was the steepest ascent out of them all, even coming from the far right side and avoiding the cliff that Samuel and I had scaled the day before. It was tough going and would be time-consuming.

I found myself riding Possum again, Ezra apparently still reluctant to let Jericho back on duty.

We snaked up the narrow trail leading to the plateau in a long, broken line, and at one point I reined the palomino to a halt to give him a rest.

The clatter of shod hooves on pebbles alerted me that another rider was coming up behind me.

"Well, it wasn't Anson," Virginia said, riding up the trail and wiping her sweaty forehead. Saint Christopher trotted at Buck's heels, his tongue lolling to the side.

I quickly glanced around to make sure no one else was close by. Luckily we were alone.

She pulled Buck to a stop beside me and threw one leg over her saddle horn to rest her calf muscle like an old pro. "He is definitely not involved in your little murder."

"Tell me you didn't ask him what he was doing two years ago," I said.

If she was busy blatantly grilling each member of the crew about where he had been during the time of the killing it would be like holding up a big sign that she knew about it.

"Do you think I'm stupid?" She examined my face. "Don't answer that. And, no, I didn't. I asked if he was married or single."

"I don't see how that is going to help us out," I told her.

She took a drink from her canteen. "That's why I asked him if he had any kids, where they went to school, that sort of thing."

"Maybe you should leave the snooping to me and Samuel," I suggested.

"I'll have you know that Anson told me he used to work for Mr. Cotton several years ago," she said, shoving her canteen back inside her saddlebag. "But that he wasn't here two years ago for the spring roundup because his wife was about to have their second child and she didn't want him to be gone. He was working at the feed mill in Polson at the time."

I pulled myself up short. Surprisingly, her reasoning seemed sound. After a pause I gave her a cautious look. "Did you believe him?"

She slid her leg down and shoved her toe back in the stirrup. "He said he still works there now, but he wanted to come on this last roundup so he could say goodbye to Mrs. Cotton."

It was flimsy, but better than nothing. Honestly I'd never really thought Anson, with his broad shoulders and wide, earnest face, was involved with the murder. It was a cruel thought, but Anson didn't seem like he was smart enough to be partners with a successful, large-scale poacher.

I let air puff out my cheeks wearily. "I guess that leaves only five. Maybe this isn't such an impossible task after all."

A gunshot cracked through the still air and Virginia and I looked at each other with alarm.

A moment passed, then another shot rang out and echoed across the slope of the mountain like a faraway thunderclap. Then there was silence.

"Was that a gun?" Virginia asked.

"Yes, but it was a long way off," I told her.

"Whoever it is had better hope Mr. Lamb doesn't catch him," Virginia said.

"Let's get going. I think Samuel has a radio, so maybe he heard something."

We urged our horses up the steep trail fast, and as we rounded a blind corner I had to pull Possum up short to keep him from ramming into another horse.

Dan sat astride the big roan gelding called Rooster. Dan's face was red, his ear pressed to the radio in his hand.

"Say that again?" he said, keying the mike.

The radio squawked. "I said who's shootin'? That ain't you, is it Dan?"

"You've got my gun, still, Mr. Lamb," Dan said into the radio as he rolled his eyes in our direction. He released the key on the radio. "As if he didn't know that. Why's he pegged me for being trigger-happy?"

"Maybe you should ask Mrs. Cotton's bull about that," I said.

Dan flipped a strand of dark hair from his eyes with a smirk. "Smartass."

He keyed the radio again. "Anyway it sounded like a rifle to me, Mr. Lamb."

The reception was terrible, but somehow they managed to understand each other.

Mr. Lamb's voice howled from the speaker. "I want to know who's shootin'."

A long pause gave Dan time to glance up at Virginia and me, and I could see his face was flush with anger. Nobody confessed over the radio.

Dan shook his head. "He's never going to find out which one of us it was. But I'm going to get blamed for it anyway." He keyed the mike again. "Anson, are you firing?"

The radio chirped. "Sweet Mary mother of God, you got to be kidding me. Mr. Lamb would put me in the ghost camp if I did."

Dan shook his head and replaced the radio on his belt. He squinted up through the trees and nodded to the south. "That's where the shots came from, but it was quite a ways away. Nobody is supposed to be up on the first fork, are they?"

I shrugged. "I thought we were all riding up here on the third fork today."

Dan kept his eyes trained on the trees like he could magically part them and somehow manage to see all the way across the valley. Finally he gave up and dropped his head. "Could be Mrs. Cotton is relaxing her policy on hunters accessing the ranch. Probably somebody trying to get an early jump on the season."

"Season doesn't open until October twentieth," I said.

"Bow season is open now." He eyed me carefully. "You and I both know bow hunters always lie about it and bring a gun with them."

"If they are dishonest," I said.

Dan slowly grinned. His brown eyes crinkled at the corners. "You sure do have a black-and-white idea of things."

"No, I've got a right and wrong idea of things," I said.

He smiled so devilishly it was plain he was mocking me. My face must have been a billboard of indignation. Dan took in my expression and laughed at me outright. "Okay, Mrs. Allen Hunter. Why don't you take point?"

He nudged Rooster to the side and made a grand, sweeping gesture for me to proceed.

Something about his teasing look disarmed my irritation and I shook my head at him as I rode on.

Virginia followed close behind me as we gained ground. It was just the two of us and when I glanced back, I could see that Dan lingered in the same spot.

I craned my neck to see what he was doing, and saw him staring off towards the area the shots had come from, his face puzzled.

"How did he know Allen's first name?" Virginia asked.

I was busy studying Dan's odd behavior and had to shake myself back to the here and now. "What?"

"Mr. Lamb introduced you to the crew as Mrs. Hunter, but he never said Allen's first name. How did Dan know it?" she asked me.

A sudden jolt of worry surged through me.

It felt exactly like cold lake water coursing over the top of my head.

I looked back at Virginia. "That's a really good question."

Virginia watched Dan for a moment with a speculative look on her face.

Finally, she let out Buck's reins and gave him a kick. "Let me know when you figure it out."

I let her pass me on the trail and when I looked back to see if Dan was following us it came as a nasty shock to see that the trail was completely empty.

Dan was nowhere in sight. Where had he gone?

It took me a moment to get my composure back. How did he know Allen's first name?

Nothing sparked a memory, no matter how hard I thought about it. As far as I knew, I'd never seen Dan before in my life. He didn't look at all familiar to me, and try as I might I couldn't call to memory anything helpful. Sitting in the middle of the trail staring at the ground wasn't doing me a bit of good either.

Finally I urged Possum on and followed after Virginia.

It didn't take us long to find the others.

Burris, Samuel and Ezra sat astride their horses in a small circle beneath a giant ponderosa pine, enjoying the shade for a moment. For late September it was sweltering.

Hot days, cold mornings. Welcome to fall in Montana.

Burris smoked a cigarette hurriedly, keeping a wary eye on the trail. "Tell me if you hear Mr. Lamb coming. If that old bastard sees me smoking he'll cut off my thumbs with a hacksaw."

"Ouch," I said. "Mr. Lamb's that tough on smokers?"

"He's worried I'll burn down the forest or something. I swear the man is like Smokey Bear, PETA and Sally Jewell all rolled into one."

"Who's Sally Jewell?" I asked.

Burris shrugged. "Secretary of the Interior."

"We are about halfway to the plateau," Samuel said impatiently. "Burris figures if there are any cows at the top they will be hidden pretty well, and we should all meet at the summit, spread out and start riding down in a line to force them out. It sounds half-crazy, but there it is."

I felt my enthusiasm crumble. "It's a pretty steep mountain to ride straight down like that."

Burris took one long last drag from his cigarette and carefully flicked the tip with his middle finger until the ember died. "It's the fastest way. We'll be up here all day otherwise."

"Yeah, but I'd like to make it home without going ass over teakettle off the front of my horse," Samuel said.

I gave him a worried look. His tone was harsh and his manner was sullen. Had he figured something out and was waiting for a moment to deliver some more bad news?

Virginia was already heading up the trail, giving us all a spectacular view of her horse's backside. She had long since abandoned any pretense at being friendly to the rest of the crew and ignored anything that wasn't to do with cows.

If it weren't such a pain in the neck, I would have almost admired her single-minded determination.

After she disappeared up the trail I looked back at the others and saw Ezra staring at me blatantly. His white streak of hair looked even more pronounced in the daylight, giving him an otherworldly appearance.

I stared back at him unapologetically.

He watched me for a moment, then turned his mount away and followed after Virginia silently.

When he was out of sight I heaved a small sigh of relief.

"That guy give me the creeps," Samuel said.

Burris picked a small bit of tobacco leaf from his front teeth. "Yeah, but nobody knows more about horses than he does."

"How does he know so much about these horses in particular?" I asked. "Has he worked for Mrs. Cotton before?"

Burris nodded. "He used to, a long time ago. At least a half dozen years have gone by since he's worked here. Ezra handles the stock at the sale barn in Three Forks these days. The Headwaters? You know it?"

"So how did Mrs. Cotton get him to give up his day job and come all the way up here?" I asked.

Burris chuckled. "He's looking for his next favorite cutting horse. He had his eye on Jericho, until you smashed him up. Ezra knew the Cottons pretty good, and he knows that Nash always had an eye for nimble horses. When he found out Stephanie was selling all her stock, he came up here to this roundup so he could garage sale the herd."

With that, Burris flicked his reins and rode up the hill after Virginia.

In spite of myself, I felt relief surge through me with the knowledge that Ezra was probably not the man we were looking for. He was an unsettling person, at best, and I was glad I wouldn't need to poke into his private life anymore.

That meant we only had four men left to question.

Samuel frowned and seemed to be mulling something over.

He had been on the verge of belligerent since I'd arrived. Most likely it would be pointless to try and talk to him while he was so agitated, but I wanted to at least give it a try.

"Dan knows Allen's first name," I told him.

He shrugged an elbow. "So?"

"So, did you tell him?"

"I didn't tell anyone."

"Not even Mr. Lamb?" I asked.

"Sure, I told Mr. Lamb. But I had to in order to vouch for you."

Maybe the foreman had mentioned it in passing. It was possible. The fact that Dan knew Allen's first name was unsettling, but it was also possible it meant nothing at all.

The idea that Dan could be our killer seemed implausible to me. Maybe because he had saved my neck by shooting the bull before it crushed me. But also because he was likeable.

How could a bad guy come across as such a friendly human being?

Easy.

He could be a bald-faced liar.

As much as it pained me to do, so I had to put Dan squarely in the "possible suspects" category.

The job here was to be suspicious, and objective.

"What?" Samuel asked as he watched me go through my mental calisthenics.

"This isn't as easy as I thought it would be, that's all," I admitted. "At least Virginia found out that Anson wasn't here at the time John Hill disappeared. He was working at a feed mill in Polson."

"So that leaves five total strangers we need to sort through," he told me with a stern look.

"Four. Don't forget Ezra was in Three Forks."

"So four men we need to turn inside out before one of them skins us alive."

"When you say it like that . . ."

"Marley, I appreciate your determination," Samuel said.

"But?"

"But this is above our heads. You and I are not law enforcement."

I brushed at a stain on my worn shirt. "I know."

"So I thought about it last night and I decided I'm quitting and getting the hell out of here," Samuel said.

My mouth dropped open. "You're what?"

His tone was incredulous. "The fact that you are surprised by someone acting sensible should freak you out just a little."

"I don't understand," I said. "There are only four guys left to check out."

"You've been trying for almost three days now to connect the dots on this picture and you still don't know if it's a jackass or a teeter-totter."

"Right now it looks more like a jackass to me," I said.

"I'm not asking your permission or getting your opinion, I'm telling you what I'm going to do. Everyone else is headed up to the plateau and I am going to ride down to camp while they are gone and pack my stuff."

"You are leaving now?" It came out a bit more desperate than I wanted.

"I'm driving down to Livingston and I'm calling Todd Ramsey so he can put me in touch with Allen."

"We can sort this out. I just need a little more time," I said.

"You need to come back to reality-land," Samuel said harshly. "I know you think you have this under control, but from where I stand, this situation is so far gone there is no way anyone but cops or Feebs will be able to get a handle on it."

"Feebs?"

"FBI," he said. "I want you to come with me. You and Virginia."

"I can't," I said instantly.

He shook his head. "Yes you can. Dammit, this isn't the time to be stubborn."

The image of Samuel cradling his pistol and rocking back and forth like a frightened child suddenly replayed itself in my mind. As I watched him trying to reason with me, I noticed both his

239

hands were shaking. His eyes were wide with fear, and I knew almost instantly that I'd grossly overestimated the amount of pressure he could handle. It looked like he was on the verge of snapping.

"You know as well as I do that the minute there are police running around up here the guy who shot John Hill will disappear and we will never see him again," I said.

"That's not my problem," Samuel told me. "And it isn't yours either."

"What about doing what's right so I can figure out the truth?"

He pointed two fingers at me. "That's an excuse. Is it worth getting killed over? Is that what you believe?"

"I'm not leaving," I said, my voice hard.

Samuel studied me, his lips working side to side furiously. "I can't make you be intelligent. It's your funeral."

He reined his horse around hard.

"Wait," I said, not wanting him to leave with such bitter words still hanging in the air. "You should call Bruce Duvekot at the Helena Fish and Wildlife branch office. He'll know what to do."

"Bruce Duvekot. Anything else I need to know? The name of the funeral home you prefer?"

"Sam—"

"Don't go off alone with anyone from now on," he said over his shoulder. "You and Virginia need to stick together until I can get in touch with the authorities. Alright? Don't ask any more damn questions. Leave it alone."

"Samuel," I started to say.

"Don't argue with me," he said sharply. "It was a mistake not to get the hell out of here the moment we found the dead guy at Fischer Lake. Do me a favor, and don't say anything to anyone about me bugging out. The less they know the better."

Gus sat on the ground next to Samuel's horse, his ears cocked forward, his dark eyes darting between us with concern. Our tone must have betrayed the tension. Gus looked confused.

I knew how he felt.

"I might be able to have someone back up here tonight. But more than likely it won't be until tomorrow morning. Can you stay out of trouble for that long?" he asked.

I could see from the fierce set of his jaw there would be no negotiation. He'd already made up his mind.

"I can try," I said.

"You'll have to do better than that," he snapped. "Promise me you won't put yourself at risk."

"I never mean to put myself at risk," I said with a lilt to my voice.

"This isn't funny, Marley. All you have to do is keep your mouth shut for twenty-four hours. Do you think you can do that?"

"Keep my mouth shut," I said. "Sure. I can do that."

His look betrayed his doubt. Without another word Samuel rode down the slope, and Gus paused for only a moment before loping after.

They were gone in an instant, vanishing between the shadows of the trees.

As I watched them disappear a wave of anxiety gripped me. I suddenly felt so alone it was like a vise squeezing my lungs. The only person I could count on now was my husband's spoiled ex-wife, whose finest achievement was graduating top of her class at finishing school and who had once worked part-time selling real estate.

Perfect.

I took a deep breath and did what I could to shake off the sudden feelings of helplessness. I waited at least five minutes longer than I should have to see if Samuel would change his mind and come back. But I already knew the answer to that question.

Then I turned Possum up the mountain trail, and rode after the others.

CHAPTER 20

By lunch we had managed to bushwhack only a quarter of the way down the mountain. Ira, Dan and I had taken refuge from the hot sun beneath a thick stand of aspens to knock back our hunger with the meager food we'd brought along. The horses rested with their heads bent down, munching the dry fall grass placidly.

I hadn't seen Virginia for over an hour, and God only knew what trouble she was getting into. I realized reluctantly that I'd started to think of Virginia as my responsibility. If anything happened to her on the roundup, I would probably feel terrible about it, in spite of our past differences.

Ira leaned back against a tree trunk and stretched his arms with a groan. "I could use a nap."

"Take one, we won't tell," Dan said.

"You were the kid in grade school always asking the smarter kids to let you cheat off their tests, weren't you?" I asked Dan.

"Who says I wasn't the one they were cheating off?" he replied.

The three horses lowered their ears at each other. Horse-speak for you are starting to bug me.

My horse, Possum, took the opportunity to bite Dash on the flank, and Dan's horse, Rooster, swished his tail with irritation and pulled back so he wouldn't be caught in the middle of the argument.

"Jesus he's mean," Ira said, watching the disagreement between them. "Glad I don't have to ride that hotheaded palomino."

For the first time I really looked at Possum's shoulder and noticed that his brand was nothing like the others. Dash and Rooster both wore the OO on their left rear flank, like all the other horses on the ranch, but Possum was branded with something completely different.

"Well no wonder," I said. "He's the new guy. See? JF Bar means he came from another ranch, not the sale ring, right?"

Dan wiped his mouth on his filthy plaid shirtsleeve and stood up, cramming the last of his lunch inside his saddlebag. "Let's get back to work. Marley, why don't you and I take one last look at that meadow just up the hill and make sure we didn't miss anyone. Ira, take a snooze."

"Promise you won't squeal on me?" Ira asked, leaning back and tipping his hat down over his eyes.

"Lazy-ass," Dan said.

But Ira looked so comfortable settling in for a catnap not even I had the heart to deprive him.

"We promise," I said.

"And tonight back at camp, for the privilege, you get to do our dirty dishes," Dan said.

Ira peeked out from underneath his cowboy hat and gave us a wink. "Deal."

Dan and I mounted up and Possum trotted back to the clearing with both ears plastered flat, eyeing Rooster like he was considering which body part to bite next.

"What's got into you?" I asked the feisty palomino.

As we reached the clearing I could see at once it was deserted.

"This was a waste of time," I said. "You didn't really think that Ira would forget to check this place out top to bottom, did you?"

Dan didn't respond. He'd reined to a halt behind me and wasn't moving.

I scanned the clearing again, and some sixth sense told me something wasn't right.

A chill ran up between my shoulders and it was as if the air was suddenly charged with electricity.

"Dan, did you hear me?"

He didn't say a single word and the hairs on the back of my neck started to tingle a warning.

I turned around slowly in the saddle.

He stared at me in silence, holding a small pistol in his right hand, the barrel pointed straight at my face. He rested the butt of the pistol on his saddle horn casually, like he was holding nothing more dangerous than a fishing pole.

"What—"

"No, don't yell," he said quietly. "I'm not going to shoot you. I just needed to get your attention."

I stared back at him, every muscle in my body tensed. "You've got it."

I should have been more afraid but that wasn't the first thing I felt.

The fear would have to wait it's turn. At that moment I was furious.

He nodded towards my stirrup. "Show me your feet."

"My feet?" I asked. "If you like my boots that much you can have them."

He quirked a small smile. "Show me your soles."

My lace-up Roper snagged for a moment as I tried to wiggle it loose, but finally it slid out of the stirrup and I lifted the bottom of my boot.

He scanned it quickly and seemed satisfied. "Alright. I'm going to put my pistol away now. But if you try to escape I will draw and shoot Possum before you can get ten yards."

It took everything I had to keep my temper under control. This was not the time to be belligerent. "Just tell me what you want."

"I want you to ride to Fischer Lake."

"What if I say no?"

His face gave away nothing. "Then I will knock you over the head and take you there quietly."

He wasn't in a hurry, or desperate, and I absolutely believed him.

The pistol vanished inside his jacket pocket and when he pulled out his empty hand he gestured up the mountain. "Ladies first."

Every fiber of my body urged me to spur Possum hard and make a run for it. But I knew if I did, we wouldn't make it very far.

I decided to go along with him, but the moment he made his first mistake I wouldn't hesitate to act.

"Maybe you would like to explain what you are really after," I said.

"No talking. Just ride."

Reluctantly, I urged Possum uphill towards the lake, occasionally glancing back to see if Dan was getting careless. His vigilance was disheartening. He shadowed me expertly and never let me out of his sight.

The going was rough, and we were forced to skirt around scree slopes and thick brush the horses couldn't handle. It took us almost forty minutes to reach the edge of the lake, and when we did I felt my entire body break out in a cold sweat.

"That's good right there," Dan said. "Tie up. We do the rest on foot."

I eased out of the saddle and looped the reins loosely around a short stand of willows, purposefully leaving the end untied so that Possum could pull free easily. If he wandered down the mountain without me, someone might see him and get suspicious.

"Marley, tie him good."

My eyes squeezed shut by their own accord.

Dan was too smart to let me get the upper hand in anything.

If I was going to make it out of this I had to be quick.

It pained me to do it, but I bent down and tied the reins tight, giving them a tug so he could see that I'd done it.

I stood up and let my hands fall to my sides. "Now what?"

He stood a few yards away with both hands inside his jacket pockets. Almost casual, like taking a hostage wasn't anything to get excited about.

"I had the kid figured out the first day," he said with something akin to amusement.

"The kid?"

"Sam. He's some turnip from body recovery, isn't he? Him and that dog of his."

My heart hammered hard but I kept my voice neutral. "I never met him before."

"And you, of course. I had you pegged ten minutes after you showed up. But I can see you don't remember me at all," he said.

"Remember you?" I asked. "I've never seen you before in my life. How could I possibly remember you?"

"It's Virginia I couldn't quite get," he went on.

"Dan, what the hell do you want with me?" I snapped.

He nodded towards the lake. "Show me."

I shook my head. "Show you what?"

He pulled the pistol out of his jacket and pointed it at the ground. "You know what. Start walking."

He was taking me to John Hill's body. Probably because he was going to put me in the lake right next to him.

I started moving, but with each step scanned the ground for a fist-sized rock I could hurl at him if I got the chance. If it came to it, running was the worst possible move. I'd seen Dan shoot the Brangus bull square on the head, and that had been from a draw. His pistol was already out. He would have plenty of time to aim.

There was no way I was making it out of this alive.

When we were only a few yards from the corpse I stopped on the lakeshore.

Dan looked at the ground, toed the thick layer of rocks speculatively and glanced at me with confusion. "You've got to be kidding me. I saw your boot tracks in the dirt, over there, just inside the tree line. Why are you stopping here?"

"Because this is the spot," I said.

"He's here? Under all this?" Dan knelt down and started searching the ground, flipping the rocks frantically with his free hand like he was digging for something.

Something about his desperate moves jarred me into awareness. He wasn't here to kill me at all. He brought me here so I could show him where John Hill had died.

It all came together in a flash.

It was almost too incredible to believe. The bits and pieces of information were careening wildly inside my head like startled birds and it took every ounce of concentration I had to sort it out.

"You are John Hill's partner," I said.

His eyes flicked up. "Dan Hobart. High Country Taxidermy. I run it. Or, I did until everything went to hell. I am surprised you don't recall."

Realization slammed into me, nearly taking my breath away. "I've talked to you on the phone before. You called me to ask about bobcat trapping permits and regulations."

He stood up and gave a slight bow, almost like he was introducing himself. "And you are the game warden's wife."

"You are the son of a bitch."

He stared at me quizzically. "The son of a bitch?"

"She called us and left a message on the tip line. John's girlfriend."

"Mickey?" He frowned. "When did she call you?"

I felt the blood drain from my face. "Two years ago. She said you killed your partner."

He let his head fall back and stared up at the sky with a look very much like remorse. "Mickey was always a bit jealous of him. She never liked me at all, and came up with some pretty wild ideas about John's down time. But how could she have possibly thought I would ever kill my own partner?"

My brain shifted gears so fast I was sure smoke came out my ears. "You came up here to find him, to find out what had happened."

Dan looked down at the pistol in his hand and slid it back inside his jacket pocket.

"This was the last place I saw him alive." He sat down on a wide boulder and slumped with sadness.

Even through my anger and confusion, I could see he was devastated. It was too soon to feel relief just yet, but his manner told me I was probably not in danger at the moment.

Dan's eyes welled with moisture. "He wasn't just my partner. He was my friend."

"Mickey Tipton," I said with my eyes wide. "That's who called us. I remember now. That raspy voice."

"She preferred Winston lights. As if the 'light' made a bit of difference."

I could see her in my head. Her wild hair. Her crazy eyes.

"She was the cleaning lady for my Fish and Wildlife branch office in Helena. She's the one who called us."

Dan looked grieved. "It sounds like something she would do. You people sure took your time following up on it."

"No wonder our investigator could never catch you and John," I said. "Mickey probably kept you well informed about what he knew about your activities."

"Not as much as you would think," he said. "After John disappeared, at least I knew he hadn't been arrested."

My eyes lost focus as I sorted through it, thinking hard. "You cleaned out his garage, and destroyed all the evidence before we could search his property. Did you bury it all under a slab of concrete outside the garage?"

He straightened a bit. "Yeah, I did. Probably not the best place for it. But I was in a hurry, after all."

"Then you closed your taxidermy studio and left Helena."

"And hoped like hell he would get in touch with me. But he never did. A couple months after he dropped off the planet I thought he might have ditched out on me, given up the life and gone off someplace to start over. But I knew he would always let me know where he was. We were partners."

"And this was the last place you saw him alive?" I asked.

"We worked the spring drive together a couple years ago. One evening I came back to camp and he was gone. All his gear, packed up. No word. No nothing."

"Why didn't you come back up here to look for him sooner than this?" I asked.

"It wasn't until I saw the Cottons were selling out that it made me really think about that spring drive all over again, and it seemed so damn strange that he took off without even checking with me first. I came up here to see if I could find something, anything. When I saw you and Goldilocks up here snooping around I knew right away what you were doing."

"How could you have possibly known?" I asked.

"Your cousin from Denver?" he said. "Come on. Is that the best thing you could come up with? Any idiot could see that was a lie."

I vowed to slug Virginia in the jaw the moment I saw her again.

"So, where is he then?" Dan asked. "Not under all this rock, I'd bet."

He looked forlorn and seemed smaller somehow.

"In the lake," I said. "He was shot in the forehead. Then whoever it was, they put him inside a sleeping bag, dragged him into the water and filled up the bottom of the bag with rocks so it would sink."

Dan nodded wretchedly, his color gone. "Alright then."

He looked like a man with nothing left to lose. I backed up a few steps. "You should know Samuel is on his way to Livingston. He's bringing back Allen and an investigator, so it would be best for you to let me go right now."

"Marley, John and I made a very profitable career out of poaching elk velvet for the Taiwanese and bear gallbladders for the Chinese, and we never got caught. You think I don't know how long it will take him to get back here with a warden?"

"He might be quicker than you think."

He stood up from the rock, shook his head sadly and stared at the lake with heavy eyes. "I'm sorry about the gun. Nothing personal, you understand?"

"As long as it stays in your pocket I'll feel a lot better about it," I said.

"I want you to stay here for one hour after I'm gone. Make it an hour and a half. After that you can ride back to camp. I don't want to see you unsaddle your horse at the corral before me. I know I promised not to shoot you, but it would be in your best interest not to trust that."

"Count on me not trusting you," I said.

"Will you make sure he gets buried properly?" he asked, still watching the water. "You could do that much for me."

"Do you know who killed him, Dan?" I asked. "Is that why you are here? Looking for revenge?"

He shook his head slowly, like it almost weighed too much to lift. "Revenge is a kind of wild justice, which the more man's nature runs to, the more ought law to weed it out."

"I . . . I don't understand."

"Sir Francis Bacon. He warned about the need for revenge, and since I started walking on the wrong side of legal I sort of made a promise not to take it too personally when bad things happened to me. John knew what he was into, working with me. We both understood the risks. It's up to people with badges to find out who killed him. I want no part of it. Just bury him in a Christian cemetery, at least"

"At least," I said, feeling my gut tying itself in knots.

He seemed on the verge of leaving. But until I saw him ride away there was no chance I'd get my hopes up.

After what seemed like hours but was more like a few minutes, Dan finally ended his mourning, backed away until he was a few dozen yards from me, turned and walked to his horse quickly. He didn't bother to check on me as he climbed on Rooster and galloped down the mountain.

I waited thirty minutes before sprinting back to Possum and riding after him.

CHAPTER 21

I saw the small herd of cattle before any riders came into view, and when I pulled Possum up short beside the Red Angus heifers, he blew a sigh of relief.

He was coated in sweat, and he deserved a rest I was panting from exertion too, my legs shaking with the effort of keeping me in the saddle during the steep descent.

Virginia appeared from the trees and when she saw me she rode straight at me, her face furious.

"Where, exactly, have you been? The rest of us are out here working and taking up your slack."

I tried to catch my breath. "Dan was the dead guy's partner."

She threw both hands out at her sides. "Dan who?"

I stared at her. "Dan. Mr. I shot Mrs. Cotton's bull. The one who wears hiking boots and the big red jacket?"

She snorted with irritation. "So?"

"Virginia. Dan was John's partner in their poaching scheme."

"Did he kill the guy, or not?" she asked.

"Don't you want to know what just happened?" I asked.

"Did he suffer a sudden attack of conscience and confess to murder?"

I dropped my chin to my chest with frustration. "Not even close. He was trying to figure it out just like I was."

"So you still don't know who we are looking for." Her tone was laced with disapproval.

"Not a clue," I said.

"Well, was he here when his partner disappeared two years ago?" she asked. "Maybe he remembers if there was anyone else on this crew here at the same time."

I grimaced. "It didn't exactly come up in conversation, because he had a gun pointed at me at the time."

"Marley, you had him right there. What's wrong with you? I cannot believe you are that stupid," she said, wheeling her horse away. "And you think that I'm the amateur."

A surge of anger shot through me. But it was followed instantly by a surge of self-pity. I'd come so close to figuring out who had killed John, but that chance had slipped out of my grasp.

All at once I realized Samuel had been right. I was in way over my head. If I were a well-trained law enforcement official I could race back to camp and catch Dan before he vanished.

But that was impossible. By the time I made it to the valley floor Dan would be long gone and I doubted very much he would hang around Montana after this.

The situation had deteriorated about as far as it could, and there was nothing left to do but finish the roundup, and hope that if John Hill's killer was really among us, he didn't figure out I had been searching for him. Hopefully I would be able to follow Samuel's advice and would manage to keep my mouth shut for a full day.

One thing was certain. I was getting damn tired of feeling like a hunted animal.

It was well past lunch and reluctantly I dismounted to give Possum a much-needed breather while I dug a handful of trail mix from my pack.

Virginia had left me in charge of the small herd of cows she'd gathered and vanished into the trees.

The sun was less fierce than the day before, but it was still warm for September.

Possum hung his head low and munched a sprig of grass while I nursed my wounded pride.

"I am stupid," I said to myself, feeling overwhelmed.

What had I been thinking?

Coming to the Cotton Ranch had been a horrible mistake, and the best move I could make would be to leave immediately, just like Samuel had suggested in the beginning.

My stubborn pride had gotten me into this.

If I hadn't been so focused on solving the disappearance of the man who had inadvertently cost me my job, I would have been able to see from the start that putting myself at such risk was reckless and foolish.

I wasn't the only one at risk.

Virginia was smack in the middle of it right along with me.

A pang of guilt washed over me.

In spite of the trouble she had caused in my life, she was still a human being and didn't deserve to be in a dangerous situation against her will.

I had never said it out loud, but in my mind Virginia was a hurricane of bad judgment and poor choices. I'd considered myself better than her because in my own mind I was sensible, and she was unpredictable and selfish.

Look who was in the hurricane now.

The ground rumbled and I looked up from my pity-party session to see a long line of red noses erupt from the trees. Possum jerked away and I had to scramble to catch his reins and climb in the saddle as a huge mob of cattle descended the mountain straight for us.

Patrick popped into view at the right flank of the big herd, a wide grin spread across his face.

"How many you got?" he called.

I scanned our meager collection quickly. "Fifteen."

"We've got over a hundred at least!"

It took only minutes for the two herds to join together, and with the steep slope and thick trees, it would be impossible to get an accurate count. But I could see Patrick was right about his guess of head count. His herd was huge.

He stopped beside me, cocky and smug. "Found them all hiding out behind a stand of lodgepole pines. Scared up a big bull elk, too."

"Who's with you?" I asked.

"Albert and Burris. Ira's on drag."

I squinted up through the trees, trying to get my bearings. "How far down are we?"

"More than half," Patrick said. "Getting all these damn critters to stick together in these trees won't be fun. We could sure use you on flank."

"Left or right?" I asked, just happy to be useful again.

"Left. Get to it quick so we don't start losing them."

He spurred his horse and darted away to take point once again. I located the back of the herd and started to work my way to the left flank fast.

Ira was riding drag, looking both tired and happy. "We probably got almost all of 'em," he said as I rode by at a trot. "Maybe Mr. Lamb will let us off early."

"Best news I've had all day," I said.

"I'm forty-eight hours away from ordering pizza," he said with a wide smile.

I laughed in spite of my sour mood, and took up my position on the left flank dutifully.

It wasn't long before Virginia and Saint Christopher found me, and although I had been confidently ordering her around for the duration of the roundup, this time I sent her to Ira for instructions.

Considering the mess I'd managed to create, it might be wise to let someone else make decisions for a while.

We managed to bring the entire herd down the mountain without losing a single cow.

All of us worked together and not one straggler managed to slip away, try as they might.

The sun was still a couple hours from setting, and for the first time in days I felt like something was finally going right for a change.

Mr. Lamb was at the corral with the gate swung wide when we ambled into camp. He might have looked satisfied as the huge mob filed by, but with his craggy features, it was almost impossible to tell.

After the herd had settled in, Patrick, Mr. Lamb and Ira sat on the top rung of the corral and started counting.

I fell to the ground and put my back to the steel bars, too weary to help.

The bulls had gotten worked up about the new arrivals, and a few skirmishes broke out that delayed the whole process several times.

But finally they all settled down and after three consecutive counts, Mr. Lamb announced the total.

"Six hundred and two," he said.

"That means there are only three missing," Ira said.

I gave him a confused look from where I sat on the ground, shading my eyes with one hand as I looked up. "I thought we had six hundred and fifty? Did you flunk math in high school?"

Ira shot me a snide look. "Ezra said over the radio he and Anson had forty-five. They were riding nearly off the map to the north. They are coming now and should be here in about a half hour."

"Only three missing. That's not bad," I said.

"Well, it's not good enough," Mr. Lamb announced. "Not good enough until we have every single last one of 'em."

Ira's expression fell, and I felt a sinking sensation in my stomach and a sudden premonition of what was coming next.

"I want everyone to ride up the first fork, today, and find them last three head," Mr. Lamb said. "There's still over two hours of daylight. As soon as all the rest of you get back, saddle up and get up there. And when I say all of you, I mean all of you."

I groaned quietly, but Mr. Lamb heard me and his eyes snapped to my face. "Anyone got any complaints?"

"No, no," I said hastily. "Maybe I'll change out Possum, though. He's had a hard day."

"Take Jericho, then," Mr. Lamb instructed.

I swallowed my reply.

Ezra would incinerate me if I rode the Appaloosa again after nearly getting him killed.

But I wasn't about to argue about it in front of the foreman, and instead I led Possum back to the horse corral and pulled off the saddle. I turned him in with the others and waited for the rest of the crew to show up.

I'd let Ezra decide which horse to put me on. Even if it meant incurring the wrath of Mr. Lamb, I wasn't about to cross Ezra when it came to the horses.

The big gelding, Rooster, lazed in a doze with the others, and it was clear Dan had been true to his word and was long gone. He'd probably had plenty of time to gather his gear and escape. All the rest of us had been working the rough mountainside and he must have had camp all to himself while he loaded up his things. This ranch was so huge, even with the handheld radios, it was a miracle the crew managed to keep track of each other. Slinking away unnoticed wouldn't be that difficult.

It could take until evening for anyone to even notice that Samuel was gone too.

Feeling miserable all over again, I let my eyes wander over the horses while I waited for Ezra to arrive.

It didn't take long for the other cowboys to make their appearance. I sat down in the bed of the tack wagon and watched as the second string of cattle ambled into camp and funneled inside the corral with the others.

Even from the distance I sat, I could see the disappointment from the crew as Mr. Lamb ordered everyone back up the first fork. The groans were so loud I could hear them above the din of the herd.

The crew led their horses to the stock tank for a quick drink before heading back into the trees.

I waited for Ezra, feeling miserable. More than likely the quiet wrangler would change out his horse for one that was rested, and I wasn't about to saddle a horse he didn't give me. At least I could sit down for a little while.

The sun was low, but still cast enough light that if we were lucky, we could find the stragglers before too long. If not, maybe in the morning we could fan out and scare the last three cows out of hiding. The trucks were scheduled to arrive well before noon, so we wouldn't have much time, but it would also take time to load all the cows, so that might give us some leeway.

I wiped my dusty face with my dirty shirtsleeve, probably just managing to make a bad situation worse, and blinked grime from my eyes as I tried to focus on the pasture.

A lanky shape, leading a tired mount, appeared across the dry grass and it looked like Ezra was coming.

I planned to tell him it was Mr. Lamb who wanted me to take Jericho, even though I knew the consequences.

As Ezra walked closer my eyes drifted back to the rest of the horses. They were dog-tired from the roundup and stood together looking weary, heads bent and eyes half closed.

Simply because I had nothing better to do while Ezra took his time trudging closer, I scanned the brands on the remaining horses and noticed that all of them wore the OO associated with the Cotton Ranch.

All of them but one.

Out of idle curiosity I hoisted myself up and climbed inside the corral. Of course most of the horses were out working, but the ones remaining all had the same brand. The OO.

All of them, except Possum.

"Take Sugar Beet," Ezra said.

I jerked into awareness and blinked at the wrangler. "Mr. Lamb wanted me to take Jericho."

Ezra didn't bother to reply. He pulled his saddle off his tired horse and led him to the gate.

Sugar Beet's eyes looked bright and clear, probably because he had spent half the day resting after Samuel had bugged out.

I went to the tack wagon and retrieved a bridal for Sugar Beet, and as I was sliding the bit inside his mouth, something occurred to me.

"Hey Ezra?" I led Sugar Beet to the gate and let us both outside. "Why didn't you warn me that Possum's ticklish?"

He stared at me, his face an emotionless mask. "Because I didn't know."

"I thought you knew everything about these horses?" I asked.

He studied me. "Who told you about Possum?"

"Mr. Lamb. He said Possum bucks everyone off because his withers are ticklish."

The corner of his mouth twitched. "Don't know how he could have known it. Possum's only been here two years."

I was about to heft my saddle up and froze, looking at Ezra. "What did you just say?"

"Say about what?" he asked.

"Possum's only been here two years?" I asked. "How do you know that?"

His voice drawled as he explained. "He was the last new horse the Cotton Ranch ever bought. Mrs. Cotton got him just before the spring roundup in 2010. She thought he was perky. She told me it turned out he was just ornery."

"And she bought him two years ago? Are you sure?"

"That's what she said."

The timeline didn't make sense to me and I tried to puzzle it out. "But Mr. Lamb retired five years ago. How could he have known Possum's ticklish . . . if he wasn't here . . . ?"

I felt the saddle slip out of my hand and thump to the ground. My head reeled as Dan's words replayed themselves through my memory.

We made a living poaching elk velvet, and bear gallbladders . . .

An image flashed in my mind of Mr. Lamb forbidding anyone to shoot the bears on the mountain. He was their guardian. Their protector.

Then I recalled seeing the remains of a bear beside Fischer Lake. How likely was it that a bear carcass would be found only yards away from the spot a murder victim had been hidden?

I felt my jaw drop open.

John Hill hadn't been killed because of a business deal. It had been for a totally different reason. A reason nobody could have possibly guessed.

John had poached a bear by Fischer Lake, and Mr. Lamb had found him doing it.

"He lied. Mr. Lamb was here two years ago. It wasn't about business at all. It was about the bears," I said.

"What are you yammering about?" Ezra asked.

Everything was starting to make sense. I stared at Ezra. "It was because of the bears."

I hoisted the saddle up on Sugar Beet as fast as I could and cinched it in place. Ezra watched with a confused expression as I rode out of camp in a cloud of dust.

I didn't have time to be cautious anymore. If I was right, all the evidence of John Hill's murder was about to vanish. But if I was quick enough, I could stop him. All I had to do was get to the body first. And I now knew why all of the crew had been sent out on this wild goose chase by Mr. Lamb. It had been by design. He'd needed time to hide the body again.

And now I had to hurry or he would hide it where no one would ever find it, and all the evidence of the murder would be lost forever.

CHAPTER 22

I managed to catch sight of Virginia just inside the tree line and whooped at her to get her attention.

The rest of the crew was long gone, riding up the slope on the contrived errand Mr. Lamb had arranged. Virginia had obviously taken longer to get back in the saddle and she was the final rider straggling from camp. As I caught up to her I saw Ezra disappear into the trees far to the north of us. He had been the last cowboy left in camp. Now it was deserted.

Mr. Lamb had succeeded in clearing everyone out so he could finally finish what he had started two years ago. As I let my eyes dart over the camp, Mr. Lamb was nowhere in sight.

But he soon would be.

"Virginia, stop!"

She turned on me, looking supremely irritated. "What now?"

Sugar Beet danced beneath me. He seemed to sense my nervous energy.

"We need to go back," I said.

She blinked at me. "Back where?"

"Camp. We need to go back."

"Why?" she demanded.

"Because the killer has John Hill's body there right now and we need to find it before he can hide it again."

She stared at me with her lips pulled to one side. "Have you suffered a recent blow to the head?"

"I can't do it without you. Someone has to keep an eye open while I search," I said.

"And you want me to play scout?" she asked. "Forget it."

"Those shots we heard earlier?" I said, talking fast. "He was killing steers so we would all have to leave camp to go look for them. It's no coincidence that those cattle are missing. He wanted everyone out of the way."

"Because he is trying to smuggle out a body? That's absurd."

"Not smuggle it out," I said. "Hide it again. But this time, someplace safe. Someplace nobody would ever, ever think to look."

"Alright, where exactly would that someplace be?" she asked.

It was inconceivable that I hadn't seen it until now.

"Well?" she snapped. "Where is he going to hide it?"

"In the latrine."

"Marley, that's disgusting."

"Exactly," I said.

She gave me a sour look.

I tried to explain quickly. "Who would ever think to look there? It's too deep after it's been filled in for bears to smell any remains and dig them up, and nobody on the crew would ever deliberately search a latrine for any reason. But he had to wait until just before the last day so he could fill it in and nobody would think it was strange. The body is still in camp and if we hurry we can find it."

She looked away as she thought it over. I could see her debating whether or not she would believe me.

I did what I could to appeal to her. "All we have to do is get there first and make sure the body is really hidden in camp. Then tomorrow when I see Allen again I will be able to tell him exactly where to look for it."

"As much as I hate to admit, it does make sense," she said.

"Virginia, I swear this will be the last favor I ever ask you."

She held up one finger. "It had better be."

We broke from the tree line and galloped back to camp side by side. I didn't bother heading for the tack wagon and rode straight towards the tents that ringed the fire pit.

"Alright. What are we looking for?" Virginia asked.

"Keep your voice down," I said. "Just . . . I don't know. Go stand over there and tell me if you see anyone coming."

I pointed vaguely towards the covered supply wagon, and ignored her peeved look as she made a performance out of marching over to it in a huff.

He couldn't have already put John Hill's body inside the latrine; there was a chance someone would have seen it before now.

The body had to be in camp. Somewhere.

"Okay," I said to myself. "If I was a dead body where would I be?"

"You have no idea what you are doing, do you?" Virginia remarked.

"Well it can't be that difficult to figure out," I said. "There aren't that many places you can hide something that size."

I scanned the camp, studied the cookware, the fire pit and the supply wagon, thinking. Where could someone hide a body where no one else would see it? It had to be someplace nobody would think to look. And it had to be someplace close by. Granted, there wasn't much left of John Hill besides bones and sinew, but you couldn't leave a human skeleton lying around in a sleeping bag where somebody could accidentally stumble over it. It had to be someplace nobody ever needed to go.

My head was starting to ache. "I wish Gus were here."

"Will you hurry up?" Virginia snapped.

I darted inside each tent in turn and rummaged through them. Not one of the tents held anything larger than a wad of crusty blankets or a bag of dirty laundry. Nothing was hidden underneath any of the cots, and the only place I could think of big enough to hide a body was the supply wagon. I jogged to it and clambered inside. It was full of cans, boxes and one heavy wooden crate, but when I opened the crate the only thing inside was a steel cooler full of one slimy package of old bacon that positively reeked.

This was getting me nowhere.

Virginia pulled back the canvas flap on the wagon and poked her head inside. "Did you think to look inside everybody's car?"

"It wouldn't be in anyone's car," I said, irritated.

"Why not?" she asked.

"Everything out there is a pickup truck with a bed and nobody would be stupid enough to set a dead guy in the cab of a four-wheel drive."

She let the flap fall as she turned away, and I felt the wagon rock back and forth as she leaned against it.

My shoulders slumped. "It doesn't make any sense."

"What doesn't make any sense?"

I'd said it more for my own benefit. "It's got to be right here. There isn't any other place to hide it."

Then it hit me.

Someplace not underfoot. Someplace nobody would ever need to go.

I climbed out of the wagon fast and dropped to my knees.

"What are you doing?" Virginia asked.

"Move," I said, pushing her aside.

She harrumphed as she slid over, and I crouched beneath the wagon. I pulled myself across the ground until I was in the center of the wagon bed, rolled on my back and looked up.

Strapped to the underside of the boards, exactly as I'd thought it would be, was an old wet sleeping bag. I reached up and felt the surface. Something was inside.

The last time I'd seen this bag had been from under three feet of water. I had to make sure it was the same one.

Using both hands I struggled until the opening rotated towards me. The slippery blue material and heavy ropes resisted my efforts, but I finally managed to pull back enough fabric to see inside. Pale white bone came into view, and I knew at once it was the body.

"It's here," I said. "He hid it underneath the wagon."

"Marley," Virginia said.

"I knew it," I said, pounding the ground with one fist triumphantly. "I just knew it."

"Marley, did you say who killed him?" she asked. "Was it Mr. Lamb?"

"It was Mr. Lamb," I told her. "Why?"

"Because he is coming straight for us."

Panic gripped me and I tried to sit up. Something hard jammed into my forehead but I didn't have time to think about the disgusting implications of that at the moment.

My butt moved of its own accord and I inched my way from underneath the wagon like a caterpillar crossing a freeway.

Just as I got to my feet I saw Mr. Lamb, head down, marching around a tent into view.

He stopped dead when he saw us, frozen in place like he'd just stepped on a land mine.

"What are you gals doing here? I thought I told you all to get up that first fork and look for them missing steers," he said.

"We lost Saint Christopher," Virginia blurted out.

He stared at us with a suspicious expression. "Lost him?"

"We thought if we got some of his food we could bribe him into coming back," Virginia said, laying it on thicker and thicker.

"Saw him with Ezra," Mr. Lamb told us evenly. "Not ten minutes ago."

Mr. Lamb looked down at my jeans, squinting hard. I glanced at my knees and my thighs and saw that they were stained with dirt and grass.

He slowly looked back up at my face, and his eyes widened with a sudden flash of anger.

I snagged Virginia's arm with my hand. "We'll get to work now."

"No, I don't think you will." With one smooth motion he reached back beneath his old plaid shirt and pulled Dan's heavy pistol from his belt. He brought it up fast but Virginia and I were already running.

With all my strength I shoved Virginia inside the closest tent and dove after her. She fell on her side hard but I was already scrambling after.

"Move! Move!"

My hands and legs pumped furiously across the ground and I rolled underneath the flap out the back of the tent. Virginia clawed her way after me.

He hadn't fired a single shot, and I knew he wouldn't until he had us both pinned down. Gunshots would alert the others, and until we were in his sights he wouldn't take the chance of missing.

I kept my head down and ran for the next tent, trying desperately to keep cover between Mr. Lamb and us.

As we crouched behind our own tent, to my astonishment Virginia lifted the back flap and crawled inside before I could stop her.

My voice came out a hiss, "What the hell are you doing?"

She fell back outside from underneath the flap, clutching her purse with a death grip.

"I had to get my bag."

I was so stunned my mouth refused to work. The soft pad of footsteps told me Mr. Lamb was only a few yards behind us, and without even thinking I grabbed Virginia's arm and dragged her along with me.

There was only one tent left. We'd raced by all the others and the last tent in camp became our shelter. Instinctively I jerked Virginia's arm and pulled her into a crouch behind it. There was nowhere left to run. We had to do something fast.

I held one finger over my lips, not that it would do a bit of good, because we were both panting so hard from running he wouldn't have any problem hearing us. We both held as still as possible and I tried in vain to hold my breath.

When I heard footsteps inside the tent, I knew Mr. Lamb was inside it, and he intended to shoot us both right through the canvas.

The camp tents were sturdy and tall, and no fewer than eight stakes roped each one to the ground. But the heavy canvas would collapse if the ropes on one end gave way. I moved fast before I had a chance to talk myself out of my idea.

As quickly as I could, I clawed two corner stakes from the ground and gripped them tight with both hands.

Virginia looked at me with utter confusion, and just as I heard Mr. Lamb take a step closer, I stood up and ran.

The heavy ropes tugged the corner down as I threw all my weight against it, and the remaining stakes broke loose as I barreled forward. The entire thing collapsed.

Mr. Lamb fell inside in a heap of canvas and ropes.

I turned back to order Virginia to run for the vehicles, but when I did my heart jumped up in my throat. She was already sprinting out of camp and headed for the corral as fast as she could move.

I shouted and tore after her. "Go for the truck!"

She was faster than I ever imagined she could be, and by the time I caught her she was almost to the wooden fence that funneled the cattle inside the steel corral.

I tried to stop her but she pulled away. "What are you doing?"

She was beyond listening. Her eyes were glazed and unfocused. She was running in a blind panic, not thinking, just trying to put as much distance between herself and danger as she possibly could.

She grasped the top rung of the corral and I chanced a look back before following her.

Mr. Lamb had managed to get out from underneath the mountain of canvas and was headed for us, his bowed legs pumping.

Hiding in the herd was the worst move we could have made, and that was exactly what we had done.

Virginia practically fell inside the corral, still clutching her purse to her chest like it was a child. Tears streamed down her face and she looked around wildly, flinching when she bumped against a steer.

Cows milled around her nervously, sniffing the air and trying to escape.

They were packed in so tight it was almost impossible to move.

I managed to shove my way through to the middle of the herd and pulled her into a crouch beside me. Spooked cattle swarmed around us.

"Hold still," I said. "Don't make a sound."

"He's going to find us anyway," she said with a sob. "And we don't even have to be here. We didn't even have to be here."

"Virginia, you need to shut up now."

"I went to high school with Bobby and Gino. They were just doing me a favor!"

I stared at her, disbelief bubbling to the surface. "What did you just say?"

"I don't owe any money to Theo Thompson. I just wanted Leif to pay me my fair share."

My fists balled up of their own accord. "Your friends from high school burned down my house?"

"It wasn't like that!" she wailed. "It was an accident!"

I grabbed her by the shoulders and shook her like she was a hysterical teenager. "Virginia shut up while I think."

"He's going to kill us," she babbled. "He's really going to kill us. What is there to think about?"

"If you don't be quiet these cows will panic, start a stampede and kill us for him," I said furiously.

Something in her face shifted.

She stared straight at me like she had just seen me for the first time.

"Oh, of course," she said.

Her expression grew resolute and she stood up, straight and proud, still holding her purse.

I tried to pull her back down. "What do you think you're doing?"

She slipped out of my grasp, and before I could snag her again a frantic heifer rammed me from the side and my feet careened out from under me.

I hit the ground hard and curled into a tight ball as shifting legs and sharp hooves cut the dirt inches away from my hands and face.

Through the forest of limbs I saw Virginia's feet walk calmly away.

I managed to roll to my knees and grabbed out with both hands, using the tail of a startled cow to pull myself up.

I heard the rattle of metal against metal and realized what she was doing.

Virginia was unlocking the gate.

Mr. Lamb stood in the middle of the wooden chute holding the pistol in one hand, caught sight of her and paused. He lifted the pistol at her and aimed. "I just want to talk to you gals! No need for all this. Come on out!"

Virginia ducked back into the herd and vanished.

I searched over the backs of milling cattle but couldn't find her anywhere.

The gate creaked, and started to swing open.

Mr. Lamb lowered his arm, stared at the swinging gate like he didn't understand how it could be moving, and started to back away.

I heard a low rumble behind me, and turned to see the horned Brangus bull staring straight at me. He bellowed a warning and his bloodshot eyes rolled inside his massive skull with fury. It was almost as if he remembered me.

A steer rammed into me from behind and I bounced off his shoulder helplessly, struggling to stay upright. When I glanced back at the bull again he wasn't looking at me any longer.

His head was tilted to the side and he stared at something behind him. His bullwhip tail lashed the air.

I had to crane my neck to see what it was.

Virginia stood behind the horned bull with her handbag looped over her arm. She reached inside, grasped something with her right hand, and slowly pulled it out.

It was pink.

Hot pink.

My entire body went instantly numb. Everything seemed to happen in slow motion, and my legs moved like they were stuck in wet sand.

I heaved myself towards her, flailing madly, but she was already lifting her arm.

A terrified heifer lurched away as I half-climbed across her back trying to get to Virginia. But it was too late.

Her lips pulled back from her teeth in a primal grimace, Virginia aimed her Taser at the Brangus bull and pulled the trigger.

Two strings shot from the end and pierced the tender skin right below the bull's tail.

For one horrifying moment nothing happened at all. Then everything happened at once. The Taser hissed with electricity. The bull bellowed in pain and the entire world turned upside down.

He didn't pause to pick his targets. The bull charged with fury and gored everything in sight. Cows flew aside as two thousand pounds of pure rage exploded inside the corral.

All I could do was lunge for the bars and pray I made it before being crushed.

A living wave of horns, hooves and rolling eyes heaved with fear-driven force and there was only one place for it to go.

The gate flew open with a crash. Bellows of pain and fear filled the air with a deafening cacophony of sounds.

With one massive push the cattle spilled from the corral into the chute in an undulating horde.

It took all my strength to scramble over the backs of two steers and lunge for the fence. I grabbed the top rung and pulled my legs out of the meat grinder flooding beneath me.

A blur of blonde hair across the corral caught my eye and I saw Virginia throw herself over the top of the fence and drop with a bone-crunching thud on the other side. She stared with disbelief at the merciless avalanche of terrified cattle thundering past.

The earth vibrated as animals streamed by the swaying fence and my balance was so precarious I was afraid to move. All I could do was hope the fence didn't collapse under me.

I saw Mr. Lamb make a run for it with both arms pumping like pistons, trying to reach safety before he was overtaken. The herd was already crashing through the gate in a tsunami of horns, noses and hooves.

He didn't make it.

Just as he almost reached the fence, he inexplicably stopped dead, swayed slightly, and fell over backwards before the crush of beasts overtook him. The last I saw of Mr. Lamb was his prone form, splayed out in the dirt, unmoving. And then he disappeared from view beneath an ocean of running cattle.

CHAPTER 23

"I'm not mad at you, Bruce," I said.

I could see from the expression on his face that he didn't quite believe me.

"You've got every right to be. But maybe I'm mad enough at me for the both of us," Bruce replied.

"Because you didn't get to come along and get a piece of the action?" I asked.

The two of us sat at the same kitchen table at my new house, where only a week ago, Allen, Bruce and I had put the finishing touches on our ill-planned mission. Needless to say, it hadn't turned out exactly as we anticipated.

I slid a cup of tea across the table towards Bruce and he accepted it with a faint smile. It was late morning and I had just finished doing the very first load of laundry in my brand-new washer and dryer. Virginia had gone back to Chicago, Leif and I had gotten to spend a peaceful night alone in our new home together, and Bruce was apologizing to me for being a dope.

Things were looking up.

Bruce's expression was pained, and he carefully wrapped both hands around his cup. A ribbon of steam curled over his knuckles. "You shouldn't have been up there. I nearly got you killed, Marley."

"I nearly got me killed. Between Allen, you and me, this was truly a team effort."

For a moment he looked almost as if he could laugh. But his face clouded over again and he covered me with a guilt-stricken stare.

"A team effort," he said.

I took a long sip of my own hot tea and set the cup down softly. "The three of us had hard feelings about what happened in the past, and maybe we were all a bit hasty when we saw a chance to resolve the whole mess."

"It was still a pretty idiotic thing to do," he said. "It's lucky Leif's ex-wife made it out of there in one piece. City girl caught in a stampede? It could have been a lot worse."

"Virginia managed just fine," I said, my tone stone cold.

Bruce quirked an eyebrow, but was wise enough not to say anything else about the matter and let it drop.

Leif had been less than thrilled at Virginia's admission that she had faked the entire Bobby and Gino scheme in an attempt to squeeze him for more cash. He'd actually been quite furious. But Leif's version of furious was to scowl and say to a person in quiet tones, "I'm very disappointed in you."

He'd given Virginia a structured settlement in their divorce that only paid her a set amount each month and she had bitterly resented conforming to a budget. She thought she deserved more than he'd given her, wanted a lump sum, and thought her fake extortion scam was the fastest way to make it happen. Her plan had almost worked, because Leif had transferred the cash before I could make it off the mountain and tell him the truth about what she had done. After I'd explained the situation, Virginia had confessed everything in a teary-eyed attempt to win his forgiveness.

He had been able to reverse the transaction after hearing her confession.

The conversation had not ended well for her, and by the time Leif had straightened it out again, he wasn't referring to her as "Ginni" any longer.

Virginia never fully came out and admitted to me that she was the one who had burned down our house in a fit of jealousy. But I suspected it. It was too much of a coincidence that the fire had started in the master bedroom, probably directly in the center of the bed itself. The message had been loud and clear, if you thought about it from a woman's perspective. The arson inspector said kerosene was the accelerant. We kept a big bottle of kerosene in the garage for an old hurricane lantern, and my suspicion was that she had started the fire in a moment of weakness.

My own personal theory was that Virginia had intended to burn just the bed to make it appear that Bobby and Gino were trying to send a message to Leif, and the fire had gotten away from her too quickly to stop.

It was a good story. But I couldn't ever hope to prove it.

I mentioned my theory to Virginia before she returned to Chicago, and suggested that it would be in her best interest to stay away from Killdeer in the future. I doubted very much that I would ever see her again, after the look of shock she'd given me.

I thought it would be better if some time passed before sharing my thoughts about the fire with Leif. He was already dealing with enough trouble, and I'd noticed how tired he looked lately.

No, not tired. Weary. He was not his usual stout self and I made the decision to wait until things had gotten back to normal again before clueing him in on my suspicions.

Not that we would ever need to worry about Virginia showing up after what had happened. I doubted that she would ever come back to Montana after being chased by a crazed old cowboy with a gun.

"Douglas Lamb suffered massive internal bleeding caused by blunt trauma from being trampled," Bruce said, rubbing the back of his neck with one hand. "That and a collapsed lung."

"Is that what killed him?" I asked.

Bruce rubbed his eyes and yawned. "I think the sucking chest wound from the massive bullet hole we found was what did it."

"Someone shot him?" I asked.

"I guess Dan was setting you up to ferret out the man who killed his partner. That's why he watched your every move during the roundup. He knew you and Samuel were most likely looking for the same man he was hunting, and there at the end he just stepped aside and let you do all the heavy lifting."

"Dan wanted me to think he was grief-stricken," I said.

Bruce nodded. "In a manner of speaking, he probably was. Allen thinks that Dan believed, like you did, that someone on the crew had killed his partner. And since Dan had been working the cattle drive for the Cottons two years ago, he knew that Mr. Lamb had been there too. But he needed to know where John Hill's body was before he took his revenge, so that he could be certain he'd guessed correctly. It must have seemed like a setup to him in the beginning when he spotted you and Samuel poking into things. But then he used it to his advantage. He waited around just long enough for you to get the job done for him. When Dan was sure you and Samuel had located the body, he started to hurry things along."

"Which is why he pointed a gun at me. He wanted me to race back to camp and stir the pot."

"Which is precisely what you did. And when Mr. Lamb bubbled to the top of the pot, Dan shot him from about a hundred yards away. We recovered the weapon from the trees just outside of camp. The rifle used had been taken from a saddlebag. It belonged to one of the cowboys."

I recalled Mr. Lamb's last moments.

He had swayed back and forth before falling to the ground just as the herd overtook him.

No wonder he hadn't made it to the fence. "Dan told me he wasn't interested in retribution."

"He lied," Bruce said matter-of-factly.

"Good luck tracking down Dan," I said. "He's probably in Guatemala by now."

"Not my problem," Bruce muttered. "It's an FBI case as of yesterday. And just so you know, the body in the sleeping bag recovered at the camp was definitely the missing poacher. You said Mr. Lamb killed him because of a bear?"

My hands felt cold and I cupped them around my hot tea.

"John shot a bear while he was working the spring drive two years ago, probably to harvest its gallbladder," I said. "At least, that's what must have happened. Dan and John were opportunistic poachers and the opportunity presented itself. I think Mr. Lamb must have caught John skinning the bear and he just snapped. I don't think he even planned on killing John. It was more a heat-of-the-moment situation."

"He was protective of those bears, was that it?" Bruce asked.

I grimaced. "He probably looked at himself as the guardian of the Cotton Ranch. If I was going to speculate, I'd say Mr. Lamb felt a little bit like killing a poacher was justified. He was insanely protective of those bears."

"How about just plain insane?" Bruce asked.

"Did you hear from Samuel?" I asked. "We sort of said goodbye in a bad way. How did he seem?"

"Allen filled me in and said after he told Samuel what had happened to you and Virginia the kid almost lost his lunch. He said he felt so bad he was going to send you a puppy or something by way of an apology."

"Geez, the last thing I need is a dog," I said. "I'm still cleaning up hair from when Saint Christopher was here shedding all over everything."

Bruce settled back in his chair and let out a long, slow breath. "I'm sorry Marley. For everything."

More than likely, he wasn't talking about the roundup. No, he was talking about something else altogether.

I met his eyes with difficulty. "I'm sorry too."

"Now we know better, right?" he said with a chuckle.

"If you say so," I said.

He fiddled with his cup, his green eyes fixed on the table. "You could always come back to Helena. I hear they are hiring a cleaning woman for the branch office."

"Thanks a lot," I said.

"Really. You are eligible. You could put in for an office position again. Or, if you got off of your dead ass and went back to school, you could finish your biology degree and get a job working in the field for a change."

For one shining moment I tried to picture that scenario in my mind.

Me, wearing the uniform, working on some sage grouse study or trying to catalog chronic wasting disease cases in deer.

But after a moment of consideration I shook my head.

I'd changed too much for that. I was married, had a job I didn't hate, and could say I honestly felt like I was living someplace I belonged.

"You can't go back," I said. "You can only go forward."

Bruce smiled faintly and finished his tea. He set the cup on the counter behind him and stood up, sliding the chair backwards with his legs and scooping his hat off the table.

"Tell your husband I gave my regards."

"When he gets home again, I'll do just that."

"Where is he?" Bruce asked as he headed down the hallway towards the front door.

"Panama," I said, trailing after. "He is flying himself to Dallas this morning in his plane and taking a jet from there. He should be back home in a few days."

"I never thought you'd be married to some international business mogul," he said with a laugh.

I shook my head. "Yeah? Neither did I."

Bruce opened the front door and let in a blast of cool fall air. A few leaves dropped from the trees onto the stairs, falling like golden pinwheels.

Before he turned to leave Bruce crushed me to him with a mighty hug.

"Take care of yourself, girl. Tell that new husband of yours he better look after you."

"You don't need to worry about that," I said reassuringly. "He's a good man. Leif doesn't know any other way to be."

I closed the door after waving him down the driveway and for a moment it felt good just to stand in the house alone and listen to the silence.

There was so much to do before Leif got home from his trip.

We had to sort out the mess left over from the fire that had destroyed our old home, not to mention deal with the insurance paperwork and all the bills starting to roll in from the cleanup costs. We had to decide where to put the new garage, because Leif was adamant about not leaving the BMW uncovered. And then we had to decide what, of the furniture and dishes that had come with the new house, we wanted to keep and what we wanted to replace.

But all of that would have to wait.

After I washed the teacups and tidied the kitchen, it seemed sensible to get out the mop and bucket, swirl some soap around the floors and dust the hardwood.

Almost without thinking about it, I dug a bandanna from a box of towels in the kitchen and tied up my strawberry blonde hair so it wouldn't get in the way while I tidied up my new house.

Things got out of hand, and before I was even aware of it, four hours had come and gone and the entire house was sparkling.

I was coming down the hallway with the empty mop bucket in hand when I stopped short.

Someone was standing in my living room, I could see a shadow from the open front door, and for a horrible moment I flashed to the memory of the two pretend gangsters who had barged in on me a few days ago.

"Hello?" I cautiously peered around the corner at the end of the hall.

Relief washed over me when I saw Loy Shucraft standing in my living room, baseball cap in hand.

"Hey, Loy. You ever think of knocking?" I said, standing in front of him with my arms crossed.

He swallowed so hard his Adam's apple surged up and down. His eyes bled sadness and his face was bleached white.

"What's wrong?" I dropped the bucket where I stood. "Loy, is it my dad?"

He lifted one big paw and set it on my shoulder. "Sit down, Hun."

I didn't budge. "Loy. Tell me what it is. Is it Irene?"

He drew breath to speak but nothing came out.

I took his hand with both of mine and shook it. "Tell me."

The sheriff held out his other hand as if he was going to catch me. He couldn't seem to look in my eyes.

"Leif's plane crashed just outside of Telluride, Colorado. He lost an engine, didn't have enough power to make it, and hit the wall below the runway."

My chest felt like it was collapsing from the inside. "Don't say it, Loy. Don't say it."

"I'm sorry, Marley. I'm so sorry. He's gone."

WE WERE THE BUTCH AND
SUNDANCE OF LIBRARIANS.
THANKS BOSS.

A fourth generation Wyoming native,
Jessica McClelland is a librarian, avid archer and
spent a decade hunting dinosaurs in the
Jurassic formation in the foothills of the
Bighorn Mountains, a stone's throw away from
where the Johnson County Cattle Wars occurred.
She is the author of the Marley Dearcorn novels,
a series of murder mysteries set in
South Central Montana.